MONK'S CURSE

by Stephen Wheeler

Text © Stephen Wheeler

Cover photograph of Orford Castle, Suffolk © Philip
Moore

By the same author

THE SILENT AND THE DEAD

Brother Walter Mysteries:
UNHOLY INNOCENCE
ABBOT'S PASSION
BLOOD MOON
DEVIL'S ACRE

this one for
David Messer
Rector of All Saints, Stanton, Suffolk
who will know my many mistakes
and keep them to himself

Prologue and Obituary

(Notice pinned to the door of the abbey church of
Saint Edmund, Bury St Edmunds, Suffolk.)

*It is with deep regret and sadness to have to
announce the death of Samson of Tottington, for
three decades our abbot, shepherd and father.*

*He died peacefully in the midst of his
congregation this 30th day of December 1211 at a
little after nine in the evening, "the time when the
wolf is indistinguishable from the dog".*

*Our sorrow at his loss is tempered only by our
joy in the knowledge that he goes to a better place.
May his soul rest in eternal peace.*

✝

He was seventy-six when he died. A good age even
in these peaceful times. Samson's thirty year tenure
was one of the longest in the abbey's history. In that
time he served three kings, six popes, five
archbishops and many thousands of ordinary Suffolk
folk. His reputation spread far and wide throughout
Europe where his wise counsel was regularly sought
and valued. He was in addition a judge delegate,
baron of the realm and member of the king's high

council. Not bad for a poor country lad with no notable ancestry.

He left the abbey in better condition than when he arrived, strengthening its finances, securing its liberties and ensuring its independence. He also did many good works for the town including building schools, churches, hospitals and even an aqueduct. I suspect, too, that he deliberately chose the feast of Thomas Becket, England's greatest martyr, as the date of his departure to ensure that we were never likely to forget it: the Norfolk Trickster's final trick.

Why am I telling you all this? To stress the point that Abbot Samson was no dotard. He was in full command of his senses right to the very end. It is important to remember that as you turn the page and read what I am about to divulge.

Part One

AN INVITATION TO MURDER

Chapter One
SAMSON'S TESTAMENT

When I began these jottings some dozen or so years ago it was never my intention that they should become a chronicle. I leave such things to far greater wordsmiths than I like Gerald of Wales, William of Newburgh or even our own Jocelin of Brackland. Indeed, I wouldn't have picked up my pen this day had it not been for the fact that a few days before his death Samson called me to his bedside and told me a tale of such astonishing improbability that I felt I had to write it down if only to be sure I wasn't making it up. The events he described are supposed to have occurred some fifty years earlier and I have to admit my initial reaction was to dismiss them as the ramblings of a confused old man; it is often the case that ghosts from the past return to torment the dying in their final hours. But I repeat, Samson was fully cognisant at the end and he told his tale with such conviction that I was forced to take it seriously.

Even so I decided to proceed with caution enquiring around the abbey – discreetly - if the tale had been recorded anywhere else. But I wasn't able to find anybody who knew of it, not even Jocelin who can truly be said to be Samson's biographer. This didn't exactly fill me with confidence, for if

Jocelin didn't know then who would? In fact as I later discovered the story had been written down, but not at the abbey, and tracking it down was to become my prime occupation over the coming days.

The problem with such tales is that so much is hearsay and with each retelling facts get lost or distorted until the final version bears little resemblance to the original. Normally this doesn't matter because the events described happened so long ago that they have little bearing on the present. But that wasn't so in this case. They may have occurred five decades earlier but with consequences for people living today which could and did mean the difference between life and death.

You may have noticed a slight hesitancy on my part to begin the tale in earnest. That is deliberate. I will get to it, never fear, but I want to lay out my stall carefully first. You may wonder, for instance, why Samson chose me, the abbey's physician, to confide in rather than one of his own chaplains. I like to think it is because over the course of three decades that we knew each other I earned his trust and respect. But I suspect it was more to do with the fact that at forty-seven my eyesight was still good enough to be able to write down his words which was more than could be said for most of his other senior obedientiaries. In fact there was another reason why he chose me for this doubtful honour which had nothing to do with trust or the efficacy of my faculties and one I truly wish I didn't deserve...

'Are you sure you wouldn't rather have Jocelin hear your confession, father? He's far better at this sort of thing than I am.'

'No. Jocelin just weeps all the time which makes him hiccup. I'll gasp my last breath before he manages to stammer out his first. You can tell him after I'm gone if you wish which won't be long now.'

'Nonsense!' I said. 'This is but a passing rheum. You'll be back on your feet again in no time. How could you not with the entire convent of eighty monks praying hourly for your recovery?'

He gave me a sideways look. 'Oh dear. You know things are bad when your own doctor lies to you.'

'Father, I have every confidence in the cogency of my brothers' prayers.'

'Have you, indeed? I doubt that. Like the rest of them you'll have been casting lots to see who my successor will be. Well, I'm sorry to disappoint you all but I've no intention of popping off just yet. I'm ten weeks off completing thirty years as abbot of this place and I'm determined to get there. After that I don't much care.'

That wasn't quite true either. He cared very much what happened after his death. England was still under interdict over King John's refusal to accept Pope Innocent's candidate for Archbishop of Canterbury. That meant, among other things, that anyone who died could not be buried in consecrated ground. This is no light matter for if a body doesn't receive the proper burial rites it can affect the soul's passage through purgatory where it can get stuck and maybe never make it into paradise.

Fortunately no interdict lasts for ever and once this one is lifted all the dead will be reburied properly with all due ceremony. But for the past three years that hasn't been possible and bodies have been piling up in the fields, or placed in temporary graves, or even hung from trees out of the reach of wild animals. Nothing of that nature will happen to Samson of course, but his fear is that we may forget or even lose his body. In fact there has been some discussion as to what to do with him when the time comes. The proposal is to store him in the abbey crypt until such times as he can be transferred to the chapterhouse floor and laid next to his predecessor, Abbot Ording. But still, it must be a worry for him.

Samson turned on his cot grimacing with pain and let out a groan.

'Is it your protuberances again, father? I can give you something to ease the discomfort if you wish.'

'Opium you mean?' He shook his head. 'No, I have something to tell you for which I need all my wits sharp not dulled by drugs. And you're wrong, it's not a confession of my past sins. What I have to disclose is far more interesting - and far more disturbing. So, my good and faithful servant, draw near and harken, for what I am about to tell you will make your ears sting and your pate grow feathers.'

I could see this was going to be a long session so I pulled up a stool and sat down. What was this great revelation to be, I wondered? The meaning of life? The whereabouts of the Holy Grail? What really happened to the prince Arthur, King John's nephew?

'You've heard of the Green Children of Woolpit?'

That momentarily stunned me. Woolpit is a village some seven or so miles to the east of Bury. The church there has long been a source of anguish for Samson and the abbey. Maybe this was just a case of past devils come to haunt him after all.

'I think I've heard the legend. It was one of the stories my nurse used to tell my brother Joseph and me when we were children in order to frighten us into obeying her: "If you don't wash your hands before supper they'll turn green like those poor children" – that sort of thing. But nobody really believed it.'

Samson shook his head. 'No legend. It really happened. The green children existed. I even met them.'

Now, if anyone else had said that to me I would have laughed in his face. But I say again, Samson was no gullible dolt. If anything he was even more of a sceptic than I was. For the moment I decided to humour him.

'As I recall the story,' I said dredging through my childhood memories, 'wolves came into it somehow. But that can't be right because there aren't any wolves in Suffolk.'

'Not anymore there aren't, but there were then. Remember we're talking over half a century ago. It's where the village gets its name from: Woolpit - Wolf's Pit – you see? That's how wolves were captured in those days. A pit was dug to the depth of a man's height and covered with leaves and twigs. Then some rotting flesh was placed on the top to attract the wolf which would fall into the pit and be trapped. At one time the county was pocked with them.'

'So?'

'The children – a boy and a girl - were found in one of these pits by a local shepherd. In all probability they were after the carrion and accidentally fell in. Luckily for them it was empty. Some of these pits had spikes in the bottom to impale the quarry, and sometimes the spikes were coated with human dung to hasten the process further. The walls are sheer and impossible to scale. They must have been in there for days unable to get out. By the time the shepherd came across them they were half-starved and frozen. He rescued them and tried to quiz them to find out where they came from but they spoke no English - or any other language he recognized. He didn't know what to do with them so he took them to the local lord, a man called Sir Richard de Calne.'

I thought for a moment. 'You say the children fell into the pit?'

'Apparently.'

'And they were coloured green?'

'As I said.'

'Why would that be? I would have thought blue a more appropriate colour if they'd been there for days and were freezing.'

He shrugged. 'It's just how they were described. They were green. No-one knows why.'

'Well, let's see: the moon is green. Maybe that's where they fell from. Then there's the man in the moon who presumably has a wife. Possibly these were their children. I don't know what language is spoken up there but I doubt it is English. And let's not forget wolves howl at the moon, so there could be a connection there too.'

Samson glared at me. 'If you're not going to take this seriously...'

'Well really father,' I snorted. 'I mean - *green* children!'

He sighed and shook his head. I could see the effort of arguing was beginning to tire him. I had to remember his condition. He wasn't well and I didn't want to over-tax him.

'All right, you say you met these children. Did they look green to you?'

'Green-ish.'

This time I didn't even try to hide my scorn.

He frowned. 'You have to understand, Walter, when I saw them they'd already been living with Sir Richard for a while. By then the colour had faded somewhat.'

'How convenient. Did Sir Richard happen to mention how they came to lose their green hue?'

'Diet. At first the children would eat nothing offered them.'

'Except some rotten mutton. I know - they had the belly-ache. Turned their gills green.'

I was joking but he was serious. He shook his head. 'No, not that either. By chance they were given some raw beans which they fell upon and devoured and for a while they would eat nothing else. Gradually with time their green tinge faded.'

My jaw dropped. 'By eating beans? Raw *green* beans? Wouldn't you think that might increase their verdancy rather than lessen it?'

'I'm only telling you what Sir Richard told me.'

'Sir Richard told you this personally?'

'Not me. Abbot Ralph of Coggeshall. It was Ralph told me.'

'Coggeshall,' I said thoughtfully. 'That's a town in Essex isn't it?'

'Near Colchester. What of it?'

'That's some distance from Woolpit. How did an Essex abbot come to have the story?'

'Ralph is a great chronicler and collector of mystery tales. He's even written a book about them.'

I shook my head in despair. Green children indeed! I was beginning to think I'd strayed into an insane asylum. I visited one of those places once in London. It was quite an experience. They were all there: the Emperor Charlemagne, John the Baptist, the abbess of Whitby. All very convincing and every one of them mad as March hares. It made me start to wonder again about Samson.

'What happened to the green children once they recovered,' I continued to indulge him, 'and were bleached white?'

'The boy died. He was younger than his sister and more delicate. The girl survived and continued to live with the de Calne family for a while. What became of her after that I don't know.'

I shook my head again. But then a small alarm bell started to ring faintly at the back of my head.

'What did you say this lord's name was again?'

'Sir Richard de Calne.'

'De Calne,' I frowned. 'That name sounds familiar.'

'So it should. Sir Richard is your neighbour - or rather was. Long dead now of course. But his manor still adjoins your own. Wykes Hall at Bardwell – a couple of miles from Ixworth.'

The alarm bell was clanging much more loudly now. 'Father, I hope you're not going to suggest what I think you're going to suggest.'

'I want you to go and talk to your mother.'

'Father!'

'You should be pleased. It's Christmastide, the season for families. Oh don't pout. When were you last there? It must be months.'

'Years more like.'

'Well there you are, then. Go and see your mother, Walter. She will be delighted to see you.'

'You don't know my mother.'

He sighed wearily. 'Don't make me command you, I'm too tired. Be a good chap and just go. To please me.'

'You said yourself, all this happened a very long time ago. Why now?'

'Because a few days ago I had a visitor. A woman. She told me there is going to be a murder. I want you to prevent it.'

Chapter Two
MY OWN GYXEWEORDE

Perhaps now you begin see why I was initially nervous about disclosing the details of this matter. I mean really, green children! Have you ever heard the like? And if that wasn't enough there's also a woman, supposedly, announcing a murder *before it even happens*. What woman? And who would do such a thing? When pressed Samson wouldn't go into detail and ended the interview abruptly by turning over and snoring loudly. I did ask among my brother monks if anyone had seen a woman visiting Samson in recent days, but no-one had. You'd have thought that a lone female wandering around such an exclusively male establishment as a monastery would be remarked upon. But no. In fact there had hardly been any visitors to the abbot's palace since he took to his sickbed, and certainly none female. And as for his wanting me to prevent this purported murder - how was I supposed to do that? I didn't even know who the victim was meant to be.

Maybe Samson was going gaga after all. The trouble is while he had breath in his body he was still my abbot and I was sworn to obey him however outlandish his requests. He now wanted me to go to

Ixworth to discuss this insane matter with my mother. I was sure it was going to be a fruitless exercise. But did I have any choice?

I have to admit the prospect of a trip out of Bury was not entirely unappealing. Life at the abbey had become very difficult of late. What with the abbot incapacitated and the strictures of the interdict prohibiting all but the most essential religious rituals, everything seemed to be on hold. The only real sign of life was the work being done on Samson's beloved twin towers on the front of the abbey church.

That apart, all else was in a state of suspension and it was beginning to make my brother monks restless. I had my private medical practice and so could get away for a few hours but we had to come together each day in chapter and at mealtimes. And with the intrigues of what would happen post-Samson - who was likely to win the abbot's mitre, who was up and who down – tempers were beginning to fray. In the circumstances it would be a relief to escape for a while.

I hadn't been out of Bury town for some months and not to my home in Ixworth for much longer even though it is but a short distance away. That wasn't because Samson refused to give his permission; he was always very good where families were concerned. And human nature being what it is, few men - or women in the case of nuns - can turn their backs on their blood relatives with complete alacrity. Those of us from noble families usually find the severing of familial links easier since it is normal practice for our children to be sent away to other households in order to learn how to become proper little aristocrats. However, that didn't happen to me.

My parents kept me entirely within the family home. Not that anyone could accuse my mother of excessive cosseting. On the contrary, Lady Isabel's maternal instincts stopped abruptly at the birthing-chamber door. But she did have an affection for my adoptive-brother, Joseph. He was always the cleverer of the two of us and that above all else would have caught my mother's eye. She therefore took it upon herself to educate us personally and thus by default I received more of her attention than I might otherwise have done. In her eyes I squandered even that advantage by becoming a monk and have never been able to convince her otherwise.

Still, I was fond of the old harridan and not entirely convinced by her act of maternal indifference. She did, after all, once save my life when she deployed another of her protégés, the remarkable and enigmatic Chrétien, to defeat my old enemy Geoffrey de Saye. Surely that shows a mother's affection for her offspring? Alas, de Saye was still around though languishing in exile in the west country – and long may he remain so. Not so my mother, at least for much longer. I sometimes forgot just how incalculably ancient she was. I might not get many more chances to see her before God gathered her to his bosom - or more likely bundled her off to the other place.

All of which thoughts tumbled through my mind as they always did on the short ride from Bury to the tiny hamlet of Ixworth - or Gyxeweorde as our Saxon forebears would have known it. The house my mother inherited when my father died nestles along the banks of the Blackbourn River, a pretty little brook that rises in the higher ground south of the village and meanders its way languidly towards

Thetford a dozen miles to the north. Ixworth Hall, my family home, is the larger of two manors encompassing the village, the other belonging to the Augustinian Priory of Saint Mary the Virgin located further up the valley. Part of my mother's dislike of monasteries, and of Bury in particular, was the fact that Ixworth was once owned by the abbots of Saint Edmund's and they have never entirely relinquished their claim. My becoming a monk, and a monk of Saint Edmund's to boot, was the final betrayal. That was one reason why I didn't visit quite as often as I should: the unspoken but lingering tut-tut of disapproval. Still, if things got really difficult I could always stay with the Austin Canons half a mile up the road. At least there I would be welcomed as a returning son.

As I entered the courtyard Oswald, my mother's ancient retainer, and by then her only companion, hobbled out of the house to take Erigone's head.

'Master Walter!' he beamed. 'What a pleasant surprise. It is good to see you.'

'It's good to see you too, Oswald,' I said handing him the rein and dismounting. 'How are your knees?'

'Better since you gave me that potion last time you were here.'

'That wasn't my concoction. That was Joseph's.'

'How is Master Joseph?'

'Busy making money. Is my mother about?'

Oswald glanced hesitantly over his shoulder. 'I'm not sure she's is expecting you, sir.'

'Oh, I'm sure she is. She probably knew I was coming even before I did. Where would she be, I wonder? In her solar?' I glanced up at the window overlooking the courtyard.

'She rarely goes anywhere else these days. Her hip keeps her immobile.'

I nodded. 'Old age, my friend. It comes to us all eventually.'

I made my way to the room on the upper floor of the house and found her seated beside the hearth dressed head-to-toe in black as usual and grimacing up at me like a malevolent baboon.

'So, they've let you out for the holidays, have they? How kind of them to think of me. Where's my gift?'

'It isn't New Year for another two weeks yet,' I said kissing her proffered cheek. 'And isn't the smiling face of a child gift enough for a loving mother?'

She grimaced. 'Hard to say. I see it so rarely I'd forgotten what it looks like - unlike your brother Joseph's who visits often.'

'Joseph gets more opportunity than I do.'

'That's because he isn't encumbered by foolish archaic rules. I'm thinking of converting to the Jewish faith, by the way, following in your brother's footsteps. They have fewer rules. There, what do you think your abbot would say to that?'

She was being her usual provocative self. I dare say living alone out here she had little else to occupy her. In her day she'd been something of an academic, unusually for a woman, and she missed the cut and thrust of debate. To me it just highlighted the folly of allowing women to be educated. The female is by nature verbose; an educated one impossibly so. My mother could unravel a fart with that tongue of hers. Her reference to Judaism, by the way, is because of my brother Joseph who isn't actually my brother at all but the son of a Jewess from Syria. And it was an empty boast. When it came to religion Joseph was even more of a sceptic than she was. I wasn't going to rise to the bait.

'I doubt whether Samson would care just now which religion you professed,' I sighed. 'He's dying.'

'Oh? What of?'

'What do you think? Old age. He is seventy-six.'

'Is he indeed?' Her lip curled with satisfaction. 'Two years younger than me. I always knew I'd outlive the old goat. Did I ever mention we were once students together?'

'Once or twice.'

She nodded. 'It was at the Paris school - before he took the cowl, of course. He was a handsome buck then. Red hair and a fiery temper to match. I quite fancied the look of him myself.'

'I'm surprised you noticed such things. I thought you only ever had eyes for my father.'

'Oh it was long before I met your father,' she said flapping a negligent hand. 'Anyway, I was too much in love with learning. I didn't have time for adolescent fumblings.'

I shifted uncomfortably on my chair. The conversation was in danger of descending into the vulgar. Thankfully Oswald entered at that moment with a tray of refreshments - spiced wine for her and warmed ale for me. Having given me my cup Oswald started looking round for somewhere to put hers.

'Oh, just put it down on the floor, man,' she said impatiently tapping her stick on the flags.

'You won't be able to reach it if I put it on the floor.'

Having found a stool he placed it next to her and rested the tray on top. He then went over to bank up the fire.

'You see what I have to put up with?' she scowled. 'Insubordination. He wouldn't have dared say that to me if I were a man. I should have him horse-whipped for his impudence.'

She glowered at Oswald who studiously ignored her as he carried on repairing the fire.

'Well,' she said returning her attention again to me, 'since you've plainly not come laden with gifts, why are you here?'

'Can a son not visit his dear mother at Christmastide?'

'No. Samson sent you. And if he's doing that on his deathbed he must have a good reason. So what is it?'

I frowned. I could never be sure how many of her guesses were pure deduction and how many came from her spies, of which she had many. But now it came to it I was reluctant to begin. In the cold light of day the whole sorry business about green children and murders seemed more absurd than ever and I'd almost decided to forget it. If she hadn't asked, I probably would have done.

'It's a silly story, really,' I started hesitantly, 'about wolves and children. Something that's supposed to have happened a long time ago. I doubt there's anything in it.'

'*Green* children?'

I pouted. 'Well - yes.'

She nodded. 'I met them - the girl at any rate. The boy was already dead by then.'

Another one. What was this, some kind of conspiracy?

'So you're saying these green children really existed?'

'Of course they existed. Except they weren't green - at least the girl wasn't. Not that they could tell you what they were, gibbering and jabbering like monkeys. No-one could understand a word they said.'

'You make them sound like creatures from a foreign land.'

'Very possibly they were. Certainly they spoke no English. The shepherd who found them could get no sense out of them either, so he took them to a local knight - Sir Richard de Calne.'

'I was going to ask you about him. He was our neighbour, wasn't he? Why did the shepherd take them there?'

She shrugged. 'Why not? Sir Richard was well-known at the time. Had something of a reputation as an academic.'

'Yes, but Ixworth is closer. To get to his home in Bardwell they would have had to go through Ixworth - right past your door. Why didn't the shepherd bring them here?'

'You'd have to ask him that, although I don't fancy your chances. I imagine he's long dead by now.'

That was true enough. After fifty-seven years I doubted there was anybody left who was alive at the time other than my mother who never did know when she'd outstayed her welcome – which probably explained why Samson wanted me to speak to her. She clearly had the same thought:

'Is that why Samson sent you? To ask damn-fool questions about ancient myths?'

'So now you're saying it was a myth? Not real after all?'

'I'm saying nothing of the kind. But these old wives tales, they get twisted. Who knows what the truth was.'

'You tell me. What do you remember about them?'

'Not much,' she sniffed. 'I told you, I only met the girl and only the once.'

'Well, how old was she? You must remember that.'

'About fourteen I'd say. But she'd been living in Sir Richard's house for four or five years by then.'

'So that would have made her about nine or ten when she was found. And the boy?'

'A year or two younger.'

'Seven or eight,' I nodded.

She gave a wry smile. 'You're taking this rather seriously, aren't you? Considering it's just a silly story.'

'I'm not saying I believe any of it,' I defended. 'In fact I'm trying to see the flaw. I'm sure there must be one. The boy - why did he die?'

She shrugged. 'Who knows? Girls at that age are tougher than boys. One day he was there, the next he was gone.'

'But the girl - what was she like?'

'A hussy - quite blatantly so. I remember that much. She had absolutely no shame when it came to men. She even made eyes at Oswald here.'

I looked with astonishment at the arthritic old man who by now had finished banking up the fire and was struggling to rise to his feet.

'Hard to imagine isn't it?' she chortled. 'Decrepit old boot. But he wasn't always the wreck you see now. And as I say, the girl was a trollop. Any man, young or old, servant or knight - it mattered not to her. Even Oswald.'

I shifted with embarrassment. To his credit Oswald gave no sign of having heard us, as good servants are supposed not to. No doubt he was well used to my mother's bad manners.

'Do you want anything else?' he asked her picking up her empty cup.

'No. You can go.'

He started towards the door.

'Erm, thank you Oswald,' I said handing him my cup as he passed.

'My pleasure, master,' he smiled and left the room quietly closing the door after him.

'Mother, do you have to be so rude?' I said to her when we were alone again. 'It's a sign of graceful living to treat servants courteously.'

She snorted. 'Oswald's not a servant. He's been here since before the Ark. I inherited him along with the wine and the tapestries.'

'Then if not a servant what is he?'

'I don't know,' she smiled. 'You think of a word for him.'

I decided I'd rather not.

'This Richard de Calne?' I said trying to get back to the subject in hand. 'If he was such a close neighbour, why did I never meet him?'

She frowned. 'He wasn't the most neighbourly of neighbours. Kept himself to himself. I don't think he had much time for people. Preferred books. It was said that every day was a school day to Sir Richard de Calne.'

'He sounds just your sort of man.'

'I admit I admired him. But as for knowing him,' she shook her head. 'I can't say I ever did that.'

'Do you know if he was he married?'

She nodded. 'To a mouse. There was a son, I believe, also called Richard.'

I thought for a moment. 'All right. The boy died. But what about the girl, what did she do later – other than flirt with every man she met?'

'It was said she eventually married and went to live on the north Norfolk coast somewhere. Lynn I believe.'

'And after that?'

'After that it all sort of died a death and got forgotten. But it's not me you should be asking about all this. Ralph Coggeshall's the one for that.'

'Abbot Ralph?' I remembered Samson mentioning the name.

She nodded. 'He's the expert where green children are concerned.' She started shuffling forward in her chair. 'And now we will have to leave it there. You've tired me out with all your questions. We'll meet again at breakfast. Interrogate me then if you must.'

She struggled to get to her feet and I darted up to help her.

'You haven't told me yet why Samson is so interested in all this,' she said hobbling towards the door. 'Why he's resurrecting it now?'

'Oh, just some fancy he has. He actually thinks there's going to be a murder,' I snorted. 'Can you believe that?'

She stopped. 'Whose murder?'

'Probably no-one's.' But she wouldn't be fobbed off so easily. I sighed. 'He has this absurd notion that there's going to be a murder and he wants me to prevent it. It's somehow mixed up with these green children. Some woman is supposed to have told him. I'm not convinced about any of it.'

She frowned up at me. 'You? He wants you to prevent it? He asked you? You?'

'Amazing, isn't it? Maybe he has greater faith in my abilities than my own mother does.'

She thought about that for a moment. 'Yes, I suppose that must be the reason.'

Chapter Three
A TIMELY WARNING

Can't understand why Samson would choose me for the job? Am I such a dunderhead? I'm sure she thinks so. Mind you, I wouldn't be alone. Few men have ever matched up to my mother's high expectations, not even my father. Small wonder the poor man spent so much time locked away in his laboratorium. I'm amazed he came out long enough to father a child - only the one, mind. They never tried again.

Well I'll show her. Having fulfilled my obligation to Samson by visiting her I had intended leaving the matter there, return to Bury and forget all about green children and wolf pits. But that last comment of hers got my blood up. I decided I would go to Coggeshall and speak with this Abbot Ralph if only to prove to her that all these stories were just that: stories. But I wouldn't tell her what I was doing. I'd just look forward to seeing her face when she discovered I'd managed to wrap up the whole affair entirely on my own. Then we'd see who was the dunderhead!

I rose early next morning hoping to get away without having to see the old termagant again only to find that she was already seated at the breakfast table.

She seemed to be in the process of dis-articulating some sliced pear. I tried not to show my disappointment.

'Good morning mother,' I greeted her taking my seat at the table. 'You're up early.'

'I don't sleep well these days. An hour, two at the most and I'm shifting on my bed. Doubtless you're going to tell me this is the usual time for you monks to rise.'

'It is the hour for lauds,' I agreed. 'But that's not why I'm up. I've decided to leave straight after breakfast.'

She cocked an eyebrow. 'It's a bit early to be travelling, isn't it? The sun won't be up for another two hours yet.'

'I thought I might pay my respects to Father Aimery up at the priory before I left,' I improvised quickly.

'He won't thank you for that. Augustinians keep civilized hours, unlike you Benedictines.'

'I'm sure the good prior would be too polite to refuse me,' I smiled sweetly.

Oswald came in with a bowl of honey-sweetened porridge and a posset for me.

I could feel her eyes on me. 'It's only a couple of hours to Bury even on that old nag of yours.'

'Erigone is no nag. She's one of the abbey's finest mules.'

She popped another slice of pear between her toothless jaws and chewed. 'You could go to see Aimery this morning, come back here for dinner and still be back at the abbey before dark.'

'Why Mother dearest,' I smiled. 'I could almost believe you craved my company.'

'I see little enough of you. I may as well make the most of it while I can.'

Now I felt guilty. How did she do that? Just when I thought I could hate the old shrew she says something like that and pulls me back. And I suppose she was right. We should make the most of what time she had left. I didn't want to have to live with the knowledge that our final meeting had ended on bad terms. In any case, Coggeshall is thirty miles away. Impossible to achieve in a single day even if I left now. I would have to break my journey somewhere overnight. The only question was where?

'Melford,' she said without looking up.

'I'm sorry?'

'You could stay in Melford tonight. The master of Kentwell Hall owes me a favour. He'd give you a bed if I asked him.'

I looked at her in astonishment. 'Why would I want to go to Melford? It's miles out of my way.'

'Not that far. About half way I'd say.'

I snorted. 'Half way to Bury? Have you lost all sense of direction?'

'Half way to Coggeshall, I mean. That is where you're going, isn't it?'

My jaw dropped open in astonishment.

She frowned with distaste. 'Oh do close your mouth, Walter dear. Has no-one ever told you it's rude to chew with it open?'

I snapped my mouth shut again. 'How did you know I was going to Coggeshall? I only decided myself last night.'

She shrugged. 'A simple matter of deduction. I planted the idea in your head, it grew overnight. I guessed if you were up early this morning that's where you'd be going. Seems I was right.' She popped another slice of pear into her mouth and chewed smugly.

I pouted. 'Do you enjoy playing these games?'

'Of course. What else is there to do in this God-forsaken backwater? But I don't get the opportunity anymore. Oswald's the only person I can practice on and he knows all my tricks.'

'Which I'm beginning to learn. Well, I'm sorry to disappoint you but I've just changed my mind again. I shan't be going to Coggeshall after all.' I poured myself a decisive cup of ale and took a few hefty gulps spilling most of it down my chin.

'Oh, don't be so childish!' she said tapping the table with an arthritic finger. 'Admit it, you're eager to prove me wrong which you can only do by going to Coggeshall and solving the matter yourself. Here.' She pushed two sealed letters across the table towards me.

'What's this?' I said eyeing them suspiciously. 'Another of your tricks?'

'Letters of introduction. One for Sir Gilbert Kentwell and the other for Abbot Ralph. I wrote them last night after you flounced off to your room in a huff. Please don't make me rescind them. It'd be a waste of good vellum and Oswald won't thank you for making him scrape the ink off.'

'I do not flounce,' I said snatching up the two white oblongs. Each had a huge wax imprint of the Ixworth family crest sealing it. I wondered what they contained.

'How come you're so friendly with this abbot?' I asked petulantly. 'You despise churchmen.'

She looked sheepish. 'Ralph and I have … certain things in common.'

'Such as?'

'A shared dislike for the Mortain upstart to begin with.'

I might have guessed. The Mortain upstart. She meant King John. It was one of a number of derogatory sobriquets given to John by those who opposed his rule. My mother was one of his most outspoken critics. She'd long despised the man and made no bones about it. You see, despite appearances my mother is descended from an old Anglo-Norman family. They never really accepted the Angevins who were originally a race of French counts and therefore not of the pure royal bloodline. In my mother's case there was the added annoyance of John's high-handedness when it came to her inheritance of the Ixworth estate after my father's death. The monarch traditionally has the right to dictate to widows of my mother's rank who they were to remarry. It was a matter of politics: the king liked to know who his tenants were forming alliances with and whether they posed a threat to his government. It was also very profitable. Money changed hands before marriage vows did. From my mother's point of view it was sheer interference which she would not tolerate willingly. However, never one to let principle get in the way of making money, John eventually let her have her way and allowed her to remain an unmarried widow – in exchange for a sizeable contribution to the royal coffers. The whole experience had reinforced her already low opinion of the king and left her a permanent and implacable enemy.

'You should be careful about voicing such opinions in public,' I warned her seriously. 'It could get you into trouble.'

She flapped her hand. 'There's no-one out here in this wilderness to hear me. And even if they did, who'd listen to the rantings of an old woman?'

Quite a few people, I'd imagine. I knew for a fact she was in touch with like-minded people all over the country. It wouldn't surprise me if half the conspiracies over the last decade could be linked to her one way or another.

I dropped the letters back down on the table again. 'You seem very keen suddenly to have me pursue this matter of the green children.'

'As I said yesterday, Samson may be the greatest charlatan but he's no fool. If he thinks there's something to this supposed murder then it will be worth investigating. That is the reason he sent you to me, isn't it? To persuade you. Seems I have been successful.' She gave a smug smile.

'Could you not simply have asked me outright? Or are you so twisted now that you are incapable of doing anything straight anymore?'

'Would you have agreed if I had?'

'No.'

She grunted. 'Then eat up your porridge. You'll need something warming inside you. It's a long, cold ride to Coggeshall.'

Downstairs I found Oswald waiting for me with Erigone already saddled. It was indeed a chilly morning and threatening rain again. He had oiled a cape for me to throw over my shoulders to keep the worst of the rain off.

What was I thinking of travelling thirty miles in such weather? I must be mad. It was that woman. She'd tricked me into it although I still couldn't quite work out how. If I had any doubts about the truth of that I had only look on Oswald's face. It was filled with sympathy and regret.

'Thank you Oswald,' I said accepting the rein from his hand.

'You're welcome, master.'

I climbed onto the animal's back while he held her head for me. As he did so a thought occurred to me:

'You've been here a long time, haven't you old friend?'

'Nigh on sixty years, master. I grew my first beard here.'

'Then you must have been here when the green children were discovered. What can you remember about them?'

He seemed reluctant to say anything. But I pressed him:

'We are old friends aren't we, Oswald? You've known me all my life. You also know that Abbot Samson has asked me to investigate the children. It is possible someone's life may be at stake. Anything you can tell me about the children will be useful, anything at all.'

He paused reluctantly. 'There was an incident. It was shortly after the children first came up here. In the middle of the night your father roused me and a few of the other servants and ordered us to go with him to Wykes Manor.'

'The de Calne residence? What sort of incident?'

'There was a fire. Sir Richard was away at the time. It was one of the Wykes servants came to fetch your father.'

'It must have been a serious fire if they had to come two miles to fetch help.'

He shook his head. 'It wasn't the fire that was the problem. The Wykes servants had that out before we got there.'

'So why were you needed?'

He paused again. 'You have to understand, master, I was just a stable groom at the time, not much more than a boy myself. I didn't really know what was going on.'

'As I said, any information.'

'It was the children. It seemed they had escaped.'

'*Escaped?* But they weren't prisoners, were they?'

'It was your father's word, master, not mine. It appeared they had burned down their door and got into the piggery.'

This was sounding more and more bizarre. 'I'm not sure I'm following this. The children got into the piggery. To do what precisely?'

He shrugged. 'Torture the poor creatures. At least, that's how it looked to me. They had done their work well. The animals were all but butchered though some were still alive. It was carnage. Most could not be saved. The only thing to do was to put them out of their misery.'

I was shocked and confused. 'Are you sure about this? They were small children, weren't they, eight and ten? What were small children doing butchering pigs?'

'I truly don't know, master. But your father was very distressed about it.'

Yes, I could see that would have upset my father. He abhorred suffering even in dumb animals.

'I think what troubled him most,' Oswald went on, 'and me if I am honest, was the children's reactions. You have to understand, the scene in the piggery was horrific. It was like a butcher's shambles only much worse because many of the animals were still alive. There was blood and gore everywhere. The animals were screaming in their agony. It was enough to turn the hardiest stomach. But the children seemed … amused.'

'Amused? How so?'

'They were laughing. It was as though they were enjoying what they were doing - or if not enjoying it, at least they could see nothing wrong in it.'

'What did you make of it?'

'It wasn't for me to make anything of it, master. I was but a servant.'

'Well what was Sir Richard's reaction when he returned? Did he see it?'

'He was angry.'

'Understandably.'

'Not with the children. With your father - for interfering.'

I frowned. 'I thought you said he was summoned by Sir Richard's own servants. What was he meant to do, ignore them?'

'That's what we servants thought. But Sir Richard was not to be placated. He accused your father of meddling when all he was doing was alleviating suffering. It left a rift between our two houses. For years afterwards whenever our servants met they would fight.'

'That's disgraceful. I hope you didn't get involved.'

'It was a matter of honour, master. Our house against theirs.'

A matter of honour. Still, it might explain why I was so rarely allowed to go to Bardwell as a child.

'And you are sure about all this? It was a long time ago.'

'It is as clear in my mind as though it were yesterday. You don't easily forget something like that.'

No, I supposed not.

'Well thank you Oswald. That's very helpful.' I started to turn Erigone's head.

'Master, may I ask, are you now going to Essex?'

'I am, but not directly. I have to go to Bury first. There are one or two things I want to pick up at the abbey. Don't worry, you can tell your mistress I shall be taking the Sudbury road later.'

'She will be gratified, master. Master?'

'Yes?

'She does often speak of you, you know?'

'Oh, I'm sure of it - with disdain.'

'With the love of a mother for her son.'

There, she'd done it again. I took one last look up at the window to the solar with its flickering candlelight. No face at the window but I sensed her presence.

I sighed. 'Look after her for me won't you, Oswald?'

'With my life, master.'

Chapter Four
INTO ENEMY TERRITORY

Having reached the ripe old age of forty-seven years and four months – two-thirds of the way to my allotted three-score-and-ten - I like to think I have seen enough of the world not to be easily shocked by what goes on in it. But I have to admit Oswald's account of the piggery incident left me shaken. I couldn't get the image out of my head of those half-butchered creatures writhing in agony while two young children looked blithely on with no apparent sense of the horror of what they had done. It made me wonder again about their origin. What sort of country is it where children are permitted to laugh at the senseless torture of God's innocent creatures? I could only assume it must be some far-off dystopia where the civilized tenets of our Christian ethics had not yet penetrated. But where could that land be? And how did these children come to be in a field in the middle of the Suffolk countryside knowing no English and without anyone noticing? It defied explanation.

The more I learned about these children the deeper the mystery became. Could anybody – possibly this Abbot Ralph – shed any new light on the matter, I wondered? Whether or not he could help solve the other mystery about the anonymous woman messenger and her forewarning of a murder was another question. I couldn't for the life of me see how the two were connected. But Samson must have thought they were or else why would he have told me about them? It was a pity I didn't get him to explain himself a little better when we spoke. I resolved to try and get to see him again once I'd returned from Coggeshall. Maybe by then I'd be a little wiser.

So preoccupied was I with these thoughts that I hardly noticed the passage of time and before I knew it I was back in Bury. I didn't intend staying, just long enough to check on my laboratorium to make sure nothing was amiss and to furnish myself with a few provisions and a little money for my journey south.

I confess I was somewhat nervous about leaving for too long. I'd just recently acquired a new assistant – my third since Gilbert left to take up the position as sub-sacrist at Eye priory. I was sorry to lose Gilbert but not not entirely surprised to see him go. He wasn't really cut out for the medical profession. Too much blood and gore for his sensitive stomach. This new lad by contrast, Nathan, seems to relish the work – a little too enthusiastically if truth were known. In the space of two months he had turned my quiet laboratorium into a hothouse of activity with all sorts of exotic brews and potions. Some mornings I dreaded entering the place for fear of what I might find. This day was no exception. He had evidently taken my temporary absence as an opportunity to try out some of his more adventurous concoctions. There was certainly something very suspicious bubbling away in the bowl above my little stove.

'What's this?' I said peering warily into the pot.

'I call it Willow-wort, master.'

'I take it from that you mean it's your own invention?'

'Not mine. It's from an Arabic friend of mine. But I'm afraid his name for it is unpronounceable. You'd never get your tongue round it.'

'My dear boy,' I smiled benignly. 'I'll have you know I have step-brother who is himself half-Arabic and an apothecary to boot. I assure you there's nothing you can tell me about Arab medicine I don't already know.'

'An Arab as a your brother, master? How can that be?'

This wasn't the time for long explanations. 'Never mind. Just tell me the name.'

He enunciated the word. Twice. It began with "*Al*" but that's all I can tell you.

'Actually it's not my friend's either. He got the formula from Hippocrates - he's the father of modern medicine.'

'I know who Hippocrates was, Nathan.'

'Of course you do, master. Sorry. It's a distillation of the bark of the willow tree hence my name for it: Willow-wort. Here's some I made earlier.'

He handed me a small phial of milk-white liquid which I sniffed cautiously. It didn't seem to have an odour.

'What does it do?'

'Pain relief mostly. It's particularly good for headaches.'

Now it was my turn to demonstrate my superior knowledge. I shook my head disdainfully:

'Oh no. No no no. No no no no. No no no no no no no no.'

'No master?'

'No Nathan. Walnut is the correct herb for ailments of the head, not willow - every first year medical student knows that. Have you never heard of the doctrine of the signatures?'

I smiled with gratitude at the lad's blank stare and proceeded to enlighten him:

'It was Galen of Pergamon – who, incidentally, was the real father of modern medicine – who first propounded the theory. Let me explain: among all the plants of the earth God has hidden the correct antidote to all mankind's afflictions. They are revealed by their correspondence to those parts of the body they most closely resemble. Liverwort, for instance, is so-named because its leaves are shaped like a liver. Spleenwort for the spleen; Eyebright for the eye; Maidenhair Fern for…' I looked at his young, curious face. 'Yes well, never mind about that one. It is for us practitioners of the medical arts to seek out these signatures and apply them to the appropriate parts of the body – that is the challenge God has set us and for which our training prepares us. In the case of the walnut the correspondence could hardly be clearer. The hard outer shell mimicking the skull which in turn encompasses the soft fleshy kernel beneath which is furrowed and divided into two equal hemispheres exactly like the brain. Few herbs are as perfectly ordained as the walnut is for malefactions of the head – and that, my boy, includes headaches.'

'I thought that theory had been discredited, master.'

I stared at the boy in astonishment. 'Discredited? A theory of master Galen's? My dear child, wherever do you get such ideas?'

'From books, master.'

I smiled at him kindly. 'If Master Galen said something you can be pretty sure it is correct. This,' I held up the phial of white liquid between finger and thumb, 'is fantasy.' I offered it back to him.

'Keep it. You never know, it might come in handy. It can do no harm.'

Nor any good either. But I could tell the boy would be disappointed if I didn't take it and I didn't want to dampen his enthusiasm too early in our relationship. I shrugged and put the phial into my belt pouch, not that I thought I'd ever use it.

'Well now, how are you getting along? Anything happened in my absence?'

'Father prior was looking for you.'

'Prior Herbert is always looking for me. He thinks that with the abbot out of circulation it's his place to organize the convent. And he's right of course,' I added quickly – it wouldn't do to show disunity among the senior staff. 'How is the abbot, by the way? Any improvement?'

'Not that I'm aware, master. I'm not permitted near him.'

Was there any wonder with crazy concoctions like this Willow-wort? He probably thinks the boy's a sorcerer. I brought him up to date with what had transpired at Ixworth Hall ending with Oswald's tale about the children and the pigs.

'That sounds oddly familiar,' he said when I'd finished.

I looked at him in surprise. 'Familiar? How so? Was your father a butcher, perchance?'

'No. Mathematician. But Galen used to work with pigs. They were his subject of choice. In his lectures he used to cut the spinal cord of the living animal in order to paralyse them. Back legs first and then the front. By the end of the lesson the animals were totally immobile. It was quite a show by all accounts.'

I frowned at this gross defamation of my medical hero. 'Why would the great man do such a thing?'

The boy shrugged. 'To demonstrate the connection between the spine and the extremities, one presumes.'

'Indeed. Well I don't think vivisection was what these children were about. In their case it was sheer wickedness.'

The bell for sext started to ring at the church.

'Dear God, is that the time? You keeping me chatting with your nonsense, Nathan, I'd lost all track. I must go. I have to be in Sudbury before nightfall.'

'Would you like me to come with you, master?'

'Certainly not. You've enough to do here with all this impedimenta,' I said frowning at the steaming pots. 'Just try not to blow the place up while I'm away. And clean away your mess when you've finished, there's a good chap. It smells like a Baghdad souk in here.'

I left feeling more worried than when I'd arrived. It was worse that I thought. I honestly feared I might come back in a few days to find my beloved laboratorium gone up in smoke. Keen or not, I couldn't see Nathan remaining with me once I returned. I should have to find some way of letting him go gently. But I didn't have time to think about that now. I refreshed my water-bottle, retrieved Erigone from the stable and set off again out of the south gate of the town.

The rain that had begun earlier was falling steadily now. What weather we were having. It was turning into one of the wettest Decembers in living memory. The road, if you could still call it such, was becoming a quagmire. Poor Erigone. Few creatures on God's earth look quite so miserable as a sopping wet mule. But at least I had Oswald's oiled cloak to cover us both. We kept our heads down and persevered through the deluge as the day darkened and disappeared beneath a leaden sky. Just as I was beginning to think we might have to continue into the night I saw the first smoke of Melford village in the distance. I murmured a brief prayer of thanks to Saint Christopher for our deliverance and gently pulled Erigone's ear.

'Well done, old girl. We'll soon have you in a nice warm stable with a pocket of steaming oats to fill your belly.'

I found the entrance to the manor-house and turned Erigone's head in through the gate to amble the last hundred yards up the drive.

Kentwell Hall lies at the northern edge of the village of Melford - sometimes known as *Long* Melford on account of its ... well its *length* - in the shadow of Holy Trinity Church which sat on top of the hill. "Hall" is a somewhat grandiose title for what was really little more than a large and rather dilapidated farmhouse. Clearly not much had been done to the place in some years. Plaster was cracking, bits of masonry were falling off. It wasn't an insubstantial house and must have been impressive at one time. I wondered how it came to such a sorry state.

Sir Gilbert told me his story over a light supper of cheese and bread before a blazing fire. It seems the Kentwells had once been a prosperous local family, lords of an extensive manor that had descended from a Norman knight who had fought alongside the Conqueror. But over the generations the Kentwells had steadily fallen on harder times. They had always been a large family with many children – in itself a blessing, of course. But they were nearly all boys, generation after generation of sons all of whom needed to be accommodated by an ever-fractioning estate (a problem my family never suffered from). The estate steadily fragmented until all that was left now was the demesne – the land immediately around the house.

The present brood of Kentwell children was five strong though with more girls than usual: the oldest, a girl of about eleven years, was followed by another aged nine and then three boys in quick succession, five, four and three. Their mother, Lady Agatha Kentwell, must have spent most of the past decade in confinement and indeed was pregnant again. With three sons to accommodate and on past performance another on the way, I could see Kentwell manor disappearing altogether.

Despite their straitened condition the Kentwells were a jolly lot and could hardly have been more welcoming to me. I found a generous response to my mother's letter of introduction. They happily gave me a bed for the night together with a brass ewer of hot water to wash my hands and feet and some fresh linen.

The Kentwell children are a delight and such a refreshing relief after the horror stories of the Woolpit children. Once they learned I was a physician there was no end to the number of the ailments they invented the nature of which I had to guess by way of a mime-game to test my skills. I did my best to repay my debt of board by joining in and recommending suitable palliatives for them all. It was a good game and an enjoyable distraction from those awful events that had brought me here and restored my faith in the benignity of a good solid Christian household with so many happy children in it. I couldn't imagine any of these five torturing defenceless pigs. I left the next morning rested and refreshed, the children having completely emptied my satchel of herbs and still practising their bandages made from the torn-up remnants of old bed-sheets.

And so to Coggeshall. The second half of my journey was less inviting than the first since it took me into far more dangerous territory. Essex was a county I knew little about and largely avoided for one very good reason: its earl was Geoffrey Fitz Peter, Chief Justiciar of England and nephew of the dread Geoffrey de Saye, the fiend I mentioned earlier whose exile I had secured a decade earlier for murdering the fuller's son in Bury town. And that wasn't the end of it for both these two Geoffreys were members of the Mandeville clan whose most notorious member had been yet another Geoffrey: de Mandeville, the so-called *Scourge of the Fens*. My family had an ancient association with that gentleman too.

During the civil wars known as the Anarchy, Geoffrey de Mandeville, a soldier of fortune whose loyalty could be bought by the highest bidder, switched sides once too often and himself became a hunted man. He went into hiding in the fens of Cambridgeshire where he terrorized the local people committing murder, rape and pillage at will and was only stopped when killed himself whilst attacking Burwell Castle just outside Cambridge. It happened that the bolt that killed him was fired by my father who had been one of the castle's defenders at the time. This was the origin of the blood feud between the de Saye family and my own and for which Geoffrey de Saye has sworn revenge. Fortunately the present earl only married into the family and doesn't hold me personally responsible for my father's actions. But as the county's leading family the Mandevilles must surely claim the loyalty of all Essex's religious houses, the priory of Coggeshall included. Given all this, I couldn't help wondering what sort of reception I might get from its abbot.

Well, I would soon find out for once across the River Colne I was in Essex proper and it was but a gentle ambulation down through Coggeshall town to the priory beyond. I approached with trepidation and as it turned out was right to do so for I could hardly guess what was waiting for me when I got there.

Chapter Five
ABBOT RALPH

Coggeshall Priory is a comparatively new foundation dating back just seventy years to the time of King Stephen when his wife, Matilda (not to be confused with the Empress of the same name), relocated a dozen monks here from Sauvigny in Normandy. At that time the Sauvignacs were black-robed Benedictines like myself. It was only later that they accepted the stewardship of the Cistercian Order and adopted their signature white robe.

Abbot Ralph was so attired and nothing like I had anticipated. With his reputation as a man of letters, I imagined an aesthetic soul, unworldly and given to much sighing. Nothing could have been further from the truth. What I saw sitting before me as I was ushered into his study beside the banks of the River Blackwater was a robust, stocky man, a little older than myself, looking more like a dockside brawler than a diarist. The most striking thing about him was a prominent indentation in the middle of his tonsured pate which drew the eye immediately and wouldn't let it go.

'An injury sustained during the siege of Jerusalem,' he explained fingering it with a curious mix of humility and pride.

'I'm sorry father, I didn't mean to stare.'

'That's all right, everybody does it. I was there when the Holy City fell to the forces of Saladin and his Saracens. Mind you, I took a few of the heathen down myself before I was captured,' he added with a satisfied curl of his lip.

'And yet you evidently survived the encounter.'

He nodded. 'On Saladin's personal orders. Whatever else is said about him, he was a man of honour. He released all his prisoners just as he said he would – those of us who could pay, naturally.'

'I had no idea you led such a colourful life, father. My mother never mentioned it.'

'It was a long time ago,' he said waving me to a seat. 'How is your mother? Well, I trust?'

'Remarkably so considering her age.'

'Like the old Queen Eleanor, she will go on for ever.'

I sincerely hoped not.

'She sends her good wishes – and her, erm, prayers.'

He smiled wryly. 'I doubt that. But thank you for the thought. And my brother Samson? How does he?'

'Alas, not so well. I fear he may be on the final page of his life's story.'

'It will be an interesting one if it is I don't doubt. But we will remember him in our prayers - as we will your mother.'

'Forgive me father, but I'm intrigued that you know my mother so well given her … unorthodox … views on religion.'

'We all come to God in our own way and in our own time, my son. And,' he added obliquely, 'we have other interests that concern us both. In these uncertain times we must find our allies where we can.'

'Allies - against the king, you mean?'

He raised an amused eyebrow. 'You're very direct, Brother Walter. Are you one of King John's spies?'

'With a mother like mine? I should say not. She'd have had me throttled by now. But you are very candid yourself, father. Is that not dangerous?'

'I make no secret of my views, Brother Walter, and care little who knows them. John can do as he likes to my mortal body it won't stop me saying what I think. It is my duty to speak out against a tyrant. And for your information John is not the king - at least, not the true king. England's rightful king is dead - murdered, most probably, by John's own hand.'

'I take it by that you mean his nephew, the prince Arthur. But that's just rumour, surely?'

'Is it? Arthur hasn't been seen alive for nine years.'

'That's hardly surprising. He led a revolt against the government, and probably would again given the chance.'

'And with God's grace the next one he might even win.'

This was dangerous talk indeed. John had only become king by defeating his brother Geoffrey's son Arthur in battle. At the time John seemed the least bad option – after all, nobody wanted a twelve-year-old boy on the throne. But to many it seemed they had backed the wrong horse. There had been stirrings of disquiet ever since John lost Normandy to King Philip of France, and now there was the interdict. Since then things seemed to be going from bad to worse. I knew, for instance, that earlier in the summer the papal legate had absolved all John's subjects from their oaths of allegiance effectively giving papal sanction to open rebellion. The barons were already jumpy. Talk like this could send them over the edge.

'You surely wouldn't welcome insurrection, father?' I said carefully. 'Possibly a return to civil war? You've seen war, as have I. It's not something to be welcomed. And no king lives for ever. Wait long enough and there will be another.'

'By then it may be too late. Look around you, brother. Churches closed, the dead lying unburied in the streets. And all because of John's refusal to accept the pope's candidate for archbishop of Canterbury.' He snorted his contempt. 'Did you know that John has even threatened to hang cardinal Langton if he sets foot in England again? The archbishop, for heaven's sake, head of the church in England threatened with execution by the king who is sworn to protect him.'

'Surely it's more complicated than that. It's a struggle over who governs England – the church or the crown.'

'A struggle the church must win.' He tapped a resolute fingernail on the desk-top to emphasise the point. 'It's not just the interdict. In a few short years John has managed to lose half the empire his father and his brother took decades to build. And do you wonder? He's an interloper. He isn't fit to be king. And he bathes too much - a sure sign of vanity and moral turpitude,' he added wrinkling his nose with distaste.

'Oh, that's a bit harsh, isn't it father?'

'You wouldn't say that if you'd met him.'

'As a matter of fact I have.'

'Then you'll know the sort of man he is. Not like his brother. Now Richard was a real man, a true warrior of God. As soon as he heard Jerusalem had fallen he moved heaven and earth to recover it.'

'And nearly bankrupted the nation in the process.'

'How can you compare silver coin to the priceless treasures of the holy places? They are beyond the avarice of man.'

I could see there was no point arguing. He was as firmly set in his views as my mother was in hers. But the effort of expressing them had evidently tired him. He was repeatedly fingering that indentation on his scalp.

'Are you all right, father? Can I get you some water?'

'It's nothing. I get these headaches, that's all. Mine are like those of Hildegard of Bingen. That holy lady saw visions of the Virgin Mother.' He gave a sick laugh. 'Would I were so fortunate. I see only flashing lights and have to lie in a darkened room until they subside.'

'Have you sought cures?'

'I've scoured Christendom. Nothing works. Nor will it. My suffering is God's punishment and nothing man can devise will o'ercome that.'

'Punishment for what?'

'For not doing enough to prevent the loss of the Holy City, of course. It was just after the fall that the headaches started.'

'You don't think your injury might have something to do with it?'

'It probably didn't help. But no, this pain is divinely inspired, of that I've no doubt.'

I thought of prescribing a palliative of my own but the Kentwell children had emptied my entire satchel of herbs and I had nothing left. But then I remembered Nathan's potion. It probably wouldn't do any good but it couldn't do any harm either.

'You could try this,' I said fishing the phial from of my belt-pouch.

'What is it?'

'Oh, just something I've been experimenting with. I call it Willow-wort. I can't guarantee it will cure you but it may help.'

Ralph eyed the white liquid sceptically. 'Your mother writes that you are a doctor. Quite a good one it seems. No doubt a loving mother's hyperbole,' he smiled.

No doubt.

'I'll try it later.' He put the phial to one side before returning to the letter again: 'Lady Isabel asks that I aid you in your quest.' He looked up. 'What quest would that be?'

I briefly outlined the story of the green children.

'That's more or less the truth of it,' he agreed when I'd finished.

'You know the story?'

'I wrote it - along with many such tales. You'll find it all laid out in my chronicle.' He laid his hand lovingly on a large tome that lay on the desk beside him. 'You may borrow it while you're here if you wish.'

'Thank you, father. I shall be honoured. And you believe these stories to be true?'

'I neither believe nor disbelieve. I merely record.' He looked at me curiously. 'May I ask, what is your interest in the case?'

I hedged not wanting to disclose too much. 'It's complicated. It was abbot Samson who asked me to look into it.'

'I see. Well, ask away. I'll tell you what I can.'

'First of all, do you have any idea where the children came from? I imagine it must have been some distant, distinctly *un*-Christian land.'

'Why do you say that?'

'Their ignorance of any language known to the church. And then there's their colour – green.'

He frowned. 'There is always an element of exaggeration in these cases. It is so easy to invent in order to fill gaps in the narrative. That's why it's so important to have these things written down, to make a definitive version. Even then mistakes can be made.'

'Do you think that is what happened with regard to their colour? That seems the least likely aspect of the tale, wouldn't you say? My mother maintains the girl wasn't green at all but quite a normal colour.'

'I didn't have her good fortune to know the children personally so I cannot say.'

'But you must have speculated. Where do you think they came from?'

He sighed. 'Some believed they were spirits unable to get back to the nether world. Others said they were changelings, abandoned by their parents. Some said simply that they fell from the sky.' He chuckled. 'I shouldn't put too much credibility to these tales. They are just stories.'

'You seem to be casting doubt on your own authenticity.'

'There are many such tales around the world. I have confined my writings to these islands. But there are other lands with far stranger creatures in them.'

'Such as?'

'The *Sciapods* for one, a race of beings who purportedly live in the southern continent of *Terra Australis*. They are reputed to shield themselves from the midday sun by lying beneath their giant feet. Personally I doubt that. With such big feet, how would they get about - hop?' He chortled at the absurdity of the notion. 'Then there are the dog-headed *Cynocephales* of Bohemia; and not forgetting the *Blemmyae* of India who have no heads at all but wear their faces in their chests. In reality I doubt if any of these creatures actually exist.'

'Nevertheless, my mother insists she met the green children – the girl at any rate. And there is other corroborating evidence,' I said remembering Oswald's story. 'If you didn't meet them personally how did you come across the story?'

'From their guardian, Sir Richard de Calne.'

That name again.

'I've heard much about that gentleman. Actually that was the other intriguing aspect to the story I wanted to ask you about. Why do you think the children were taken to him?'

Ralph shrugged. 'They had to go somewhere. The man who discovered them -'

'A shepherd?'

'Yes - couldn't look after them. It would be natural for him to take them to the local lord.'

'Not that local, surely. Woolpit is seven miles from Wykes. Other houses were closer. My father's at Ixworth for one.'

Ralph smiled kindly. 'No disrespect to your father, Brother Walter, but I would have been surprised if they'd have gone anywhere else other than Wykes. Sir Richard was a remarkable man. An exceptional man. One of the most learned men I've ever had the privilege to meet.'

'The phrase I heard was that every day was a school day to him.'

'Really? I've never heard that one but it is a very apt description of the man. Sir Richard was one of those extraordinary men who was interested in everything. His knowledge on all manner of things was boundless. I imagine the shepherd knew this and would naturally have thought of Sir Richard first. I'm sure I'd have done the same.'

'How did you come to meet him, as a matter of interest? Coggeshall is a long way from Bardwell.'

A broad smile spread across the abbot's face. 'Ah now, that is another tale altogether. Our greatest good fortune. Come,' he said rising from his desk. 'Allow me to show you.'

He led the way out of his study, across the yard and into the main body of the convent. Compared with Bury the priory was a very modest affair, more like a large farm than an abbey, which made me wonder how they supported themselves. I didn't need to ask. Father Ralph was only too pleased to tell me:

'As you can see, Saint Mary's is tiny compared with a great abbey like Saint Edmund. We don't have your advantage of a resident saint to attract pilgrims so we have to rely on our own ingenuity. Like our brother Cistercians in the north we farm sheep and are beginning to make a name for ourselves in cloth-making. But it has been a long hard struggle. That is until we learned the art of brick-making.'

At this I was truly surprised. 'Bricks? Are you serious?'

'Never more so.' He chuckled with glee. 'I see I've surprised you. Good. Allow me to astound you further. Look around you. Have you noticed how many of our cloistral buildings here are faced with this miraculous material?'

I hadn't noticed, but now when I came to look – yes, I could see many of the buildings had a pinkish hue amid the flint and timber. It reminded me of the roofs I'd seen in my student days in southern France.

'But I thought the art of brick-making was lost with the Romans.'

'So it was. And it was from the many former Roman buildings in Colchester that most of our brick here at the priory originated. But that source is at last beginning to dry up. We needed something to replace it and this is where Sir Richard comes in for it was through his genius that we perfected our own technique.'

'Sir Richard was a brick-maker?'

'Among his many other skills. Without exaggerating I think it is true to say he saved our priory. Without brick-making we would likely have had to close. As it is our industry has thrived and Coggeshall brick is now to be seen all over the country. Who knows, one day it may even adorn the roofs of Bury abbey.'

'I have a feeling it already does,' I said remembering Samson's twin towers.

'Eventually we aim to roof the whole of East Anglia. And then, who knows? The world?' he chuckled.

'And now you're going to share your secret with me?'

'I couldn't even if I wanted to. Brother Alberic is the man in charge of the brick yard. He will explain all - though not quite all, I trust.'

We had stopped in the cloister where an elderly monk was waiting to greet us - or rather, not a monk. He was dressed in the habit of a monk but somewhat differently from that of abbot Ralph. To begin with his robes were not white but brown.

I have to admit I knew very little about the Cistercians there being so few of their houses in the south of England. They tend to be dispersed in the remoter fastnesses of the north where they can practice their particularly austere version of the Rule in splendid isolation. And good luck to them. I am quite happy with our soft regime of singing eight offices per day, rising at two-thirty in the morning, no warmth anywhere in the convent even in the depths of winter - and of course poverty, ever grinding poverty. But one of the ways I do know the Cistercians differ from us so-called black monks is that they do not approve of employing servants. They prefer to do all the work of the monastery themselves be it in the scriptorium or digging latrines. It is part of their drive to return to a simpler, more austere form of worshipping God. But since only the literate can become fully professed monks, over time this has led to a division between the choir monks and this second rank of lay-brothers - or *conversi* as they are called - who do the more menial tasks. Brother Alberic, as evidenced by his brown robe, was one of these.

'Well,' said Abbot Ralph having introduced us, 'I will leave you in Brother Alberic's capable hands. Doubtless I will see you later at vespers.' With that he gave one final bow before turning and returning smartly to his lodge.

'Father Abbot will be retiring for an hour,' explained Alberic watching him go. 'He does this most afternoons.'

'His old war wound,' I nodded. 'Yes, he was telling me about it. Does it give him much trouble?'

'More than he will admit. Well now brother,' he smiled. 'If you'd like to follow me.'

'Er, this really isn't necessary, Brother Alberic,' I said holding back. 'I haven't come for a tour. I have other matters to occupy my time.'

'Oh you must. Father Abbot will be greatly offended if you refuse. All our guests visit the brickyard. It's expected. You have to understand he is justly proud of what we have achieved here.'

I grimaced painfully.

He chuckled. 'Don't worry. I'll keep it as brief as possible.'

Had I known what I was letting myself in for I might have feigned a headache too. The brickyard wasn't close by. It wasn't even within the priory walls but half a mile's distance at the top end of town. And what a place it was! Never had I seen such a hive of activity. There were men everywhere clad in the same brown robes as Alberic all wearing aprons and sleeves rolled to the elbow and robes tucked up into their belts. Some were digging clay from the banks of the nearby stream, others were carting the material to another part of the site where stones and other detritus was being removed. There were kilns for smelting, forges for metal-working, carpenters' workshops, stables, whole trees being dragged by chains pulled by oxen while others were being turned into logs stacked into great piles two men high. Everywhere was activity, smoke, noise, heat and dust. My bewilderment must have registered on my face.

'Quite something, isn't it?' Alberic chuckled. 'But this is just the start.'

He led the way to a relatively quiet corner of the site where a vast covered stable stood. This was evidently where the skilled work of actual brick-making took place. Men on rows of benches shaped clay into moulds. The craftsmen were evidently highly practised in their art for their hands moved with precision and speed producing brick after brick, each one a perfect copy. They made it look easy. They made it look fun.

'Would you like to try?' Alberic asked, eyeing me carefully.

'Oh I don't know,' I hesitated. 'Could I?'

He gestured to one of the monks who stepped aside while I took his place at the bench. At first all went well. It was, after all, just a case of mixing the clay with a little water, slapping a chunk of it into the wooden frame and sheering off the excess with a knife. Rather like making pastry really. It was easy, but still I took my time to perfect my masterpiece. But when it came to remove it from its casing that's when I discovered my mistake. The whole thing fell apart in a sad gloop on the bench, much to the amusement of the men around me.

'Don't worry,' smiled Alberic. 'It happens to everyone. Getting the mixture right is part of the art.'

'Not as easy as it looks,' I frowned yielding my place again to the young man whose abilities just went up in my estimation. But looking around I could see that bricks weren't the only things they made. There were tiles for roofs, tiles for floors, and one item I was particularly intrigued to ask about. It seemed to be some kind of tube.

'Drains,' answered Alberic to my question. 'That's the advantage of brick over stone, it can be moulded into any shape you wish. You will find the entire priory sits upon a latticework of pipes like this. And not just the domestic buildings. The fields here about also.'

'Fields with drains?' I asked, astonished. 'To what purpose?

'Turning swamp into pasture, brother. Where ducks once gambled, sheep now graze.'

I couldn't fault Alberic's enthusiasm. He was clearly proud of the entire operation, and rightly so. After nearly a thousand years to have re-invented a process last mastered by the Romans was quite an achievement. And all down to the remarkable Richard de Calne, it seemed.

I followed Alberic up a little slope to an isolated spot well away from the rest of the work. Here was an area of relative calm and quiet leaving the noise and bustle down below. Here the real magic was done. I saw before me a huge earth mound perhaps eight feet wide by sixteen long. The embankment formed a pit that was gradually being filled with lines of roofing tiles each being placed with utmost precision. It looked a very delicate operation.

'The kiln,' Alberic whispered proudly. 'We fire four thousand at a time. It is an operation that takes all night, sometimes longer. The skill comes in judging the balance between moisture and heat. Too hot and the tiles explode. Too wet and they crumble.'

'I'm impressed with your knowledge, brother.'

'Not mine, brother. Leon's.'

'Leon?'

Suddenly one of the figures inside the kiln stood upright. 'Someone call my name?'

This was with a very strange-looking fellow indeed. Not a monk - that was evident from his workman's clothes. And given the Cistercians' disdain for them, not a servant either. So what was he? A skilled craftsman clearly. But there was something else about this Leon that struck me as odd. And then I had it. The wide hips, the narrow shoulders. Leon wasn't a man at all, but a woman.

Chapter Six
LEON

'Brother, may I present to you our boon and our blessing, our jewel and our joy, our manna, our miracle, our -'

'Shut up, Alberic.' Leon removed one of her gloves and extended her hand to me. 'Leon,' she said curtly.

'Er, Walter de Ixworth,' I said taking the proffered hand and noting with dismay as I did so how rough it felt.

Of course, there is nothing unusual about women doing heavy work - in the fields, say, or the laundries. But this was different. Tiling was unquestionably men's work. Yet here was this woman not only toiling like a man but apparently overseeing dozens of other men doing the same thing. And looking like a man in the process.

I'm a little old-fashioned when it comes to the fairer sex. I prefer them to be as God created them: decorative yet capable, desirable yet unobtainable. To my mind the troubadours got it right. The poetry of courtly love with ladies swooning before the gallant knight was the ideal. But from the look of this Leon she was anything but a damsel in distress. I could imagine her happily spending the night swilling ale and swapping tales with the rudest gong scourer. Even her name was masculine. All of which might have been easier to accept had she been a gorgon, but beneath the incrustations of brick-dust and dirt and the tousled hair she was a veritable Venus. Beauty and competence. It was a combination I found altogether more disconcerting.

'You're in charge of all this?' I asked looking around us.

She was immediately defensive. 'You sound surprised.'

'Well you have to admit it's a little unusual. I mean: a woman doing men's work.'

'And what exactly is men's work?'

'Well this,' I said gesturing to the surroundings.

'Monks do women's work, don't they? They cook, clean, sew. Or do you starve at your abbey and let your clothes fall to rags?'

'That's hardly the same thing. A man can do women's work – if he has to. But not the other way round. Women simply don't have the physical strength.' That, I was confident, sealed the argument.

Leon gave me a benign smile. 'Tell me brother, do you know the story of Christ's nails?'

'Christ's nails...?' I said cautiously.

She nodded. 'It's said that when the soldiers wanted to fix Christ to the Cross they could find no blacksmith willing to forge the nails so the blacksmith's wife stepped forward and volunteered to make them in his stead. You'd agree that iron forging is heavy manual work?'

'Oh but that's just a myth,' I dismissed. 'I've heard the same tale told of Egyptians. Besides, the blacksmith's wife was an old crone and you're a -'

She cocked an eyebrow. 'I'm a what, brother?'

64

I could feel my face flush hot.

'I-I simply meant that you don't look like a tiler.'

'You've met many tilers, have you brother?'

'Well clearly not since you evidently have the monopoly,' I said growing annoyed.

'We do indeed. And so it will remain as long as I'm in charge.'

Around me I heard a murmur of agreement. By now the men had stopped work and gathered around us to enjoy the entertainment of a monk being trounced by their leader. I could feel my confusion spreading from my forehead to my throat to my neck, and did not doubt everyone else saw it, too.

Leon smiled back at me with smug satisfaction, much to my irritation. Fortunately the priory bell started ringing in the distance summoning the convent to vespers.

'We should go, brother,' said Alberic touching my elbow lightly.

'Pity,' I said. 'I should have liked to stay to see more.'

'You won't miss much,' Leon said. 'We're only going to seal the chamber now. But we'll be firing it later tonight. Come back then and join us if you wish. We can always use an extra pair of hands.'

'I might just do that,' I said.

'The lady seems to have cast a spell on you, brother,' Alberic said as we hurried back down through the town.

'Mistress Leon is clearly very good at what she does,' I said over my shoulder. 'That is always something to be admired especially in one so young and -'

'Lovely?'

'I was going to say *experienced*.'

'Of course you were, brother,' he chuckled. 'But I'm afraid you're wasting your time there.'

'I'm sure I don't know what you mean.'

'Oh come, brother, anyone could see the effect she had on you. I don't blame you. Leon is a fine-looking young woman.'

I frowned annoyance. 'I assure you, brother, my interest in the lady is purely intellectual. One simply doesn't expect a woman - *any* woman - to be doing that sort of work.'

'You expect a dutiful wife in the family home keeping house for her husband with a clutch of children hanging on her apron?'

'Something like that I suppose, yes.'

'Not in Leon's case. She's not interested in anything like that – family, husband. She's not interested in men at all in that way.'

I stopped abruptly. 'Meaning what exactly?'

'Do I need to spell it out? You saw for yourself: Leon dresses like a man. She does a man's job. She even prefers a man's name. But take it from me, she has no desire in *having* a man.'

I admit I was shocked by his words. I'd heard of such things between men - we monks are always being accused of it. But between women? How? What would they do? And in any case, certainly not Leon. She was too feminine. Not in the accepted sense, perhaps, of perfumes and skirts. But I'd felt a spark between us back there at the kiln, I was certain of it. If she was in any other way inclined there would have been nothing there.

Why would Brother Alberic tell me such a monstrous lie? It had to be jealousy. Yes, I decided, that must be it. Leon got the job that he must surely have coveted for himself. Some men cannot stomach the thought of being bettered by another, and certainly not by a woman.

'I'm sure you're wrong about Leon,' I told him firmly. 'And even if you're right, Mistress Leon's predilections are of no interest to me. None whatsoever.'

He shrugged. 'I only tell you these things to prevent you making a fool of yourself, brother.'

'No you're not. You're trying to besmirch the lady's reputation, for what reason I can only guess at. Well put away your barbs, sir, for they have no effect on me. When I leave here tomorrow I shall quickly forget all about Coggeshall Abbey – and its staff. Now come along. Keep up or we shall be late for prayers.'

I quickened my step hoping to outpace him, but only managed to stumble my way down the hill tripping over my own feet as I went.

'Well?' beamed Abbot Ralph later at supper. 'How do you like our little manufactory?'

'Very impressive, father. I only wish we had something like it at Saint Edmund's.'

'Ah, but you have something far more valuable than a brick-works, brother. You have the holy king and martyr. Not everybody needs drains but we all need the intercession of the saints.'

'I was particularly impressed with your chief tiler.'

He nodded. 'Leonie is quite something, isn't she?'

'Leonie. Is that her real name?'

'She prefers Leon. She thinks it better to have a man's name in her position. I can't say I entirely approve, but it doesn't do to look a gift horse in the mouth.' He gave a knowing look.

'You must value her highly to allow her such latitude. Quite an achievement - for a woman.'

'Indeed so,' he agreed. 'But I shouldn't let her hear you say it. You're likely to get your head bitten off.'

I already had. In light of what Alberic told me I asked my next question with some trepidation:

'Is it usual for a woman to be so alone like that? Surely she has male guardian of some kind? A father, brother – husband?'

'No husband as far as I know. Although she did have a male protector – quite a celebrated one. Sir Richard de Calne – the man I mentioned earlier. If you remember it was he who helped us establish our manufactory. You could say he was the driving force.'

'Leon knew Sir Richard? She doesn't look old enough.'

'She was his ward. He trained her in the art of brick-making and taught her all she knows. You might say he moulded her to his design,' he added chuckling at his own wit.

'Rather unusual to choose a woman for such a role.'

'Leon is unusual in many ways. Her abilities surpassed everyone we had working here before. You asked earlier why I am so relaxed with her. Frankly, for fear of losing her. She's irreplaceable - a godsend, literally. You have to understand, brother, at the time the priory was struggling to survive. We had been experimenting with brick-making for some time but with only moderate success. Leon changed all that.'

'And these skills were bequeathed her by Sir Richard de Calne?'

'As I said before, he was an exceptional man. But he was also quite elderly by this stage. Brick-making is young man's work – or young *woman's* in this case. I tell you, what that girl can achieve with clay God Himself only surpassed when he created Adam,' he chuckled again. 'Leon is a true miracle worker. '

'I hope to see the miracle performed myself later this evening if you will give me leave, father.'

'With my blessing, my son. Witness the marvel and spread our fame across the world.'

Later, alone in my room, I laid Ralph's book of fantasy stories before me on the prie-dieu. It was clearly a treasured possession, hand-written no doubt by himself and bound in the finest calf leather. It was so precious I was surprised he allowed it out of his sight. But I suppose that's the paradox of being an author. A book is a beautiful object in its own right to be coddled and protected, but unless it's read it has no purpose. It is not the thing itself that has value but the thoughts of the writer contained within it. Even so, I had to take great care not to damage it in any way, and so with hesitant fingers I opened the book and began to read.

An hour later I closed it. To be truthful I found it hard going. Ralph was no Virgil. The chronicle was little more than notes written with as much poetry in it as a laundry list. God knows I have no pretensions where pen and parchment are concerned, but I had expected more of Ralph. Still, the book held a lot of interest for me with regards to the green children. In fact it contained several tales of wonder, all of them, as Ralph said set in England, and three from Suffolk.

The first was the one already familiar to me about the so-called Wild Man of Orford. I know the town of Orford well having visited there several times, so I was interested. It is an important port on the Suffolk coast with a splendid castle, fine church and well-stocked market. Ralph relates that one day some local fishermen cast their nets off the Orford coast and caught what they thought at first to be a big fish but which turned out to be a green man. The fishermen didn't know what to do with him so they took him to the castle where the constable promptly locked him up. Days passed and they could get no sense out of the man even under torture. Eventually they allowed him to swim in the estuary having first taken care to block the mouth of the river with nets to prevent him escaping. But the man was a better swimmer than they had anticipated and was easily able to dive under the nets and escape out to sea after which he was never seen again.

So much for the Wild Man of Orford. The second tale was not so much about a creature but a spirit called a Malekin. Unlike the Orford creature this one did speak and claimed to have been a child in a former life born in the Suffolk village of Lavenham. There it invaded the house of a local lord of the manor where it played pranks – mostly moving objects around.

Now, call me a cynic but it seemed obvious to me what these two creatures were. The first, the so-called Wild Man of Orford, was clearly some kind of sea creature that the fishermen had never seen before. My guess is that is was a seal. To give him his due, Ralph thought the same. As for the Malekin – well, anybody can put something down and forget where they left it. It doesn't mean a poltergeist moved it.

Now we come to the green children of Woolpit and I must say I was slightly disappointed with Ralph's account. His explanation of where the children came from was terse to the point of being useless. He suggested they might be from another land but left its location vague:

"...they came to a certain cavern, on entering which they heard a delightful sound of bells; ravished by whose sweetness, they went for a long time wandering on through the cavern, until they came to its mouth."

A colourful description but short on specifics. Where was this supposed cavern? Presumably somewhere near where the children were found in Woolpit village. But as far as I knew there were no caverns in this part of Suffolk, certainly none with bells. He then mentioned the boy dying but gave no indication of what killed him nor much of what happened to the girl afterwards. It was all tantalisingly frustrating. I wondered if I might learn more from Leon since she seemed to be one of the few people still alive who had any connection with Sir Richard de Calne. I decided I would go to the firing later that night and if I had a chance to quiz Leon on the matter. Not that I needed much persuading.

The light was already beginning to fade by the time I returned to the kiln site next to the little brook. At night it was a completely different place once all the work had stopped and the noise and activity died down. As darkness fell it was almost like religious ceremony with everyone speaking in reverential whispers - understandable really since this was the culmination of all the earlier work. And rather like the focal point of the mass it was now that the miraculous transfiguration took place - not from bread into the living body of Christ but from inanimate mud into living brick. And overseeing all was the high priestess of the ceremony: Leon.

By now the chamber was completely filled with bricks and tiles ready for firing and resembled a small untidy hillock. Fortunately the rain had kept off which I was told was the one thing that could ruin the whole venture. The covering the workers had placed over the contents of the kiln had by now been removed exposing the bricks to the elements, their nakedness shining in the moonlight like the skeleton of a large fish. Beneath the hillock was scooped out a firebox which the brothers, under close supervision from Leon, were stuffing with twigs and small logs. This, I presumed, was where the fire would be lit.

'Ah, there you are brother,' she beamed when she saw me. 'I didn't expect to see you.'

'No no,' I smiled. 'I said I'd be back and here I am. Where are we at?'

'Have you never built a camp fire before? That's what we're doing only a much bigger fire under the earth.'

I nodded. 'What can I do to help?'

'Collect more wood - and pray, brother.'

'I'm happy to do both, but pray for what?'

'That we get the temperature right. This is the crucial part of the process, to maintain a constant heat for the rest of the night. If not, weeks of hard work will have been wasted.'

'How can you tell if it is the right temperature?'

'That's where skill and experience comes in,' she grinned, 'and a good eye for colour.'

'I take your word for it.' She started to leave. 'By the way, I'd like also, if I may, to talk to you about another matter.'

'Oh? What matter would that be?'

'Green children.'

She stopped. 'What makes you think I know anything about that?'

'Your mentor, Sir Richard de Calne. I believe he took the children in when they were first discovered. You've clearly heard of them. Can we talk? I would very grateful.'

'Later perhaps, when we're less busy.'

'Of course. My apologies. I don't wish to interrupt the excellent work.'

I was glad I'd managed to secure an interview. As well as discovering some, hopefully, useful information about the green children it would give me the opportunity to gauge the sort of woman Leon really was – and nail Alberic's outrageous calumnies about her at the same time.

Pleased with myself, I joined with everyone else scouting for suitable kindling and larger pieces of fuel to stuff into the virginal mouth of the fire. When all was ready the *moment juste* arrived and Leon gave the signal for the tinder to be lit. There was a real sense of climax just as there is when the bells are rung and the Host is being raised in the priest's hands at the height of the mass. It was an exciting moment. The first flames sparked and the wood started to crackle into life, smoke billowed from under the kiln and quickly engulfed everyone in a thick blue haze. If all went well in a few hours' time we would have brick. More and more fuel was fed into the little opening as the temperature steadily rose. It was exhausting but exhilarating work.

Gradually as the darkness closed in and the torches were lit a hush fell over our little company. I began to understand why the pagans of old celebrated their religion in the open air. The combination of darkness, the night sky with its myriad pinpricks of light, the chill of a light winter breeze and the crackle of the flames as the fire took all combined to be highly evocative. I truly felt at one with nature and with my fellow men – and woman.

I could see what Leon meant by having a good eye for colour as the fire blazed turning from red to orange. This was the optimum colour, apparently, for the bricks to fire properly, neither too hot nor too cool.

Leon came over. 'Now is the watching time,' she said squatting down next to me. 'All we can do is sit and wait for the fire to work its magic.'

And so we waited. Ale was brought round with some food and then someone began a song. I can't remember when I felt quite so at peace with the world. I was also conscious of the physical presence of the woman sitting next to me: the warmth of her body against the chill night, and the light touch of her hand next to mine. I know I should have moved away, but I was swept up by the moment – and I was determined to give the lie to Alberic's words. And if I am honest I had no wish to move away. In light of what happened next I can only say in my defence that it was not entirely at my instigation. Our hands touching under the curtain of darkness. If Leon was so revolted by men she would surely have removed it. But she didn't. She left it in place just as I did.

Looking back now I can see that I was not fully myself. It was one of those moments in life when anything seemed possible. I was also feeling a little light-headed not being used to strong ale or even awake at this time of the night. At one point Leon did get up and moved away, but she was soon back again and this time I felt her even closer, her hand moving up to the back of my neck to caress it. I was thrilled. I knew I should pull away but I was transfixed, unable to move, my heart pounding in my chest.

This was madness. What were we doing? I knew I must pull away but could not. But then her hold started to tighten - not too much at first but then more. Little by little he grip grew tighter and I began to feel uncomfortable. I tried surreptitiously to ease her hand away but her grip grew even tighter. I wanted to protest but found I could not speak. I couldn't swallow. Then suddenly the hand grasped my throat in a vice-like grip. I tried to pull away but could not Leon's hand was locked so tightly around my windpipe. Frantically I tried to claw away her fingers but they were too tight. A flash of memory came back to me of that grip when we first shook hands, a grip as powerful as any man's. Panicking now, I desperately clawed at Leon's fingers trying to scrape them off and all the while the singing continued, the singers oblivious to my predicament as I silently fought for my life as my vision began to swim before me and I started to black out.

And then just as suddenly I was aware of another presence. A brief struggle followed by Leon's cry. I felt the hand being wrenched away from my throat and, merciful God, I was able to breathe at last. I pulled back coughing and spluttering.

By now the music had stopped as the others came running. All was suddenly pandemonium as torch joined torch to bathe the scene in light. I managed to struggle to my feet still gasping for air and I turned to see the identity of my saviour. As my eyes refocussed I looked in horror at Leon lying on the ground grimacing angrily up at Alberic who was standing over her, his fists clenched tightly before him.

Chapter Seven
CONFRONTING DEMONS

'What in the blazes has been going on?'

Abbot Ralph's voice, barely above a whisper, was suffused with incredulity. He looked round at each of us in turn waiting for an answer. No-one responded. The silence was deafening.

'Well somebody say something!'

As the most senior person present after the abbot I supposed it was for me to reply. And I was the one at fault having completely misread Leon's intentions mistaking friendship for something more.

In truth I felt ghastly, utterly ashamed of myself. It was my fault entirely. I don't know what had got into me. I hadn't done anything like it since taking the cowl and couldn't explain why I had now – except that I'd never met anyone quite like Leon before. And she had been quite right to rebut me. No blame could accrue to her for what happened. I could only thank God she'd managed to stop me before I made an even bigger fool of myself than I actually did.

'Father -' I began hesitantly, but Leon immediately cut across me:

'It was a misunderstanding.'

Ralph frowned at her. 'A misunderstanding? You call half throttling Brother Walter *a misunderstanding*?'

'No, just a moment -' I began, but she cut in again:

'I know. And I'm sorry. It was my fault.'

I couldn't allow this. 'No really,' I interrupted, 'it wasn't Leon's fault. It was mine.'

Ralph glared from one to the other of us. 'Well it was somebody's fault.' In frustration he turned to Alberic. 'Brother, what do you say?'

Alberic shrugged. 'It was dark. Who can say what really happened?' He gave me a look that said "I did warn you."

Ralph shook his head. 'Well it seems to me that Brother Walter, as the injured party, must be the victim. Naturally he will be seeking punishment...'

'Punishment?' I said, alarmed. 'For whom?'

'Why for Leon of course. She's the one who attacked you.'

'No no,' I shook my head vehemently. 'I'm sorry, I can't allow this. Leon isn't to blame. It was me. Entirely me. I instigated the whole thing. I'm the one who should be punished.'

Ralph narrowed his eyes. 'I think you'd better explain.'

So I did so, cringingly, choosing my words with the greatest care but still unable to avoid the ignominy of what I had done. It was one of the most painful confessions I'd ever had to make. And not privately in the confessional but in public before these three strangers. *Mea culpa. Mea culpa. Mea maxima culpa.* It was humiliating but it had to be done.

As he listened Ralph's face grew darker and darker. 'Nevertheless,' he said when I'd finished. 'Your injury …'

'Was deserved,' I interjected quickly. 'Thoroughly. A-and it's nothing. Really.' I coughed: '*Her-her-her.* You see? I'm fine. No lasting damage.'

At my words Ralph relaxed a little doubtless relieved he wasn't going to have to lose his chief tiler after all.

'Very well,' he said at last, 'we'll say no more about it. And we'll keep it between the four of us. No point in making ourselves - or Saint Edmund's - a laughing stock. But I think under the circumstances, brother, it might be best if you were to leave.'

I was expecting that. And he was right. I should leave. Frankly the whole visit had been a mistake. All I wanted to do was crawl away and pretend I'd never heard of Coggeshall and its priory.

'I'll go straight after terce,' I said. 'If I could just have a brief word with Leon before I do? To apologize,' I added quickly, 'nothing more.'

He thought long and hard about it. I was convinced he'd refuse. But in the end he agreed.

'Very well. But here in my study if you don't mind – and under supervision. I have matters to attend to elsewhere in the abbey. I'll leave Alberic listening just outside the door should he be needed. After all, we don't want any more "misunderstandings" do we?'

When Leon and I were alone we stood facing each other across Ralph's study. Despite her attack I still retained affection for her.

'Leon,' I began, 'I want you to know that I meant what I said to the abbot. I don't blame you for what happened. I'm happy to take the blame for what happened. I don't think you have anything to reproach yourself for -'

'I don't.'

'Eh? What?'

'I don't think I was doing anything wrong. It was entirely you.'

I was a little taken aback, but I managed to smile. 'You're feeling wretched – that's understandable. What you said to Father Ralph -'

'Was a lie.'

'An exaggeration, perhaps, but still -'

'No. It was you. You alone. You were mistaken in your presumptions. I never gave you any encouragement. Not for one moment.'

I was astonished by the vehemence of her tone. 'You don't really mean that.'

'I mean every word.'

'But last night at the kiln -'

'Nothing happened at the kiln. It was all in your imagination.'

But it did. I was sure of it. She was just as responsive as I was. I didn't mind taking the blame in front of Father Ralph, that was the chivalric thing to do. But in private just the two of us - a modicum of complicity wouldn't go amiss.

'You attacked me,' I reminded her.

'No. *You* attacked *me.*'

'But I'm the one with the bruised neck.'

'And I'm the one with the bruised emotions.'

'That's hardly the same thing. I wasn't trying to squeeze the life out of you.'

'To me it was just as suffocating.'

My jaw fell open. Suffocating? The merest brush of hand on hand? I must remember that next time I take a patient's pulse. Maybe Alberic had been right after all. Maybe she really did hate men.

'That's not how I remember it.'

She looked me in the eye. 'Brother, I never asked for your attentions. To be truthful I found them ... unpleasant.'

Unpleasant? I winced at the word. My only intention had been to try a reconciliation before I left, but clearly she didn't want it.

'I'm sorry you feel this way,' I said haughtily. 'I had hoped we might at least part as friends.'

'I don't think that's possible.' She stood aside. 'And I think now you should leave.'

I drew myself up with as much dignity as I could muster. 'Very well. But before I go there's the matter of the green children.'

'I don't know anything about them.'

'I think you do.'

'No brother. Once again you are mistaken.'

She evidently didn't want anything more to do with me for any reason however innocent.

'Then there's nothing more to be said.'

'No, nothing.'

I was wasting my time. So be it. Still reeling from her words, I stomped out the door past Alberic who was waiting in the corridor with a self-satisfied look on his face.

An hour later Erigone was saddled and we were ready to go, and by now I couldn't wait to leave. Abbot Ralph was there to see me off, more for form's sake I think than because he wanted to be; it would have set tongues wagging if I'd left without his blessing. He was clearly embarrassed by the whole episode. And he was right to be so. Monks are supposed to be above such things, although I am sure he must have come across worse during his time in the Outremer. But then the Greeks are more sophisticated than we are in the west. My visit had been a complete disaster. I'd not learnt anything about the green children I didn't already know and I'd made myself a laughing-stock into the bargain. But Ralph, God bless him, was prepared to be magnanimous.

'I'm sorry things have ended the way they have, father.'

He gave a philosophical shrug of his shoulders. 'These things happen. I only hope we have been able to provide you with the information you were looking for.'

'Some. I still have a few questions – but,' I added quickly, 'they can be answered elsewhere. This, however,' I held out his book on visions and miracles, 'I found very useful.'

'Keep it a little longer if you wish. I have a copy.'

I doubted that was true, but I kept it anyway. It was probably his way of apologizing for what had happened.

'Thank you father. I'll place it in the abbey library when I've finished with it. You may find it there whenever you wish.'

'Is that where you're headed now? Back to Bury?'

'Not immediately. I thought I'd pay a visit to Bardwell first. It's quite close to my mother's house at Ixworth.'

He looked surprised. 'You intend visiting Wykes?'

'Is there any reason why I shouldn't?'

'None, except I doubt you'll find much there. The house was completely destroyed in the fire.'

'There was a fire?'

'Yes, didn't you know? The place was completely gutted a year or two back. As far as I know no-one lives there anymore. Lady Margaret de Calne and her son moved away.'

'Do you happen to know where they went?'

'I'm afraid I don't. The family have other manors, I believe. Doubtless they went to one of them. Well,' he said, impatient to see the back of me, 'fare you well Brother Walter. Be sure to give my regards to your mother when you see her.' He was about to go then stopped. 'Oh, by the way – that white potion you gave me.'

'The Willow-wort?' I'd almost forgotten about it.

He nodded. 'Yes. Very good.'

'It cured your headaches?'

'No. But I gargled with it and it did wonders for my sore throat.'

My route back to Suffolk took me up through the high street and past the parish church. Even from up here smoke from the brickworks was visible rising above the rooftops - a painful reminder of the previous night's events. But I did wish them all well and hoped my presence hadn't disrupted the good work of the abbey too much. I didn't suppose I would never see any of them again. It would take me a long time to get over my embarrassment.

Before I got a few yards further, however, I heard the sound of hoof-prints behind and turned to see Brother Alberic astride a mule pounding up the hill towards me. Damn. Of all of them he was the last I wished to see. No doubt he was coming to gloat.

'I hope you don't mind, brother,' he said panting to catch me up. 'I have some business to conduct in Norfolk. I thought we could ride together.'

'I'm not actually returning to Bury today, brother,' I said haughtily.

'Well then, until our ways part?'

Did I have any choice? There was only one road north and we either rode together or yards apart pretending the other wasn't there, which would have been absurd. And he had just saved my life I should remember.

'I feel I owe you an apology, brother,' I said humbly. 'It seems you were right about Leon.'

'I did try to warn you. To be truthful I'd suspected something of the sort might occur.'

He suspected she might try to strangle me? Goodness me, what were these people?

'She utterly rejected me and now thinks I'm a hopeless rake. She finds me … unpleasant,' I said remembering her word with pain.

'Well, you can put it all behind you now. The important thing is that you achieved what you came for in Coggeshall.'

'Not really. Father Ralph was only able to help me so far. There is still much to do.'

'Does that mean you'll be coming back?'

To be humiliatingly rejected by Leon again? I didn't think so.

'No. My work at Coggeshall is done. The remainder of my investigations will be in Suffolk.'

I explained briefly about the green children of Woolpit.

'Yes, I heard you asking Leon about that. It is, of course, one of Father Abbot's tales. You've read his book?'

'Some of it.'

'And your conclusion?'

It was the question I had been asking myself. On the one hand all the tales in Ralph's chronicle seemed preposterous and even Ralph sounded sceptical. I got the impression much of it was written tongue-in-cheek. On the other hand Samson, my mother and Oswald all insisted the children existed. I didn't know what to think.

'I'm trying to keep an open mind. In truth I'm only really investigating for the sake of my abbot who is close to death. It is by way of fulfilling his final wish. I'll continue up to a point, but I'm not sure how far I will go.'

'And are you at that point yet?'

'Not quite.'

He nodded. 'Actually, we're passing quite close to the location of one of Father Ralph's stories now.' He pointed to his left. 'Just beyond that wood lies the village of Stisted. You recall the tale of Thurkill Ploughman and his visions? '

'I'm not sure I read that one.'

'Oh, it's a particularly entertaining one with a sting in the tail.'

'Remind me.'

He was happy to do so: 'A villein of Stisted called Thurkill is supposed to have had a vision of Saint Julian – don't ask me which Julian, he didn't specify. It could have been Saint Julian of Antioch who, you may recall, was sewn in a sack filled with scorpions and cast into the sea to drown. Or Saint Julian the Hospitaller who was foretold to kill his own mother and father and later did so. Or maybe it was Julian of Toledo whose only claim to fame was that as archbishop he persecuted Jews despite being one himself.'

'You're starting to sound as cynical as Abbot Ralph, brother.'

'Not at all, I merely try to fill in the omissions. At any rate, whichever Julian it was summoned Thurkill to go on a journey with him into the underworld.'

'And did he?'

He held up his hand for patience. 'Our hero prepared himself well for his journey washing his body from head to foot before climbing into his bed - much to the annoyance of his wife.'

'No doubt she would have liked the same consideration when he climbed into her bed,' I suggested.

Alberic smiled. 'Now who's being cynical? The following Friday night Saint Julian – whichever one it was - duly arrived to take Thurkill's soul into the underworld leaving behind his body which became rigid and motionless on his bed.'

'To the continued annoyance of his wife?'

'Indeed. Thus Thurkill remained for two days, neither his wife nor his priest could rouse him. Then on Sunday evening he suddenly sat bolt upright, opened his eyes and uttered the word, *Benedicite,* which he later claimed never to have heard before. He then revealed to his priest and his family something of his experiences in the underworld. But it was all muddle and confusion. So the following week Saint Julian appeared to him again and ordered him to recount his experiences properly which he did before the entire village in Stisted church. The revelations were sensational and covered all persons irrespective of rank or order describing the fate of their deceased relatives in the afterlife – much to their chagrin.'

'But were they convinced?' I asked.

Here Alberic raised a cautionary finger. 'I said there was a sting in the tail and here it is: in the course of his revelations Thurkill also confessed that he had not paid fully his dues to the church for that year and described in great detail the punishment he had already received for his deception whilst in the underworld.'

'Thus hoping to avoid further punishment in this,' I nodded. 'So you think he invented the whole affair just to get out of paying his dues.'

Alberic smiled. 'That is one interpretation.'

I thought I was beginning to understand Alberic a little better. Perhaps his cynicism explained why his career had not progressed beyond that of a lay-brother. The work of a converso is heavy, more suited to a younger man than someone of Alberic's age. Given the opportunity I think I would prefer singing psalms than digging latrines. But not Alberic it seemed.

'Tell me brother, how long have you been in at the priory?'

He thought for a moment. 'It must be getting on for a quarter century.'

'And you have never wished to profess? To become a choir monk?'

'No brother, I have not.'

'Any particular reason?'

'I suppose the short answer is that I did not wish to be confined to the abbey. As you see I have the freedom to come and go.'

I shrugged. 'I am professed yet I have the same freedom.'

'Then let us simply say I am simply content with my lot.'

Perhaps. Or maybe he lost his faith somewhere along the way. He didn't strike me as being particularly religious. What can a monk do when that happens except hold tight and hope it may one day return? Having to live in a closed community like Coggeshall priory whilst believing it to be based on a falsehood must be torture. Yet what alternative is there? It would be nigh impossible to leave and start again, especially at Alberic's age. I think under those circumstances I might be bitter too. Despite myself I couldn't help feeling a twinge of sympathy for the man.

'Twenty-five years, you say. Forgive me, but you must have had a life before Coggeshall in that case.'

'Before that I was with the monks of Rievaulx Abbey.'

'Yorkshire,' I nodded. 'I thought I detected an accent. Rievaulx is another Cistercian house?'

'Aye, and a very fine one.'

'Do you miss it?'

He thought for a moment. 'No.'

We had come to a fork in the road and Alberic halted his mule.

'Well, this is where we must part company, brother. I go this way and you go straight on for Sudbury.'

'Then I wish you well with your business in Norfolk, brother.'

'The same to you with your quest in Suffolk, brother.'

I watched him go and I can't say I was sorry to see the back of him. His rendition of the Stisted tale had merely increased my own scepticism about the green children and all of Abbot Ralph's tales of supernatural happenings. I just wanted to finish my investigation now as quickly as possible and put the whole business behind me. I couldn't know that it had hardly yet begun.

Chapter Eight
DOUBTS INCREASE

What did I really think about the green children? Despite my increasing misgivings there did seem to be some element of truth to the tale. The difficulty lay in separating truth from fiction. I don't think my mother would have lied about meeting the girl if she hadn't really done so. Well yes, actually, she would if she thought there was some mileage in it, but it's difficult to see what that could be. Certainly Oswald had nothing to gain by making up that awful business about the pigs. So, scrub away all the flimflamery about them being green and what are we left with? Two vulnerable young children who appear overnight apparently from nowhere, stick around for a while and then vanish again. Interesting, but what they had to do with this purported murder and Samson's mysterious woman I had absolutely no idea.

The key to the affair seemed to be Sir Richard de Calne. It kept coming back to him yet he remained an enigma. Leon might have been a useful source of information having known him personally but after what had happened in Coggeshall that avenue was well and truly blocked. Still, I was intrigued to learn more about this latter-day Aristotle, he sounded a fascinating character. Was it possible for one man to be expert on so many matters? Living so close to Bardwell, I was surprised I had never got to know him.

Well, I could start to put that right and the first place to look was surely his former home of Wykes in Bardwell. It was there that the children were supposedly taken when first discovered and where they remained for some time – the girl at least since the boy died soon after arriving. The hall had burned down, Ralph said; that was indeed unfortunate. But surely someone in the village must know what happened to Sir Richard's widow and son. I resolved therefore to go there once I was back in Suffolk, and I have to say I was never so relieved to cross the border into my native county. Had I known what was waiting for me when I got there, however, I might not have been quite so sanguine about it.

I took the same route back as the one out and spent another delightful evening with the Kentwells of Melford. The children were just as lively as before running around the hall and leaving mayhem in their wake. It's at times like this that I wonder what my life might have been if I'd married and had a family of my own. I think I would have made a good father – strict but kind, stern but fair.

Who am I kidding? I'd probably have been just as soft with my brood as Gilbert Kentwell was with his.

They were quite a handful. All five scamps pounced on me as soon as I arrived and had me playing "pickle-in-a-saucer" - with me as the pickle, naturally. This wasn't my choice. I just never seemed to be quick enough to catch the ball. They had clearly refined their technique and had me darting about until I was too exhausted to stand up and collapsed on the floor with the children piling in on top of me. Just as the first time, Gilbert Kentwell would take no money for my stay, but as I departed I left three punnets of sweetmeats I'd purchased on my way through Sudbury. I left next morning tired and battered but happy.

It occurred to me as I left Melford that to get to Bardwell it was as quick to pass through Woolpit as through Bury. It seemed too good an opportunity to miss to visit the village where the children were first discovered. I had no pressing need to go back to Bury immediately so Woolpit it was.

The abbey has a long and tortuous history with this village. Samson had mentioned it many times over the years and always with a slightly disdainful curl of his lip. The church was originally given to Saint Edmund by King Ethelred, called Unready, but was subsequently taken back by the present king's father who wanted the tithes for himself. This had much aggrieved the abbey for these tithes had hitherto been used to pay for the care of sick monks and they had long wanted them restored. Samson had even gone on a special mission to Rome when still a novice to try to secure the church for the abbey. He'd succeeded in getting the pope's approval but on his return journey was accosted by ruffians which made him too late to save the church. Had he done so he would no doubt have been hailed a hero, but Abbot Hugh exiled him to Castle Acre as punishment for not asking his permission to go. The church remained a thorn in the abbey's side thereafter until it came back into our possession once Samson was himself elected abbot.

All this to-ing and fro-ing caused much anguish for the folk of Woolpit and we Bury monks have not always received the welcome there we might otherwise expect. I was therefore a little apprehensive as to what sort of reception I might get. Fortunately on this wet December morning there were few people on the street. But I did manage to find one man - a labourer seated under an awning with his shovel and his pick displayed to advertise his availability for work. I decided it was prudent not to mention that I was from the abbey.

'God be with you, my man. My name is Brother Walter. I'm a physician. Are you looking to hire?'

He looked me up and down. 'Leech, eh? I don't dig graves.'

'I don't wish to bury anyone,' I said indignantly. 'My patients survive. Well, most of them at any rate. You are a local man, I take it?'

He nodded. 'Aye. Woolpit born and bred.'

'Then you'll know all about wolf pits. I believe they are a feature of the village?'

'Mebbe I do.'

'Well, do you or don't you? Could you take me to one?'

'Mebbe I could.'

Clearly a man of eloquent simplicity.

'Mebbe a ha'penny will help?' I said deliberately mocking his accent.

He grinned a sparse set of yellowing fangs. 'Mebbe it will.'

I fished the crescent-shaped piece of silver from my belt pouch and placed it in his gnarled palm. He bit it, pressed a thumbnail into it, licked it. Satisfied it was silver, he heaved himself off the bench and led the way down a track to the side of the inn. I tied Erigone to the market pump and followed him just as the rain was starting to fall again.

We sloshed our way a good quarter mile through the drizzle across an open field and then up behind a small wooded copse. Just as I was beginning to wonder if we were ever going to get anywhere he suddenly stopped and turned to face me.

'Well?' I said.

He pointed to a shallow, grassed-over depression between us. 'Wolf pit.'

I gazed at the rain-filled puddle with dismay. 'Is that it?'

The man just grinned which I took to be affirmation.

'Are you sure? It's not very deep. I thought they were supposed to be the height of a man.'

'That wor deeper – once. Dangerous thing, wolf pit. Sheep falls in, breaks a leg.' He sucked on his teeth. 'Best thing to fill 'em in.'

I'd come all this way for this? A puddle? I sighed. 'When was it filled in?'

'Oh, must be ten year or more ago.'

'You didn't think to tell me that before I tramped all the way up here?'

'Didn't ask how deep it wor. Asked if I knew of one. This is one. Wolf pit.'

I frowned my annoyance. 'I take it then you don't trap wolves this way anymore?'

For a moment I thought he was having a heart attack but it turned out he was just laughing.

'Bless you brother, han't been a wolf seen in these parts for nigh on twenty year.'

'Because you caught them all?'

94

'Because they got frit.'

Frit. Though a native of Suffolk myself, I was having difficulty with his exceptionally broad accent. Let me see. Frit. *Fright* maybe?

'You're saying the wolves got frightened and ran away? Frightened of what?'

He looked at me as though I were half-witted. 'Frit of what will happen to 'em if he stay, acourse.' He explained: 'Farmer kills the he-wolf, see? Sticks his head on a pole. She-wolf sees it and gits.'

'I see. The bitch-wolf gets frit – er, frightened - by the sight of its decapitated mate and runs off. Is that the idea?'

He shrugged and nodded his head. Obviously.

It occurred to me that I'd seen something like this before. Jays hung spread-eagle along fences to warn their mates what will happen to them if they don't leave the crop alone.

'And did it work?'

The man smiled coyly. 'Can't see no wolves, can 'ee?'

'No, I suppose not.'

I was wasting my time here. I had hoped I might get some inspiration from visiting the location where the children had purportedly been found but there was nothing here to see. I wasn't entirely convinced this puddle was a former wolf pit. I only had the man's word for it. But there was no point arguing. I was just getting wetter and colder.

'Thank you for your trouble,' I said and started to leave. 'Oh, one more thing before I go: do you know of any caverns hereabouts? Possibly with bells?'

He looked at me as though I were mad.

'No. Well thank you.' I started to leave again.

'That it, then? Don't want to hear about the chil'en?'

I came back. 'Children?'

'Aye. The green chil'en. That's what most pilgrims come for. They comes for the shrine first then they asks about the chil'en.'

The shrine. I'd forgotten about that, too. Woolpit church had one to the Virgin, I remembered Samson telling me about it. Apparently the Holy Mother once made an appearance here and the villagers commemorated the event with a statue of her in the church. My labouring friend was turning into something of an impromptu tour guide of local points of interest, it seemed.

'So you've done this before? I'm not the first?'

The man gave me a sly grin. 'We all needs to earn a crust, brother.'

Hm, and tour-guiding was easier than digging graves. I sighed and found the other half of the penny. He tested it the way he had the first half and pocketed it.

'All right,' I said with increasing impatience. 'What can you tell me about the green children?'

'That's easy. There worn't none.' His face creased into another long breathy cackle.

I was taken aback. 'I assure you it's well documented. I've even met people who knew them.'

'So have I. So's every man you meet about these parts. Ev'y one on 'em lied.'

Now I was really irritated. 'How could you possibly know that?'

He shook his head with pity. 'Only one person ever saw them chil'en - that shepherd. And he never saw 'em neither.'

'Why would he make it up?'

'Why do you think?' He rubbed his fingers and thumb together in the time-honoured fashion. 'Money brother.'

'You mean for the same reason you do?'

His smile faltered a bit at that. 'You asked to see a pit. I showed you a pit. Never said that was the one where the chil'en was found.'

'Was it?'

'Mebbe it was. Mebbe it wasn't. They do say at the full moon two figures can be seen hov'ring over this spot. A wolf howl and next day they find the pit opened up again like it wor them chil'en trying to dig their way back inside. And it all happens right here.' He pointed to the puddle.

I must admit I felt a slight thrill at his words. Could it be that this hollow really was where the children were actually discovered after all? I tried to visualize the scene: an autumn evening, the sun beginning to set. The shepherd going home to his supper after a hard day's work in the fields hears the scratching at the bottom of the pit and goes to investigate. He approaches cautiously, fearful of what he might find at the bottom. But instead of a snarling wolf he sees two children staring back at him. The pit is too deep to pull them out. He runs home and comes back with a ladder, and together with his wife they help the children climb out and...

By now the man was chuckling quietly away to himself.

I frowned annoyance. 'You're making it up. I don't believe this is where the children were found.'

'Not me, brother - you. You want to believe it – it's writ all over your face. See, that's what the pilgrims come for. The thrill. I just gives 'em what they want.'

'So which is it?' I said finally losing my patience with him. 'Did the green children really exist or didn't they?'

The man shrugged. 'It's your penny, brother. You choose.'

Infuriating man! I wish now I'd not met him. Taking advantage of gullible people like that. It was disgraceful. I had a good mind to speak to the abbot about him.

But in all honesty, could I blame him? As he said, he was only telling people what they wanted to hear. And he was right: there is something about these tales that thrills the imagination. I found I wanted to believe in the green children, so much so that I was prepared to overlook the obvious flaws in the story: their sudden appearance from nowhere; their lack of a language; all that nonsense about only eating green beans; and above all, their green colour. Indeed, the more ludicrous the claim the more I wanted to believe it.

Thurkill of Stisted clearly understood this principle. If he had simply said he couldn't pay his dues he would have been put in the stocks until he did. But by inventing such a fantastical tale of descent into the Underworld he had his entire village eating out of his hand. You had to admire his audacity. I'm willing to bet he never did pay his Church dues.

It wasn't the first time I'd come across this phenomenon. Like many people I'd been on pilgrimage to Our Lady of Walsingham. There the monks sell phials of milk purportedly from the Holy Mother's breast. Now, clearly it can't all be milk from the Holy Mother's breast. Over the years it would have amounted to gallons. The monks admitted to me privately that the "milk" was, in fact, chalk suspended in well water and replenished daily. Indeed, most pilgrims already knew this, and if they didn't beforehand they certainly would once they got their precious cargo home. But it made no difference. They venerated this faux milk as though it were the real thing and were happy to do so – because they *wanted* it to be so.

My labourer friend didn't believe in the green children and was happy to tell me so confident that it would make no difference. That put him firmly into Alberic's camp of sceptics. On the other hand the two people I would expect to be sceptical – my mother and Oswald – insisted that the children really did exist. So who was right? I didn't know what to think anymore. And now I was utterly soaked through for my trouble. I therefore decided to go into the church for some spiritual revival - and hopefully dry off a little.

Saint Mary's, Woolpit, is a regular country church, slightly bigger but otherwise not so very different from my own at Ixworth – except for one thing: the south-east corner was given over entirely to the veneration of the Holy Mother. High up in a prominent position was a wooden Madonna – carved, by the look of it, by some local artist and rather naïvely, but no less evocative for that. She was dressed as the Queen of Heaven in silk robes and crowned with a diadem of gold-leaf. All around were candles lit to enhance the mother-of-pearl halo that adorned her image. Her hands were held out in a gesture of welcome. It was at once an image of peace and awe. After the wolf pit in the field I found the image strangely calming and refreshing.

And I wasn't alone in my admiration. In front of the shrine was a middle-aged couple gazing up in wonder at the holy image while the priest kept up a running commentary in reverential whispers of the various miracles that had been performed. To illustrate the point, hanging conspicuously from the ceiling above the shrine was an impressive array of discarded crutches and callipers of the miraculously cured.

Seeing a sodden monk shaking himself like a dog and dripping on the tiles behind the south door, the priest quickly took his leave of the couple and came over. He was a mousy little man with his hands drawn up to his chest as though guarding something precious.

'Are you local, brother?' he whispered.

'Yes. From the abbey,' I whispered back. 'Brother Walter. Abbey physician.'

'Ah,' he nodded. 'Then you are welcome indeed. I am Father Thomas, guardian of the shrine.'

'I see we are in the same business, Father,' I said nodding to the display of redundant medical aids.

He inclined his head. 'We all try to impart God's healing in our different ways, brother. Was there anyone you particularly wished to have mentioned in the prayers today?'

I thought of Samson and then of the man and his wife who were now on their knees before the shrine, hands clasped together in prayer. It seemed a pity to disturb them.

'Perhaps not today.'

'Then shall we…' He gestured towards the priest's door.

Outside in the churchyard the rain had stopped at last although the grass was very wet and soaked the hem of my robe.

'If not for devotion to our blessèd lady, may I ask was there any other reason for your visit, brother?'

I didn't want to admit I'd just been trudging across fields on a fool's errand. 'Not really. I just happened to be passing and thought I'd drop in. I'd never visited the shrine of Our Lady of Woolpit before.'

'Then you must come and visit her well.'

'Her well?'

Thomas nodded. 'Oh yes. A holy well. When the Holy Mother visited here a spring sprouted spontaneously from the very ground upon which she placed her foot. The waters have miraculous healing properties – especially good for ailments of the eyes.'

I was about to decline but then I thought of Jocelin:

'Could it restore the blight of old age? I have a brother at the abbey for whom reading has become impossible. It would be a great blessing if his sight could clear again.'

'If anybody can do it, brother, it is the Holy Mother,' he nodded with enthusiasm. 'Please. Follow me.'

He led the way through a gap in the hedge to a corner of the churchyard where sure enough a spring bubbled up through the turf. Here a large stone had been placed with another smaller version of the same Madonna statue as the one in the church perched on the top. Next to it was a cup and some pottery bottles. At Thomas's suggestion I sampled a cup of the liquid and immediately pulled a face.

He gave a slight chuckle. 'You sense the power already.'

'I sense the taste. Sulphur?'

He nodded again. 'From the very bowls of the earth. I can supply you with a bottle at a nominal cost.' He began offering a bottle with a practised hand - but then on second thoughts: 'Take it with my compliments,' he smiled. 'The money would go to the abbey in due course in any case.'

I graciously accepted his gift. After the Kentwell children and my labourer guide I didn't have much money left in any case. Besides, I was sure he wouldn't miss my small offering. What with the shrine, the well and the green children, I could see why Woolpit was such a prosperous village - and why so many kings and abbots wished to claim it.

By now the elderly couple were emerging from the church with expressions of sublime peace on their faces. They thanked Thomas for his help, greeted me and took their leave.

'Have you been the priest here for long, father?' I asked watching them go.

He frowned a little nervously. 'I am not the parish priest. That honour goes to Father John. He's away at the moment.'

'Then you won't know the legend of the green children?'

At their mention he seemed to relax a little. Evidently I wasn't an exchequer officer of the abbey as he had feared after all.

'Bless you brother, everyone in Woolpit has heard of the green children. And it's no legend I assure you.'

'You believe it to be true, then?'

'Why yes, naturally.' He seemed amused that I should doubt it.

'Tell me then, what's your theory? Everyone seems to have one.'

The man smiled indulgently. 'I think it's only too clear who those children were, brother. Angels.'

'Angels?'

He nodded with confidence. 'Indeed. Attendant upon Our Lady when she visited, they got lost on their way back to heaven and were left behind.'

It was a novel take on the subject.

'But the people. Who do locals say they were?'

He frowned. 'You have to understand, brother, these are simple farming folk. To them the world is filled with inexplicable wonders. They need the help of a guiding hand to explain and show them the way.'

'A shepherd you mean – like the one who found the children?'

'Or a shepherd of men,' he smiled modestly.

'Er yes, quite. This shepherd though took them to Bardwell. Why do you think he did that?'

'I believe his priest at the time advised him so.'

'But Bardwell is miles away. Surely the abbey is an easier road.'

Thomas grimaced uncomfortably. 'I'm sure I don't have to remind you, brother, of the history of our relationship with the abbey. It has not always been the easiest, particularly at that time.'

Yes, I could see that might be the case. But it still didn't explain Bardwell's connection with Woolpit. Maybe Abbot Ralph's explanation was the right one after all and Sir Richard was such a well-known local sage that he was the obvious one to go to when anything out of the ordinary like this appeared.

'Well thank you father, you've been most kind. And please,' I said taking my last coin from my purse and pressing it into his hand. 'For the water.'

He accepted the penny with grace. With the rain starting to fall again I bade him farewell, pulled up my cloak and turned Erigone's head northward once again.

Chapter Nine
THE MASTER OF WYKES

My next stop was Bardwell village. Compared with Woolpit this was a tiny hamlet barely a dozen houses and a church. If you didn't know it was there you could easily miss it. A little too far to the right of the Thetford road and a little too far to the left of the one to Norwich, it was on nobody's itinerary - which made me wonder even more why a shepherd from Woolpit should know of the man who lived here.

I'd always assumed Bardwell's obscurity was the reason Joseph and I never spent much time there as children, but I realised now that wasn't the only reason. It was also because of the bad blood between our two houses, ours and the de Calnes. According to Oswald this seems to have been at the instigation of Sir Richard de Calne, but I wondered now if there was an element of contrivance to keep us apart. There was a mystery here that grew deeper the harder I dug and one I was determined to uncover.

Despite its size, Bardwell boasts no less than three manor courts all under the suzerainty of the abbey in Bury. The same Blackbourn brook that runs past my mother's house passes just to the west of the village on its way to Thetford where it empties into the Little Ouse. At its closest point to the village it touches the edge of a field where, I was reliably informed, the hall known as Wykes once stood. This was the home of the de Calne family. Or rather, it was. Through the curtain of rain I could see that Abbot Ralph was right: the hall had indeed burned down leaving little more than a blackened shell behind. As I stood in what once must have been the courtyard, the building looked a sad remnant of what must once have been a substantial manor house. Half the roof had gone as had the north wall and all of the windows. Fires happen frequently and unexpectedly as we know only too well in Bury, but rarely with such total devastation as this. I wondered what could have caused it and why the hall was never rebuilt.

I tied Erigone to the remnants of a gate-post and picked my way gingerly over the uneven, sodden ground. As I drew nearer the building my nostrils were assaulted by an overwhelming stench of rotting flesh. It crossed my mind that this was the rotting corpses of the people who died in the fire but I immediately dismissed the idea as absurd. Besides, Ralph told me that Sir Richard's wife and son didn't die in the fire but had moved away to another of their estates, although he didn't say where.

My contemplations were interrupted by the sound of running feet behind me and I spun round to see a young priest, his robes held high above the ground, comically hopping and zig-zagging his way across the field towards me.

'Oh, brother!' he said breathlessly as he approached. 'I'm sorry, I saw you from the church. You must be Brother Ulric.' He offered his hand in greeting. 'Ivo of Uffington. I'm the curate here.'

'Walter of Ixworth,' I said taking his hand.

He snatched it back. 'Not Ulric of Salop?'

I shook my head. 'Afraid not.'

'Ah well.' He smiled affably and extended his hand again. 'Pleased to meet you Walter of Ixworth.'

'Pleased to meet you. Uffington…?'

'In Oxfordshire. Vale of the White Horse…?'

I shook my head.

'It is a long way away. Ixworth - that's…' he pointed vaguely.

'The next village.'

'So it is. You'll have to forgive me, I'm new here. Not got my bearings yet. So you're not here about the clock?'

'Clock?'

'Our water clock. Surely you've heard about that? I thought everybody knew about our clock.'

'Sorry to disappoint again. Actually I've come about this,' I said nodding to the ruin. 'I assume it's the de Calne residence?'

'Wykes Hall,' he nodded and pulled a face. 'Ghastly isn't it? Hard to imagine it was once a great house. Bit of an eyesore now, I'm afraid.'

'More of a *nose*-sore I'd say. What is that smell?'

'That was Alan's idea, I'm afraid. Alan's the priest here. I'll show you if you like – that's if you think you can bear it.'

He led the way into the shell of the building. With each step the smell grew worse so that I had to cover my nose with the sleeve of my robe wondering what I was being led into. Then I saw what was causing the stink. Piled up against the walls of what once must have been the central hall were corpses – dozens of them all wrapped in shrouds. But that did nothing to mask the smell of putrefaction. It was a distressing sight to see. Saddest of all were the dozens of tiny bundles huddled together that I presumed were children and babies.

'Who are they all?' I asked in awe.

'Various former residents of the village.' He pointed to one bloated parcel. 'That I know is Dorcas, Alan's old housemaid. I recognize the tablecloth she's wrapped in. She was carried off by the shivering fever last Christmastide. Over there's Hugh our grave-digger. Got drunk one night, fell into an open grave and skewered himself on his own pick. Others I'm not so sure about,' he frowned. 'The old and the sick mostly. I've sort of lost track.'

'Didn't you think to label them?'

He shrugged. 'Didn't think we'd need to. No-one expected the interdict to last this long. It's been over three years now. With the churchyard out of bounds they had to go somewhere and this seemed the most convenient place. An amazing number of people die in three years, you don't realise.' He shook his head despairingly.

'At the abbey we have a pit,' I told him. 'The servants cover the bodies with earth. It helps with the rat problem - and the smell.'

'Ah well, now you've said the magic word haven't you, brother? *Servants*. We don't have any. It's only Alan and me. And strictly-speaking we shouldn't be handling the dead at all. It's against the rules.'

'Nobody takes any notice of the rules.'

'Alan does. A stickler for the rules is Alan.'

Someone needed to have a word with this pedantic priest. Samson would certainly have something to say about bodies being left exposed and unrecorded like this.

'Where's Father Alan now?'

'He's away at the moment visiting his family. He'll be back in a day or two.'

I'd be long gone by then. But I made a mental note to speak to the prior about him when I got back to Bury. Not that I thought he'd do much. If anyone was more regulation-minded than this Father Alan it would have to be Prior Herbert.

I looked around the rest of the hall. There wasn't much to see. It was barely recognizable as a building let alone a residence. The place was cold, dark, black and wet.

'Look, can we get out of here?' I said puckering my nose. 'I'm beginning to feel faint from the stench.'

'Of course - sorry. I've sort of got used to it. Don't notice it anymore. Come up to the house. I've just brewed a fresh batch of mule.'

'You brew your mule?' I said with alarm.

'That's what I call it. Fortified wine really. I make it from dried grapes. Powerful stuff, if I do say so myself.'

'Why do you call it your mule?'

'Because it has a kick,' he grinned.

The priest-house in Bardwell stands further up the slope at the edge of the road and below the church of Saint Peter and Saint Paul. Like most village manses it's a hovel, barely more than a single room with a hearth. But it was warm and cosy this day with one or two surprisingly nice touches – like a vase of winter-flowering plants on the table. Ivo or Alan – or, I was beginning to think, probably both - had clearly made an effort to turn this hutch into a home. And he was right about his mule. It did have quite a kick.

'Tell me more about this clock of yours,' I said settling down comfortably with a cupful before the fire.

'It's a time-piece. For summoning the faithful to prayer. The bell rings at the appropriate hour powered entirely by the motion of falling water.'

'What's wrong with an old-fashioned mass dial?'

'Nothing when the sun shines. But what do you do on dark winter days like today, or when the sun goes behind a cloud? Our clock keeps regular time come rain or shine, night or day - when it's working, that is. At the moment it's broken.'

'Well there you are, then,' I said. 'God's clock doesn't break down. And I'd imagine few villages could afford such a device even if they knew how to build one.'

'But most villages don't have a living genius – or rather a dead one.'

'I take it you're referring to Sir Richard de Calne?'

His face spilt into a broad grin. 'I am indeed. How clever of you.'

I shook my head. 'Not clever at all. I've been hearing a lot about him recently. Actually, it was Sir Richard I came here to ask about.'

He crossed his ankles. 'Ask away. What do you want to know?'

'Anything you can tell me really. Did you ever meet him?'

'No, he died before I came. It was some time ago. There can't be many people left in the village who knew Sir Richard personally. Actually, you've probably met most of them already.'

'Already met them? Oh, you mean in the hall.'

He pulled a face. 'Sorry. Bad joke.'

'I understand he left a widow and a son. You don't know what happened to them?'

'I can tell you they no longer live at the hall,' he grimaced. 'That's about it, really. But look, if you really want to know about Sir Richard the best way is to show you his creation.'

'His creation?'

'His clock.'

Inwardly I groaned. I was tired after my journey and the mule was beginning to have its effect. I still hadn't quite caught up with the loss of sleep the night of the firing. The last thing I wanted was to look at rusty old bits of machinery.

'I should really be going,' I said putting down my cup. 'It's getting late and I still have a couple of miles to go.'

'You don't have to, you know? You could stay the night. No really, there's a spare bed if you want it. Alan's away so you can have his.'

I wasn't entirely sure Alan's bed got used that often.

I grimaced. 'Thank you for the offer, but Ixworth is just down the road. And my mother's expecting me.'

God, did I really say that?

He seemed genuinely disappointed. 'You'll stay for supper at least? It's an evil night out there. There's plenty of mule left.'

I realised I'd drained my cup. It was a good strong brew that had already gone to my head. And I was very hungry. I shrugged and nodded.

'Splendid! I'll kill the fatted calf – not literally, of course. Just one of the hens.'

After supper which was surprisingly good, he took me over to the church. Not a huge building. It consisted of just a nave and a chancel with no side aisles. No tower either, just a bell-cote with a single bell. Immediately beneath the bell and inside the door, however, was a true marvel: a huge structure that loomed up before us like a leviathan. I don't know what I was expecting but not this. The thing was massive. How it got constructed in such a tight space was itself a miracle. By torchlight the clock seemed to go up and up and disappear into the bell-cote with only the bats for company. It occupied so much of the nave I wondered that there was any room left for the congregation.

The main component, apart from the vessels containing the water, appeared to be a wheel with other wheels embedded inside. There were chains and ropes and a whole phantasmagoria of flutings, spirals and whirligigs that I don't have the vocabulary to describe. Suffice to say it was a work of beauty and elegance – and magic.

'Good, isn't it?' Ivo beamed like a proud parent.

'Remarkable,' I agreed. 'You say it sounds a bell on the hour?'

'That's right. It's hooked up to the church bell so it makes quite a racket when it gets going. Saves me having to pull a rope I can tell you. It's all done with these gears, do you see? As some rotate one way the others turn the other.'

He moved the giant wheel and they all began to rotate as he described. The bell at the top sounded once.

'The whole thing's powered by these urns filled with nothing but God's pure water. As one urn empties it fills the next which empties and fills the next - and so on. All I have to do is keep the highest urn topped up and it'll keep going indefinitely. At least it would if it was working properly. Trouble is one of the blades has snapped off and we need someone to come and repair it.'

'Brother Ulric?'

Ivo nodded. 'He's a monk at Saint Albans. He built a similar machine there and is one of the few people capable of understanding ours. I'm absolutely hopeless at anything like that.' He had a sudden thought. 'I say, I don't suppose you're any good with mechanicals are you?'

I shook my head. 'I can barely work out how to get in to my own laboratory.'

'Pity. Only we've got the plans, you see? We managed to save them from the fire - along with all the other stuff.'

I hesitated. 'Other stuff?'

'From the hall. Oh, just a lot of dusty old documents. Quite a lot actually. Blame Alan for that. I wanted to save the furniture and the artwork – some beautiful pieces there were from all over the world. All gone up in smoke. Tragic really. But Alan was insistent. The library came first.'

'Where are these papers now?' I asked feeling a slight frisson of excitement.

'In one of the outbuildings.'

'I don't suppose there's any chance of seeing them?'

He shrugged. 'Don't see why not.'

It was a treasure trove. A vast collection of books and papers on every subject from history to astrology to medicine to some new-fangled mathematics called *Al-Gebra,* an Arab concoction that looked like a jumble of meaningless numbers to me. All Sir Richard's notes on his cornucopia of experiments were here as were all his books in Latin, Greek, even Arabic script. I'd never seen anything like it. It was an extraordinary collection that rivalled anything we had at the abbey and might very well contain all the knowledge of the world. And it was just sitting here in this ramshackle wooden shed in a Suffolk churchyard open to the elements. It was little short of miraculous.

And then my eye fell upon one document in particular. What drew my attention was that it was one of the few written in English. I was quickly disappointed, however, as I realised it was just a history of the final days of the Anarchy, no mention of green children. But then why would someone like Sir Richard, a man devoted to the study natural philosophy and science, be interested in history? Tentatively, I began to read.

Everyone knows the history of those evil times, even those of us born decades after they ended. They were the most momentous years in our parents' lives and they never stopped talking about them. When the Conqueror's son, King Henry I, died in 1135 he left only a daughter, Matilda, as his legitimate heir to the throne. But England had never been ruled by a woman before, the idea was unthinkable. So Henry's nephew, Stephen of Blois, grabbed the crown with the support of some of the

Norman nobility. But Matilda declined to give it up without a fight and the result was the period of civil war known as the Anarchy which only ended when Matilda's son, Harry fitz Empress, was old enough to win back the crown from Stephen.

Sir Richard's document began just after the nineteen-year-old Harry landed in England with his army at the beginning of 1153. King Stephen's own son and heir, Prince Eustace, tried to force a showdown laying waste a vast tract of East Anglia – and, incidentally, sacking Bury abbey in the process. But then while still at the abbey Eustace suddenly died of food poisoning. Naturally it was assumed that his death had been caused by Saint Edmund as punishment for this sacrilege. Certainly the monks thought so - Eustace wouldn't be the first royal to feel the sting of the saint's displeasure. But the consequences were cathartic. Devastated by the loss of his only son, King Stephen gave up the struggle to keep the crown and named Harry as his heir. A year later Stephen too died and Harry fitz Empress was duly crowned King Henry II of England on 19th December 1154 at Westminster Abbey.

So far so good. But what made my eyes nearly pop out of their sockets was the final paragraph of the document. It transpired that while Prince Eustace was staying at the abbey his regular chef had suddenly become indisposed and was replaced by one Jean de Tille who turned out to be none other than Sir Richard de Calne's own cook. It even recorded his fee: seven shillings and five-pence-three-farthings, an enormous sum for such a simple job.

The implications were obvious: that this Jean de Tille somehow hastened the demise of Henry's principal rival for the throne. If true it called into question the legitimacy of the entire Angevin dynasty. In the wrong hands the document could do untold damage to King John and possibly plunge the country back into civil war.

'Have you read this?' I asked Ivo trying to keep the excitement out of my voice.

He glanced over my shoulder and pulled a face. 'A bit dry for my tastes. Is it interesting?'

'Not really.' I smiled and rolled the scroll up again. 'As you say, a bit dry.'

Ivo looked around the piles of mouldering documents with disdain. 'I keep telling Alan to get rid of it all. But he won't. Not even the family want it.'

'The family? You mean the de Calnes? You've spoken to them?'

Ivo put his hand to his mouth. 'Oh dear, have I put my foot in it? Too much mule at supper, I'm afraid,' he flapped a languorous hand. 'Alan will be furious if he thinks I've peached.'

Now my pulse was really starting to race. 'Ivo, do you know where they are?'

He shook his head. 'I've said too much already.'

'I promise I won't tell.'

But he wouldn't be drawn further. No matter. The de Calnes would keep. This document was far more important. I didn't know what to do with it. All I knew was that it couldn't remain where it was. I had to get it somewhere safe.

It was pitch black by the time I'd saddled up, and very cold. But at least the rain had held off. Erigone's breath was blowing clouds of mist as was my own.

'Are you sure you won't stay?' said Ivo with genuine disappointment. 'It's a frightfully bad night.'

I shook my head. 'It's only a couple of miles to Ixworth. And I know the road. '

He held something out for me to take.

'What is it?'

'Something to keep you warm.'

It was a bottle of his "mule".

'You've been very kind. I can't thank you enough for your hospitality.'

He flapped his hand. 'Oh, I was glad of the company. If you get part way and change you mind you can always come back.' He stepped away from Erigone and made the sign of the cross. 'God be with you, brother.'

'And with you, my friend.'

I set off into the night. Although I'd told Ivo I'd be going to Ixworth, my real intention was to ride all the way to Bury. It was only a few miles further on and I wanted to get there as soon as possible with my precious cargo. It was the only place I could think it would be safe. It shouldn't take me more than an hour – two at the most, and I knew the route well enough. Even so, one road looks like any other in the dark. My lamp lit barely a yard or two in front of us. As long as I stayed between the verges I surely couldn't go wrong.

To keep my spirits up I began to recite the office of compline, but after a while I became aware of an echo. At first I thought I was imagining it or that the sound was bouncing off walls. But out here there were no buildings on the open road.

I stopped and listened but heard nothing. No, it must be my imagination. I started walking again. But as soon as I did, it started up again.

I stopped and turned round in my saddle: 'Hello? Is anybody there?'

No reply.

I started walking again but the echo started too. Each time was the same: We stopped - it stopped. We started - it started.

I called out again: 'Ivo, is that you?'

I got no further. There came a rushing sound, a flurry of wind and Erigone suddenly whinnied and collapsed beneath me throwing me forward and over her withers. I found myself sprawled with my hands and knees on the gritty road surface a sharp pain in my hands as I hit the road. My lantern went out. We were in complete darkness. As I scrabbled to get up I felt something wet and sticky on my fingers. Blood. I quickly felt around for Erigone's head. Blood was streaming from a gaping wound in her neck.

Now I was aware of someone else on the road, no longer an echo but a definite separate presence. My knife was hidden beneath my robes somewhere but I couldn't waste time hunting for it.

Another sound - to my left this time and I instinctively dropped to the floor just as I heard the swish of something pass close over my head. I lashed out but immediately felt a sharp pain in my shoulder making me cry out.

I didn't wait for any more. Whoever my attacker was I couldn't fight him in the dark. If only I could tell how close I was to Ixworth. I peered hard into the darkness but I couldn't see anything. Then just as I was about to give up the moon appeared in a break in the cloud and disappeared again. But it was enough. I recognized this part of the road. We were just a few hundred yards from my mother's house.

Injured or not, I knew I had to remount Erigone or die.

Somehow I managed to clamber back up onto her back and digging my heels into her flanks I bolted across the open field for all I was worth desperately hoping my assailant didn't know enough to follow. Against the whiteness of a cloud I could just make out the shape of Ixworth Hall looming out of the darkness. I have never been so grateful to see the old place. Without stopping we crashed through the gate and stumbled, bloodied and broken, into the yard and I hammered on the door for all I was worth.

Chapter Ten
A MATTER OF NO IMPORTANCE

'You've no idea who it was?'

'I didn't wait to ask.'

My mother nodded her head slowly. 'I've got men out scouring the road but I doubt they'll find anything. Whoever it was will be long gone by now. Did you lose anything? Anything of value?'

'Only my dignity – and my mule.'

'Your mule?'

'Not Erigone. I meant -' I shook my head. 'Never mind. How is she, by the way?' I asked Oswald.

'Quietly eating her way through a pocket of hay. I had one of the stable lads clean her wound. She'll be fine.'

My mother frowned irritably at me. 'What were you doing out on the road in the middle of the night, anyway?'

'Coming here, of course.'

'Alone? In the dark? Rather stupid wasn't it?'

'It's only two miles from Bardwell. I didn't expect to be set upon by a madwoman. Ouch! Be careful, Oswald. That stuff stings.' He was bathing my wounded shoulder with vinegar and water.

'Sorry master.' He squeezed out the rag and started again more gently this time.

My mother leaned towards me. 'Woman?'

'What?'

'You said "mad-*woman*".'

'Slip of the tongue. I meant "man".'

'Do you know any woman who would want to do such a thing?'

'No, of course I don't. Ee-yow! Oswald! Do that again and I swear I'll strike you.'

My mother tapped her stick impatiently on the flags. 'Don't take it out on Oswald, he's only trying to help you.' She peered at my cut shoulder. 'Ach, it's a flesh wound. I've had worse injuries slicing vegetables.'

'When did you last handle a vegetable?'

'When I gave birth to an ungrateful child.' She tutted and shook her head. 'They say doctors make the worst patients.'

When Oswald had finished inflicting torture on my shoulder, I gingerly replaced my robe. It had a nasty tear where the knife went through.

'Would you like me to sew it up for you, master?'

'No, it's all right. I'll get another from the stores when I return to the abbey.'

'He meant the wound,' said my mother.

I looked at her aghast. 'Stick needles in me? Are you mad?'

'It will stop the bleeding and prevent infection.'

'Will it, indeed? Just remind me, who is the doctor here?'

But the wound was weeping blood. And my shoulder was sore. Oswald held up a needle and thread provocatively between finger and thumb.

I pouted. 'Will it hurt?'

'Not if I use a thimble.'

'Hurt *me*, not *you*,' I scowled at him. 'Oh very well.'

I shut my eyes while he did the job, and I must admit he was remarkably delicate. I hardly felt a thing. When he'd finished my mother squinted at my newly-embroidered shoulder.

She nodded. 'Very neat. Now, what's this document you've discovered?'

She meant the Eustace document. I'd managed to secret it among my things when I left the Bardwell priest-house. I doubted if Ivo would miss it. But what it contained was explosive, far too dangerous to leave just lying around for anyone to find. However, given my mother's political predilections, I was loathe to let her see it. Foolishly in my initial confusion I'd already mentioned it to her.

'I'm not sure I should show it to you.'

'Fine. Keep it. Next time she might succeed.'

'Next time *who* might succeed?'

'Whoever your assailant was this time. Obviously that's what *she* was after.'

'I already told you, it wasn't a woman.'

She sniffed. 'So you say.'

I pointed to my shoulder. 'Do you really think a woman could have done this to me?'

'Huh! I could.'

I just glared at her. Anyway, I didn't think it was obvious at all. Nobody knew I had the Eustace document - how could they? I'd only just found the thing myself. But I had nearly lost it in the scuffle and was terrified of losing it again. On the other hand if I left it here my mother would only examine it once I'd gone with or without my permission.

'All right you can look at it. But only if you promise not to start a rebellion with it.'

'Pff! Rebellion!' She hobbled over to the table, smoothed her reading stone over the crumpled parchment and silently mouthed the contents herself.

'Well?' I said when she'd finished.

'Interesting. But I can't see the baronage of England rising up over a simple case of food poisoning.'

'Hardly simple. It's virtually Sir Richard's admission that he murdered the heir to the throne.'

'Eustace was never heir to the throne. He had no political party.'

'He was still a prince of the blood royal.'

'But not Angevin blood. Now if it had been King John's blood...'

'Mo-ther,' I warned.

She flapped a dismissive hand. 'Where did you say you found it?'

'Among Sir Richard de Calne's papers. There's a shed full of the stuff at the priest-house.'

'Relating to what?'

'All manner of things. Books, legal documents. Hundreds.'

'So why did you take this one?'

'Because in my naivety I thought the murder of a royal prince might be important. And if it was the reason I was attacked tonight then clearly I was right to take it – although I don't believe it.'

'Why not?'

I demurred. 'I just don't that's all. It's not what caused the trouble.'

'Why?' she asked suspiciously. 'What else has happened?'

'Nothing.'

'Walter. This is important. Tell me everything that happened since you left here.'

She'd only hear it from Father Ralph if I didn't tell her. So I related what happened in Coggeshall – a carefully edited version of it. As she listened a knowing smile slowly spread across her wizened old face.

'You can wipe that smirk off your face. It's not what you think,' I finished irritably.

'What I think is that you've already been attacked once - and by a woman despite your denial.'

I shook my head. 'It wasn't Leon attacked me tonight.'

'How do you know? It's pitch black out there, it could have been anybody. What you mean is you don't like the idea that a female could have got the better of you. Or is there some other reason you're trying to protect this person?'

'What other reason could there be?'

'You tell me. Why do men usually lose their wits when a woman is involved?'

'In case you've forgotten, mother, I'm a monk. The charms of the opposite sex have no affect on me.'

'You're still a man, aren't you? Or did they remove your stones at that abbey along with your brains?'

'Mother, please.'

She flapped her hand again. 'A woman is just as capable of sticking a knife in your ribs as a man. I

124

certainly could. And from the sounds of this Leon she is more than up to it. What sort of woman takes a man's name and dresses in men's clothing? I'm surprised Abbot Ralph permits it.'

'He depends on her. He's afraid she might leave the abbey.'

'Does she ever leave? Other than to waylay lovelorn monks, I mean.'

'Yes – no. Oh, I don't know. Why?'

'Because if she does then it may be the answer to your question.'

'Which question is that? There have been so many.'

She held her hand open reasonably. 'Didn't you tell me it was a woman who went to see Samson?'

'You're not suggesting that was Leon too?'

'Why not? You said yourself no-one could remember seeing a woman at the abbey. They wouldn't if she was dressed as a man.'

Much as I hated to admit it, what she was saying made sense. It was winter now, the dead season for building work. But all last summer craftsmen had been working on Samson's towers, including roofers. Leon could easily have been one of them and gone unnoticed. I had assumed she was a man when I first met her. My brother monks, in so far as they ever notice anything, would likely do the same.

'All right, let's assume for the moment it was Leon who visited Samson. That makes it even less likely that she would want to attack me. What am I to her? She didn't know I existed until two days ago.'

'And you didn't have the Eustace document until tonight. Don't fall into the trap of assuming

125

because you are attracted to this woman she's innocent. Maybe she has some connection with Sir Richard de Calne. Something you don't know about.'

I pulled a face.

'She does, doesn't she? Come on. Out with it.'

'Sir Richard was her mentor for the brick-works,' I said shyly.

She looked at me with exasperation. 'Well for heaven's sake!'

'But that's got nothing to do with poisoning the heir to the throne.'

'Maybe she thought the document was something else. Maybe there *is* something else that you missed.' She tapped an arthritic finger on her hairy chin. 'I think you ought to go and have another look.'

I looked at her in amazement. 'You want me to return to Bardwell? Along the road where I was just nearly murdered?'

'Not tonight,' she frowned. 'Tomorrow when it's light. It's only the next village, you'll be quite safe. Take Oswald with you if you're worried.'

I looked at the shrivelled old man before me. He must have been seventy-five if he was a day. He gave me a nervous smile.

'Mother, much as I value Oswald in so many ways...'

'I mean as a second pair of eyes, not as your bodyguard,' she said impatiently. 'He can look out for you since you're clearly incapable of doing so yourself.'

'He may not want to come with me.'

'Well, let's ask him, shall we? Oswald, will you accompany Master Walter to Bardwell tomorrow?'

126

'Yes, my lady.'

'There. He wants to go.'

I looked doubtfully at the elderly retainer. 'I'm not at all happy about this.'

'Then stay here and wait for another attempt on your life. Maybe it'll be third time lucky. Don't let your prejudices cloud your judgement, Walter. Forget that this Leon is a woman and think of her as a potential murderess.'

More easily said than done.

'I don't know if it's relevant, master,' said Oswald stepping forward, 'but while I was seeing to Erigone I found this caught in her harness.'

He produced something which made the blood drain from my face.

'What is it?' asked my mother hobbling over.

'It's a piece of leather, my lady.'

'Do you recognize it?'

I nodded. 'It's from a glove. The type of glove tilers wear.'

'Tilers like Leon, you mean?'

Reluctantly I nodded again. 'Yes.'

I spent the night in my own bed, a luxury I hadn't enjoyed for many a year. But I couldn't sleep. I was too preoccupied with the events of the past few days. Could it have been Leon who attacked me tonight? She had done so once and had seemed unaccountably hostile towards me afterwards. I could accept her rejection of my amorous advances, but to follow me into the wilds of the countryside and attack me again? It seemed so … disproportionate. I'd have preferred to think it was a common highway robber. But on his own? In the middle of the night? I knew that stretch of road. It was just a track between two villages, not a busy route-way even in daylight. You could wait weeks in the winter for an unwary traveller to pass and die of boredom first.

I rolled over and shut my eyes again but now images of the Eustace document loomed behind the lids. What puzzled me was that it existed at all. Regicide is not the sort of thing you would want to keep on record for others to find. Even after death it could have ramifications for your children – royals are not known for their forgiving natures. Apart from anything else it seemed so out of character. If Sir Richard was this great academic that everyone claimed he was, what was he doing assassinating princes? I supposed the two things need not be mutually exclusive, but with everything else he had going on in his life, it was hard to think where he found the time.

My arm throbbed and I couldn't get comfortable. If it wasn't so cold I might have got up and made myself a soothing poultice. I could only hope that there were no more surprises awaiting me at Bardwell the following day. I lay awake on my cot looking up at the rafters. I was sure I saw pigs flying overhead as I dozed.

Next morning Oswald was already waiting in the yard with two of my mother's best palfreys saddled and ready to leave.

'I took the liberty master, I hope you don't mind.' He handed me one set of reins. 'I didn't think you'd want to take Erigone in her present condition.'

'Thank you Oswald. I'm just sorry, old friend, to have to burden you with all this.'

'Oh, it will be pleasant to be away from the hall for a while. I don't very often get the chance anymore. Lady Isabel is virtually housebound these days.'

'How will she cope without you?'

'Very well, master,' he assured me.

I turned to see the aged beldam standing in the porch.

'You'll be back by this evening?'

'Before if possible. I don't intend being out after dark again if I can help it.'

'Then you'd best get a move on. Here.' She held out a small parcel wrapped in sacking. It felt unexpectedly heavy.

'What is it?'

'My reading stone.'

'I don't need a reading stone. My eyesight's fine.'

'Take it anyway. Some people's writing is like ants walking through ink. You don't want to get there and find you can't read it.'

I didn't really want to take it. Reading stones are heavy lumps of polished glass that magnify anything beneath them. Useful for reading but no good for writing which was why Jocelin had to give up writing his chronicle when his eyes grew too dim to focus. I dare say the same will happen to me one day. But at the moment they were fine – as long as the handwriting isn't too small. What is needed is some way of suspending the stone in front of the eyes thus leaving the hands free to write – just the sort of problem Sir Richard de Calne might have turned his mind to. Who knows, maybe he already had and I would find designs for some solution among his papers at Bardwell. Now that really would be something worth finding.

'Have a safe journey,' said my mother stepping back. 'And Walter – do be careful this time.'

Her words drifted over the rain-soaked stable-yard as we ambled out, and for the first time in my life I had the feeling she was genuinely concerned.

Chapter Eleven
AN UNNECESSARY MURDER

Some people when they get nervous clam up. Others can't stop talking. I'm in the latter camp. When I'm jittery I chatter, incessantly, about anything. Not a wise thing to do when one is trying to be inconspicuous. But I couldn't help myself. Poor Oswald must have felt his ears were being burned off. The weather didn't help either. The rain had eased at last but had been replaced by mist, the sort that freezes on contact with cold surfaces and over time builds the most exquisite crystals of ice. Beautiful to look at, but this kind of mist also obscures anything further than fifty feet away. At one point I was convinced I saw a figure with his hand raised ready to strike only to find when we got to it that it was a dead tree with a single crooked branch. The mist didn't thin until we passed the first house on the outskirts of Bardwell village. A few more steps and we were standing at the top of the slope gazing down the valley slope towards the river.

'What exactly are we looking at master?'

'Wykes Hall – or what's left of it. Don't you recognize it?'

'It looks different somehow to when I last saw it.'

'Well it was nearly sixty years ago. And of course it is different. It's just a burnt-out shell of a once-proud house. And didn't you say it was in the middle of the night when you were called? Anyway, it's not somewhere you'd want to visit now, not with its current residents.' I told him about the bodies stacked up awaiting burial after the interdict.

'I hope I don't die before then. I'd hate to end up as rat fodder.'

'Don't worry, Lady Isabel won't let that happen. She'd have you garnished in a pastry crust first. Oswald *en croute,*' I chuckled.

A flock of rooks that had been nesting among the ruins rose like a spiral of black smoke and then swooped low over the river cawing as they went. I shuddered. They looked like an ominous portent.

'Come on, it's too cold to stand about out here. We'll go up to the house and find my new friend Ivo.'

It was still early morning and the priest-house was in darkness as we rode into the yard. Something wasn't right. All the windows of the house were still shuttered and there was no sign of life. I could hear the pig in its pen complaining to be let out and next to it a cockerel crowed from inside the coop. Everyone wanted the day to begin which it should have done by now.

I hammered on the door: 'Anybody about?'

No reply.

Oswald nodded to the roof. 'There's no smoke, master.'

I looked up. He was right. Had there been a fire the smoke would have escaped through one of the gaps at the top ends of the gable. There was none.

'It's still early,' I said hopefully. 'Maybe he's not up yet.' I banged on the door again. 'Ho Ivo, it's me, Brother Walter!'

Still nothing.

'Perhaps he has been called away,' suggested Oswald.

I tried the latch. It lifted easily and I pushed the door away from me but didn't enter. The inside of the house was cold and dark, not the warm welcoming place I had known the previous night. It was also silent. Eerily silent. And then as my eyes adjusted to the gloom I could begin make out a figure seated on a chair with his back towards us.

'Ivo?'

He didn't turn round. Maybe he was asleep, or possibly drunk from consuming too much "mule". No, I didn't think so. An unpleasant shudder went down my spine.

'Wait here,' I said to Oswald and cautiously stepped across the threshold. I looked quickly round the room but all seemed as I remembered it the night before. I then walked round to the front of the seated figure where I was met by an appalling sight. It was Ivo all right. His throat had been cut from ear to ear and the front of his cassock was completely drenched in blood. He was quite dead, his eyes staring fixedly ahead of him at the empty fire-grate in an expression of vague puzzlement.

I was so shocked that for a moment I couldn't move as the full horror of the scene overwhelmed me. Then in the corner of my eye I saw something move and from out of the shadows another figure suddenly roared and lunged at me. I wasn't quick enough to leap out of the way but I saw the flash of a blade and instinctively put my arm up to protect myself managing to block the first thrust. The impact pushed me backward as my attacker raised his knife a second time but somehow I managed to block that too. The two of us then fell to the floor and rolled a couple of times. As I went down for the third time something else crossed my line of vision. There was a dull thump, a brief cry and my attacker collapsed across of me. Unsure whether he was conscious or not, I pushed myself from under him and looked up to see Oswald standing over us with something heavy swinging from his hand.

'Lady Isabel's reading stone, master,' he grinned.

My assailant was a young man in his mid-twenties. Oswald's blow had knocked him out cold. We turned him over to get a better look at his face.

'Who is he?' I whispered. 'I've never seen him before in my life.'

'I know who he is,' said Oswald. 'He's the Bardwell priest.'

'Father Alan?' I glanced quickly at Ivo's corpse. 'You don't think -?'

'No,' said Oswald. 'He didn't do this. He's wearing oilskins and they're are soaking wet like ours. The curate's been dead for hours. I'd say he arrived just before us.'

I felt the young man's face.

'Yes, you're right,' I said. 'He's ice-cold. Ivo said he'd been away. He must have thought I was the murderer.'

'That's not all,' said Oswald nodding towards Ivo's corpse. 'Have you seen his hands?'

I went over to look. I hadn't noticed before but his wrists had been tied to the chair arms and his fingers were missing - all of them. They'd been severed at the second knuckle.

I shuddered. 'Dear God. Why would anybody do such a thing?'

'Only one reason I can think of, master: torture.'

A moan from Alan as he started to come round.

'It's all right,' I said going over to him. 'You're with friends. No-one's going to hurt you.'

He sat up holding his head. 'What happened?'

'You've had a bit of a bump on your head, that's all. You'll be fine.'

Suddenly his eyes widened. 'Ivo?'

'He's with God now,' I said as gently as I could.

At my words the young man's face crumpled and he sobbed: 'Who did this?'

'We don't know – yet. But we will find out. That I promise you.'

I sent Oswald off to find the village reeve while I lit a fire. There is nothing like a good fire to get the blood flowing again. I also pulled a sheet from one of the beds to hide the body from view. I said the appropriate prayers for the dead and would have liked to close his eyes but I know from experience that's almost always impossible. They continued to stare ahead, accusing, querying, unseeing. The severed fingers I found lying among the rushes below where they had been amputated and I wrapped them discreetly in a piece of rag out of view. All the while I did this Alan sat staring into space. He'd stopped sobbing, thank goodness, but now he was silent, drained of emotion.

'How are you feeling, my son?' I asked him gently.

He didn't reply, just sat staring in bewilderment. But I couldn't leave him like that. There were things that had to be done.

I sat down beside him. 'Now listen to me, Alan. The reeve will be here shortly. Before he comes you must tell me all you know.'

'But I don't know anything. I've been away. I came back this morning to find…' He covered his face with his hands and started to whimper again.

'No, don't start that again,' I said pulling them away. 'We have to get your story straight.'

'My story?'

'Have you looked around? Is there anything missing? Could this have been a robbery?'

He just shook his head.

'No,' I agreed. 'That's because this has nothing to do with robbery, has it? It's because of something quite different.'

He glanced at my face then quickly looked away. 'I don't know what you mean.'

'Yes you do. We both know what I'm talking about. I'm a monk. I live with eighty other monks. I know what goes on. Two young men living together. I don't judge, but some of the villagers might. That's what's happened, isn't it? Admit it. Someone in Bardwell has taken exception to your relationship with Ivo and in your absence exacted retribution. That's right isn't it?'

Alan's face blushed crimson. 'No, it is not.'

'Yes it is, of course it is,' I persisted. 'Name your persecutor and I promise I will have him

136

arrested. Ivo will get justice, I'll make sure of that. But you must give me a name.'

'I can't give you a name because there isn't one,' he blurted angrily. 'It's a lie.'

'Which part is the lie? The part about the persecutor, or the part about your relationship with Ivo?'

'All of it!' He hid his face and started sobbing again.

I let him go. No, that wasn't it. It may be true but that wasn't the problem. Ivo's torture had nothing to do with moral outrage. It might have been easier to deal with if it had. At least we would have a reason. But I had nothing to go on. Why torture Ivo in such a hideous way? What could he know that would warrant such an atrocity?

Then another thought struck me, an appalling thought. What if it was because of me? Coming so quickly after my visit Ivo's death was surely a dreadful coincidence if that's all it was. Could his murderer be the same person who had attacked me on the road? Having failed with me he – or she – returned here to torture and murder Ivo? Please God, I earnestly prayed, let it not be because of me. But the answer would have to wait for the sound of horses on the cobbles outside brought our interview to an abrupt end.

Bardwell's reeve was a young man in his early thirties. I knew his face as soon as he walked through the door although I couldn't remember his name. His father had been reeve before him which meant he probably knew my mother – a fact he confirmed almost as soon as he arrived:

'I've known the Lady Isabel since I was a child. A fine lady.'

'Thank you,' I smiled. 'I'll tell her you said so, Reeve…?'

'Wodebite. Robert Wodebite.'

'Ah yes. I think I knew your father.' This was going to be easier than I thought.

Nevertheless, Reeve Wodebite's professional eye roamed around the room taking in its details. I must admit it did look a bit of a mess. In our scuffle Alan and I had knocked over the table which I'd had the forethought to right before the reeve arrived, but I could do nothing about the broken flower vase which lay on the floor next to it. He also couldn't have failed to notice my torn robe and Alan's bump on the head that was swelling by the minute.

Reeve Robert's eye alighted on mine. 'Can someone tell me what happened?'

'Well Robert, it's like this,' I began. 'Father Alan here has been away visiting his family and returned this morning to find his curate as you see him now.'

I lifted the sheet just enough to reveal Ivo's body beneath. Second time round was no better than the first. All that blood down the front of him, and those staring eyes. Not that it put Robert off. He bent low to examine the body closely paying particular attention to the neck-wound and mutilated hands. As soon as he'd finished his examination I covered up the body again.

'What happened to his fingers?' Robert asked quietly.

I discreetly opened the bloodied parcel for him to view. He nodded and I put them away again.

'Any idea who did it?'

138

'None whatsoever. It's a complete mystery. I arrived this morning shortly after Father Alan to find Ivo exactly as you see him now. Nothing's been touched, by the way. Everything's exactly as we found it.'

The reeve nodded. 'May I ask why you're here, brother?'

'I came to see the curate last night and returned again this morning. We had some unfinished business to conclude.'

'What was the nature of that business?'

'Oh, just a private matter.' I didn't want to go into all the business about the Eustace document at this stage, much less the green children.

'A bit early to be paying a social call. Did you know the deceased well?'

'No actually, we only met last night.'

'I see. Were you two alone together?'

'Last night, yes. This morning I came with my man Oswald, here.' I indicated Oswald who stepped forward to identify himself.

'And the curate was alive and well when you left him?'

'Perfectly. We'd shared a little light supper together and then I left.'

'What time was that?'

'I really couldn't say. Oswald, what time did I arrive at Ixworth Hall?'

'After supper, master.'

'So quite late?'

'Yes.'

'I see,' he nodded. 'And this morning when you arrived - was Father Alan already here?'

'We arrived more or less at the same time.'

'But not together?'

'No.'

'So he could have been here already?'

'I don't think so. He was still in his riding clothes.'

'I see.' He nodded towards Alan. 'How did he get that lump on the head?'

'Oh that - that was Oswald's doing, I'm afraid. Alan mistook us for intruders - a perfectly reasonable mistake under the circumstances. Curiously enough, we did the self-same thing, didn't we Oswald?'

'Yes master.'

I smiled benignly at the reeve.

'And is that how you got your injury?'

'My injury?' My shoulder. I'd all but forgotten about that. 'No, that's an old injury,' I said hastily covering it up.

'Not that old by the look of it. The stitching's still fresh.'

'Well if you must know, I was attacked last night on the road.'

'Was that before or after your visit here?'

'After. I was on my way home.'

'I see. Did you see who your attacker was?'

I shook my head. 'A common highwayman I presume. It was too dark to see anything.'

'A highwayman? On the Ixworth road? At night?'

'I know it sounds unlikely but that's what happened.'

'I see.'

I was growing tired of all this questioning. 'You keep saying you see. You see what? Look Reeve Wodebite, what are you getting at?'

'Well brother, I'll tell you. To me it looks like either Father Alan and his curate had an argument this morning before you arrived and the curate came off worst, or...'

'Or?'

'Or you were the one who had the argument, over some private business you seem reluctant to divulge, the curate chased after you and in the ensuing fight he was killed.'

I looked at him aghast. 'Really? And I suppose Oswald helped me bring the body back here this morning?'

'That is a possibility.'

'No it isn't, it's a nonsense. Why would I strap Ivo's lifeless body in a chair and chop his fingers off? Why would anyone?'

'That I don't know - yet.'

'I've told you what happened. The three of us found Ivo as you see him now. None of us murdered him.'

'Then who did?'

I opened my mouth to answer but Oswald tapped me on my arm:

'Master, there's something outside you ought to see.'

'Can't it wait?' I said irritably.

'I think you should see. Really I do.'

I turned to Robert. 'Is that all right with you? Or do you think I'm going to run away?'

He made a conciliatory gesture and I followed Oswald out into the yard. The outbuilding containing all Sir Richard's books and papers stood with its door hanging off its hinges. Inside the contents were strewn everywhere.

'Good grief! It looks as though it's been hit by a tornado.'

'Someone was certainly hunting for something, master.'

'And from the mess I'd say they didn't find it.'

'What do you think it was?'

The obvious answer was the Eustace document since it was the only thing missing. It might explain why I was attacked and possibly why Ivo was murdered. It was the only thing that made any sense.

The same thought must have occurred to Oswald: 'Do you think Lady Isabel will be in danger?'

Of course she now had the document. 'I don't know. But we won't take any chances. As soon as Reeve Wodebite has finished with us here we'll make our way back to Ixworth.'

'I'm afraid that won't be possible, brother.'

I turned to see Robert standing behind us flanked by two of his two guards.

'I shall have to ask all three of you to accompany me to the sheriff's office. There are still one or two questions that need answering.'

'To Bury? But we can't. We have to get to Ixworth.'

'Not today, brother.' He motioned to the two guards who stepped forward. I backed away thinking I might run after all. But Oswald had his hand on my arm.

'I think we should, master.'

Recalling these events years later I am amazed at how relaxed I seem to have been. But I suppose so much was going on that I didn't have time to react rationally to each episode. One becomes overwhelmed by the sheer magnitude. But I can see now that the torture of Ivo was one of those pivotal moments when everything that came before was supplanted by everything that came after. Like the wheel of fortune turning, once over the peak each moment that passed gathered speed and momentum as we rushed ever faster onwards. But whether we ended up at the bottom broken or at the top whole was in the hands of God alone. We could only wait and see.

Part Two

THE CURSE

Chapter Twelve
A MISCALCULATION

Who was doing these dreadful things? I refused to believe it was Leon. I know I'd only known her a short while but I pride myself on being a good judge of character. She just wasn't the murdering sort, and certainly not in the hideous manner of Ivo's death. All right, she did attack me in Coggeshall, but that had been self-defence. And if she truly was Samson's mysterious visitor, why would she announce what she was going to do beforehand? It just didn't add up.

The problem was at the moment I had no other suspects. I might have a better chance of finding one if I could see some connection between all the different elements. The only common factor seemed to be Sir Richard de Calne. The green children had been taken to him; Leon had been his protégée; and the Eustace document had been found among his possessions. Somehow all these things were linked. But how?

There wasn't much I could do about any of it until I'd sorted out this mess with Reeve Robert. I couldn't blame him for suspecting the three of us of being involved in Ivo's death. I'd have done the same under the circumstances. But it was for the sheriff to decide these matters and I was confident I could persuade him we were not involved. I mean, he couldn't really think me capable of torturing and murdering someone in such a cold-blooded and hideous fashion.

Could he?

Sir Peter de Mealton and I are old friends. We first met a decade earlier shortly after he was appointed High Sheriff of Norfolk and Suffolk. Admittedly it was not the most auspicious of introductions. A London stall-holder had been accused by the then papal legate of murdering his clerk. It's a long and complicated case that I can't go into now, but basically Sir Peter and I disagreed on one particular detail: whether the stall-holder was guilty or not. Sir Peter thought he was, I thought he wasn't. It turned out in the end that I was right and the man was acquitted thus affirming the rule of law in Saint Edmund's town to the great credit of its chief law officer, Sheriff Peter. However, being right doesn't always endear one to one's superiors, especially one as vain as Sir Peter.

He's an interesting chap, our sheriff. His family were minor gentry from Cambridgeshire who were fortunate enough to have backed the right side during the Anarchy – that is the Empress Matilda, mother of the eventual winner, Henry fitz Empress - and done quite well out of the settlement. Sir Peter has since built upon that initial success by gaining property and preferment and growing immensely rich in the process. He needed to be given his expensive tastes. I dare say he knows my mother's predilections concerning King John but has a quaint old-fashioned deference when it comes to women of noble birth. I think also he has a grudging admiration for my family. He knows about my father's involvement in ending the reign of terror perpetrated on the people of Cambridgeshire by the outlaw Geoffrey de Mandeville. Sir Peter therefore tends to tolerate my occasional forays into the murky world of crime - albeit with a slightly jaundiced eye.

And the esteem is mutual. I have always admired sheriff Peter's taste in clothes which are never less than eye-catching. Today, for instance, he was attired in yellow stockings, scarlet tunic and a gold-tasselled cap. It is a combination probably better suited to a younger man, if to anybody at all, but I wouldn't be so rude as to point this out, and certainly not while standing before him in his office in the guild hall alongside Oswald and Alan each of us suspected of murdering poor Ivo. Lounging arrogantly against the wall and learning the tricks of his father's trade was Sir Peter's twelve-year-old son, also called Peter, a miniature version of his father in every way but for the beard, which omission no doubt he will correct in time. Reeve Robert Wodebite who had escorted us from Bardwell was also present.

Sir Peter looked up at me from behind his desk, one expensively-shod toe tapping the floor impatiently. He had already noticed, I was sure, the rip in my robe which was still gaping open, and Alan's bump which had not only not gone down as I had hoped but had swollen to even greater proportions and was now an angry bulge on the side of his head.

'I might have known it would be you,' Sir Peter growled between a perfect set of white teeth. 'Soon as the reeve told me a monk from the abbey was involved I guessed. What have you been up to this time?'

I explained, in my most obsequious tones, the salient features of the morning's events: how Oswald, Alan and I all arrived at the priest-house in Bardwell at roughly the same time to find Ivo with his throat cut and showing clear signs of having been tortured.

'Tortured in what way?'

'His hands were tied down and the fingers hacked off.'

Sir Peter winced. Behind him his son gave a nervous giggle.

'What, all of them?' Sir Peter looked down his own immaculately manicured fingers.

I nodded. 'All ten.'

'But why?'

'Presumably he had some information his tormentors wanted.'

'What information?'

I shrugged. 'Whatever it was we must assume he didn't get it or the curate's agony wouldn't have lasted as long as it did.'

'And you have no idea who perpetrated this barbaric act?'

'None, except it wasn't any of us – although ...' I added quickly, '... I can quite see why Reeve Robert should think it might have been.' I smiled benignly at the young man.

'Why exactly were you there? It was early morning, wasn't it? Not a time to be making house-calls, is it?'

I'd been anticipating this question and despite having had the entire journey from Bardwell to Bury to think of an answer I still didn't have one – at least, nothing convincing.

'As I'm sure you know, my lord,' I bluffed, 'the church at Bardwell is in the gift of the abbot of Bury. From time to time Abbot Samson, like all devoted shepherds, likes to visit his flock in order to make sure all is well and they are in need of nothing. Given the abbot's current indisposition, it was my honour on this occasion to fulfil that role on his behalf.'

No, not very convincing, but it was the best I could come up with. Frankly, I'd have been surprised if the sheriff was taken in by it. He wasn't:

'Bollocks. You're a physician. Overseeing church property is the job of some other abbey officer - the sacrist, isn't it? Why you?'

I shrugged. 'Purely as a matter of convenience, my lord. My family home at Ixworth is but two miles distance from Bardwell. We are neighbours. I could kill two birds with one stone – er, so to speak. A visit to the Bardwell church and to my mother. I'm, erm, very fond of my mother.'

An inspired piece of extemporization if I do say so. But any stray bolt of lightning at that moment would have cloven me to the chine for the lie it was.

'But I beg you to consider, my lord,' I went on hastily, 'what possible motive would I have for committing such a crime?'

'I don't know – and I'm not sure I want to.' He looked at me with distaste. 'What exactly was the nature of your relationship with this ... curate? The reeve here tells me you two were together in the priest-house - alone.'

Behind him young Peter was sniggering.

'Maybe we should ask the abbot?' I said growing rather irritable. 'After all, it was he who sent me.'

Now, Sir Peter may dress as a clown but he's nobody's fool. He is in fact an astute political animal. It was coming up to January, the month when royal appointments are made for the coming year. Reappointments are usually automatic but can never be taken for granted, especially where King John is concerned. As Judge Delegate and member of the King's High Council, Abbot Samson was in a position to influence the royal mind. Ill as he was, Samson still wielded considerable influence. Sir Peter knew this. My mentioning the abbot was thus another piece of inspiration.

Besides, there was another point: Samson had always made it clear to the sheriff that he regarded cases involving members of the clergy a matter for the abbey's courts and not the secular authorities. Of the four people involved in this case, three were clerics: me, Alan and Ivo. Add to this the abbot was also sick abed and would likely take it amiss if his chief physician were suddenly shut away in the town lock-up and unavailable for consultation. I was hoping Sir Peter would rather not get tangled up in all that if he could possibly help it – at least, not until his own position was confirmed. That was the message I was trying to convey. Astute as he was, I'm sure he got it. It was just a question of how best to disentangle himself.

Sir Peter sat back in his chair and stroked his neatly cropped beard thoughtfully. 'You say the curate had his throat cut? I've seen this before. It creates lot of blood. Was there much?'

I saw immediately where he was going with this. 'Oh indeed, my lord, gallons. It had cascaded down the front of Ivo drenching his tunic, dripping on the floor.'

'I imagine it went everywhere.'

'Indeed it did.'

Sir Peter nodded sagely.

By now Reeve Robert had also realised what the sheriff was up to: 'But if the killer had been standing behind his victim, my lord...?'

'There would still be blood. It would have been impossible for the killer not to have got some on him at least.' He waved a hand at us. 'None of these has any on them.'

I helpfully held up the palms of my hands and nudged Oswald to do the same. Poor Alan. He was still looking pale from the morning's revelations. This graphic description of his friend's injuries was making him faint. Sheriff Peter snapped his fingers and a guard instantly produced a chair for him to sit.

But Robert was not to be put off quite so easily: 'What about their own injuries? Obviously some kind of altercation took place.'

The sheriff flapped a dismissive hand. 'A bump on the head and a torn sleeve. You can get that falling out of bed. No, I'm inclined on this occasion to agree with Brother Walter.'

'But my lord!'

Sir Peter held up his hand for silence. 'I've made my decision. We will hunt for the murderer of this curate elsewhere. And when we have caught them,' he added looking directly at me, 'they will feel the full force of the law. You've done your job well, master reeve, rest assured it will be noted. But for now that will be all. You may go Brother Walter,

Father Alan, and erm...' He twiddled his fingers at Oswald. 'You.'

Oswald and I quickly helped Alan out of his chair before the sheriff could change his mind. Reeve Robert blustered, but there was not much more he could do. He marched out of the room followed by his guards.

'Er, Brother Walter. Just before you go.'

I flinched. 'My lord?'

He waited until we were quite alone then leaned forward and lowered his voice. 'I don't in fact believe you did do those things you described, but that doesn't mean you are entirely off the hook. You have a way of being where you shouldn't be. So if I find you were involved in this business in any way however minutely, I will personally hang you from the scaffold by your clerical balls. Clear?'

'Perfectly my lord.'

Behind him, young Peter sniggered.

Having been dismissed I quickly ran down the stairs after the others.

'Oh, Robert!'

The reeve stopped. 'Brother Walter?'

'I hope you don't take umbrage back there,' I said catching him up. 'You know I am as keen to find Ivo's killer as you are.'

He gave me the friendliest of smiles. 'I know that, brother. And I was only doing my duty. It's nothing personal.'

'I'm relieved to hear it. I'd hate for us to fall out.'

'We won't do that. But I will find the murderer. And if it does turn out to be you, I will have you.' He smiled again, quite amiably, before turning on his heel and marching off.

Oh good, I thought watching him go. The sheriff and now the Bardwell reeve both with me in their sights. Could things get any better? I made some sympathetic noises to Alan and left him in Oswald's capable hands to return him to Bardwell and then get himself back to Ixworth. The sooner Oswald was on his way the sooner he could inform his mistress of what had taken place and warn her to be on her guard. The murderer was still at large and whatever it was he was after he didn't seem the sort to make allowances for age or sex. I told him I'd follow just as soon as I was finished at the abbey.

Unfortunately it was going to take longer than I had hoped. When I got to my laboratorium Nathan was already waiting for me at the door. The look on his face was sour.

'What is it?' I asked him. 'What's happened now?'

'It's Abbot Samson, master. He's dead.'

Chapter Thirteen
AN EASY MISTAKE
TO MAKE

It was the news I'd been dreading. Had it happened a week earlier I might have abandoned the hunt for the green children in good conscience. But too much had happened since. Now I wanted to get to the bottom of the whole shoddy business myself. But would I be allowed to? At least with Samson still in charge nobody could question what I was doing. Now I wasn't so sure.

He was laid out on his bed in the abbot's palace with a single candle burning at his feet and a small posse of monks kneeling along either side of him reciting the prayers for the dying. If that wasn't miserable enough, Jocelin was also there ringing his hands and weeping copiously.

'Oh W-walter,' he said coming quickly up to me as I entered. 'You're too l-late I'm afraid. He's g-gone. I'm s-so s-s-sorry.'

Tears rolled down his cheeks. He looked terribly distressed. I placed my hands on his bony shoulders and muttered a few words of sympathy.

'Oh, p-please don't be k-kind,' he sobbed. 'I sh-shan't be able to b-b-bear it.'

Poor Jocelin. Of all the monks at the abbey he would be saddest to see Samson go. Their relationship went back many years to a time long before I came to Bury. As a young novice Jocelin had been in the care of subsacrist Samson as he then was who mentored him and taught him the Rule. After Samson's elevation to the abbacy Jocelin became his chaplain and even wrote a brief history of his life and times. I read it once and was impressed by its honesty leaving out nothing even when it was unfavourable to Samson. Usually such accounts are mere sycophantic hagiographies. It was a measure of both Jocelin's literary genius and his confidence in Samson's legacy that his was not. Unfortunately because of his failing eyesight Jocelin had to end his chronicle a decade earlier thus omitting some of the more interesting events of recent times - including my own contributions which I have endeavoured to record here.

With so many bodies crowding round the bed it was dark and stuffy in the room so I asked if we might open one of the windows.

'To p-permit the s-soul to escape more f-freely,' nodded Jocelin with enthusiasm. 'Of c-course, you're absolutely r-right, Walter.' He strode purposefully to the windows and flung open the shutters instantly bathing the room in light and air. The posse of monks shivered and shrank back.

'That's better,' I said smiling at them.

Jocelin isn't the only one who will grieve for Samson. Throughout Christendom churchmen and churchwomen as well as statesmen, noblemen even princes will mourn the great man's passing. Some, no doubt, will welcome it. Thirty years Samson had been abbot of Saint Edmund's with only Baldwin, the Conqueror's abbot, having a longer tenure. You can't hold such an important post for so long without making enemies along the way.

But what concerned me was what was likely to happen now. Few of my brother monks would remember a time when Samson wasn't there, and fewer still when there was no abbot at all. The last time this happened was before Samson's election when the abbacy was vacant for two years. That was under John's father, good King Harry. Kings, of course, are quite happy to have a vacancy, for a while at least, since the income which normally would go to the abbot goes instead to them. But it is not a satisfactory arrangement and it is in everybody's interest to have a capable man in charge of so powerful an institution as the abbey of Saint Edmund. Unfortunately this time the vacancy was likely to continue for some time, at least while the interdict lasted since among all its other restrictions we would not be permitted to elect a successor. In the meantime responsibility for the day to day running of the abbey would fall to the prior and I couldn't imagine Prior Herbert taking much interest in green children. In all likelihood the entire matter would be dropped and just as I was beginning to make progress. It really was most inconsiderate of Samson to choose now to expire.

But wait. What was that? I was sure I heard something. Was this, as Jocelin suggested, the sound of the soul leaving the body? Indeed, can souls be heard or yet seen as they pass on? It is a question many scholars and churchmen have asked so far without a satisfactory answer. Presumably souls have weight however ethereal. It must be possible to detect them once outside the body.

Another sigh.

With every other soul in the room praying and Jocelin busy whimpering, nobody else seemed to have noticed. Was I imagining it? I went closer and placed my ear to the dead man's mouth. I was sure I felt something on my cheek. The death rattle perhaps? I leaned closer still until my ear hovered a fraction above Samson's lips.

'For God's sake get Jocelin out of here. His wailing is killing me.'

Jocelin caught his breath and spun round. 'Did he speak? D-did I hear my n-name? God be p-praised, a m-miracle!' He crossed himself ferociously. 'Walter,' he said placing both hands on my arm. 'What did he s-say? Did he g-give you his b-blessing?'

'He mentioned you, my friend.'

'D-did he r-really?' Jocelin's eyes filled with tears of gratitude.

Samson's lips moved again. I leant over him.

'Erm - he wishes to consult with his physician. In private. He asks that everyone else should leave.'

The monks kneeling by his bed stopped their chanting, exchanged affronted glances but did not move. They'd had been there all day, probably for several days, kneeling in witness. They glared resentfully at me and I couldn't in all conscience blame them. They'd been doing all the work and now they were to be dismissed without so much as a thankyou. But it was not unreasonable request. I was, after all, Samson's doctor as much as anybody else's. As it happened I was also executor of his Will and needed what little time Samson had left to settle his affairs. At least, that's what I told them. All nonsense of course. I knew for a fact that Samson had his Will settled a decade earlier and as far as I knew had never altered it. Still, the monks had no option but to obey the man's dying request and started to leave followed, eventually and with great reluctance, by Jocelin.

'You will c-call me if he asks for me, w-won't you W-walter? P-promise me.'

'I will my friend.'

'The very m-moment he asks.'

'Upon the instant. You have my word,' I said gently closing the door after him.

'How are you feeling, father?'

'How does a dead man feel? Thirsty.' He nodded to the bookcase opposite. 'There's a bottle of Scotch fire water behind that copy of Abbot Anselm's *Cur Deus Homo.* Fetch it for me, there's a good chap.'

Whisky - or *uisge beatha* to give it its Gaelic name, meaning "water of life" - certainly lived up to the name as far as Samson was concerned. Before he'd finished his second cup he was sitting up in bed and looking more animated than I'd seen him in a long while. He took another gulp of the evil-tasting brew and smacked his lips.

'That's better.'

'We thought you were gone, father.'

'I told you last time I have no intention of going anywhere before I've completed thirty years. Baldwin managed thirty-two. I intend giving him a good run for his money. Mind you I very nearly died of boredom. Where've you been? I've been lying here for days with nothing to do but listen a lot of smelly old men droning on.'

I pulled a stool up and sat down. 'I did as you asked and spoke to my mother about the green children.'

'And?'

'She more or less confirmed what you said about them.'

He grunted. 'So you believe me now? I've not lost my wits after all. No doubt she sent you on to Coggeshall where you met Father Ralph. He would have confirmed it as well.'

'I read his chronicle. I couldn't decide if he truly believed in them or whether he simply enjoys a good yarn.'

'Ralph got the story direct from Sir Richard de Calne. Not the sort of man to make up a tale like that if there was no truth in it.'

'That wasn't all he got from Sir Richard. Father, why you didn't tell me Leon would be there?'

He frowned. 'Who?'

'Don't pretend you don't know who I mean. The woman who came to visit you. The one who supposedly warned you about this murder. Leon – Leonie.'

He started fiddling with his bedspread. 'Is that her name? I never knew.'

'Yes you did. She's been working on your towers for the past year. You must have spoken to her a hundred times.'

He grimaced as though in pain. 'This last year hasn't been good for me. I've not been well and -'

'She tried to kill me.'

He shot me a look of disbelief. 'Nonsense. Why would she?'

'I don't know. I was hoping you'd be able to tell me. And that's not even the worst of it.' I told him about Ivo's murder. As I did so his face grew blacker and blacker.

'I know Bardwell. I know the curate there. He had nothing to do with the green children. I shall pray for his soul.'

'So he's not the intended victim? The one Leon told you about?'

'No of course not. There must be another explanation.'

'I think there might be.' I told him about the Eustace document.

Samson frowned. 'I remember this. It was in the final days of the Anarchy. I was still a novice but I remember the other monks talking about it. They thought it was Saint Edmund's doing, of course, as punishment for Eustace ransacking the abbey - a theory King Henry was keen to endorse. Had he lived, Eustace would have been our next monarch and Henry fitz Empress would have been an unknown French count. King Eustace the first – can you credit it?' He shuddered. 'Seems we have Sir Richard's cook to thank for saving us from that. Strange, though, that he should have documented it.'

'From what I can see Sir Richard documented everything.'

'But a dangerous thing to leave lying around.'

'Which is why I removed it. And Just in time, it seems.'

'You think that's what the murderer was after?'

'I don't know. But I'd imagine a document confessing to the poisoning of the heir to the throne would be worth killing for.'

He grunted. 'Where is this document now?'

'I gave it to my mother for safe keeping.'

'Was that wise?'

160

'Oh, I think she's safe enough. Nobody else knows she has it.'

'That's not quite what I meant.' He gave me a sly look. 'We've never really talked a lot about your mother have we?'

'About her questionable associates? I'd rather not know.'

'She always was wayward in her views even as a young woman. Did she tell you we studied together?'

'She may have mentioned it.'

He nodded. 'Paris before the Flood. Women could in those days. No longer, thank goodness. Education is wasted on women. Gives them ideas above their station.'

'Some might say it's a good thing. Educate the father and you educate one man. Educate the mother and you educate the entire family.'

He looked at me sideways. 'You've changed your tune. Or has Leon changed it for you? She has, hasn't she?' He smiled. 'I knew there was more to that business in Coggeshall than you were admitting. What did you do to her?'

'Nothing that warranted murder.'

He gave a knowing grin. 'You wouldn't be the first monk tempted by a pretty face. Your mother turned a head or two in her day. That's another good reason for keeping them away from schools. Took quite a shine to me too as I recall – I bet she never told you that. I admit I was tempted.' He chuckled. 'Just think. I could have been your father.'

The thought appalled me.

'We've had some interesting times together, you and I, wouldn't you say?'

'We have indeed, father.'

He closed his eyes. 'Well, don't sit around on your arse chatting to me, you've still got work to do. Find this murderer before he strikes again. Now,' he yawned, 'if you don't mind I think I'd like to sleep a little. Dying is an exhausting business.'

I got up to leave wondering how many more such meetings we'd have before he finally did give up the ghost.

'By the way, I've been meaning to ask you. You remember when I was elected abbot and we had to present our choice to the king for his final approval? You were among the thirteen chosen to go, as I remember.'

'As you were yourself, father. You were on the short-list of three candidates.' I started to leave.

'Indeed, but I couldn't vote for myself. I've never asked you this before but how did you vote? For or against?'

I stopped but didn't turn round. 'The vote was in secret, father,' I said over my shoulder.

'I know, but it can hardly matter now. Be truthful. I won't mind.'

'I thought Prior Hugh was the right man.'

He grunted. 'That's what I thought.' As I stepped through the door I could still hear him chuckling: 'Me as your father. Tee-hee. Tee-hee-hee. Tee-hee-hee-hee-hee!'

Jocelin was waiting just outside the door and jumped up as I exited.

'W-well?'

'He wants a jakes.'

The other monks exchanged glances. 'What for? He hasn't eaten anything in days.'

'It's probably his protuberances. They get engorged and it feels as though the bowels are full. Indulge him.'

The monks shrugged and went off to look for a bucket.

'He does look th-thin,' agreed Jocelin as we descended the stairs together.

'Of course he's thin, brother, he's wasting away. That's what dying men do.'

Jocelin's eyed started to well up again.

I sighed. 'I'm sorry, my friend. Look, I need to get another robe. Will you walk with me?'

We crossed the Great Court of the abbey together and he waited outside while I exchanged my torn habit for another at the laundry. As I emerged I happened to glance up at Samson's half-finished towers. They gave me an idea.

'Tell me brother, have you been into the church through the west door recently?'

'With all that b-building work going on? I should s-say not. You t-take your l-life into your hands g-going anywhere near that sc-sc-scaffolding. Why only l-last w-week one p-poor f-fellow f-f-f ...'

'But nobody's working there at the moment, surely?' I interrupted.

'M-most have gone home f-for the s-season. But there are a few m-masons still ch-chipping away.' He mimed tapping motions.

'Any roofers?'

'Plenty of r-roofing tiles. G-good quality, too.'

Yes - and I knew their origin.

'I think I might just take a wander over there.'

'Is th-that what father abbot was a-asking you to do? To s-see how his l-life's p-project was progressing?'

'In a way I suppose, yes.'

'H-how typically s-selfless. To wish to finish his g-great p-programme even as he l-lay d-dying.' Jocelin's eyes were filled with love and admiration.

Samson and his twin towers. He had been building them ever since I first arrived at Bury. I couldn't remember a time when there wasn't scaffolding up at one corner or the other of the west front. Somehow the work never quite got finished. As ever the problem was money: whenever he'd amassed enough for some building work to progress something more urgent would come along and the funds would have to be diverted elsewhere. As far back as when he was subsacristan he had been forced to hand over the money he had collected to the abbey's Jewish creditors rather than for the towers. That was really down to poor financial management by Abbot Hugh but I don't think Samson ever forgave the Jews for it and coloured his attitude towards them.

There were long periods even when he became abbot when no building-work was was done at all and the scaffolding rotted in its post-holes, King Richard's incarceration in Germany being the most notable when the country was milked dry to pay his ransom. This latest spurt is Samson's final attempt to finish before he is gathered to God's own great Construction Project. The builders were back and among them, it seems, was Leon. But not at the moment. In winter all building work stops – something to do with the temperature lime mortar needs to set. But as Jocelin said, there were a few masons on site carving the intricate designs for the gargoyles. Having parted with Jocelin at the cellarer's gate I went over to the church front and found one of them.

'Stand there, brother, and I'll immortalize you,' said the man, chisel and mallet poised ready in his hand.

'Have my face preserved in stone?' I shook my head. 'I think not, my friend. Besides, I've better things to do than stand and pose for you.'

'You don't have to wait. I already have your image in my eye. Just say the word and rainwater will be pouring from your gaping mouth come Passiontide.'

'No thank you. My ugly face has terrified enough people for these past five decades without inflicting it on them for the rest of eternity. But let's see - who else have you got here?'

I started searching through the various carvings lying about. It looked like the aftermath of a battle. Bits of bodies, severed heads, arms and legs, lay next to each other as though hacked off in some hideous Battle of Armageddon. Each was destined for a different corner beneath the eves of the roof. Abbot Samson in his mitre I recognized. Over there must be Brother Wirem with his crooked front teeth – cruel of the carver to have him grinning like that. But who was this grotesque hidden beneath a piece of canvass?

'Don't you recognize your prior?' the man said coming over.

'He looks as though he's vomiting. Why did you carve it that way?'

'I try to capture something of the personality of my subjects as well as the features.'

'And that's how you see Prior Herbert, is it? Spewing? How would you represent me, I wonder?'

'Oh, wide-eyed with innocence and wonder, brother - and handsome of course,' he grinned.

'You tell me that now and when I see it on the roof I'll be cross-eyed and picking my nose.'

'Now that's a thought,' he grinned.

I nodded at the prior's rendition. 'Herbert won't thank you for that.'

'He won't know till it's up.'

'Then let's not spoil the surprise.' I covered the face up again.

The man wiped the dust from his brow. 'Did you come just to admire, brother, or was there something you wanted?'

'Actually, I came to talk about bricks.'

'Sssssss!' The man crumpled as though I had just shot him a bolt to the chest. 'You know how to wound a man, brother. We don't mention that word here. We masons are artists. Every scratch of the chisel is like a brush-stroke on canvass to us. The mason's skill is divinely inspired. Bricks are the devil's work.'

'I don't agree. I've witnessed their manufacturing. There is great artistry in brick-making.'

The man was agog with horror. 'How can you compare dull clay roofs with the splendour of a church vault, brother? Do you have your eyes closed when you go into your quire each day? Maybe I will do you cross-eyed after all for you obviously cannot see straight.'

'I wouldn't call Margaret's Chapel "dull". That's got a tiled roof. It's very colourful, quick and cheap. I think brick may well become the building material of the future.'

'And have my children starve because their father no longer has work? Cruel, cruel hurtful man.'

'Oh, I don't think you have much to worry about. Brick can't match these splendid monuments,' I said nodding to his sculptures.

'Too late for flattery now, brother. The damage is done. I am mortally wounded. I may never lift a chisel again.'

'I think you will,' I grinned. 'Actually there was something else I wanted to ask you about. Does the name "Leon" mean anything to you?'

His face dropped even further. 'Is there no end to the suffering you wish to inflict? The person you speak of is my nemesis. If anybody will drive me to the begging bowl it will be that lady.'

'So I'm right, she has worked here?'

'She has and no doubt will again in the coming season – God smite her.'

I was impressed. If Leon could inspire so much fear she must be good at her job.

'I don't see her face here with all the rest.'

'That's because I save my best work for my greatest enemies.'

He seemed at first a little reluctant to show me but his artist's pride got the better of him. He took me over to another corner of the yard and threw off a tarpaulin. Beneath was a handful of giant sculptures. Not many heads this time, just a few well-executed examples that clearly took time and great skill to perfect. And there she was, staring back at me: the unmistakable face of Leon. At first I thought it was a lion – appropriately enough. But then I saw it for what it was and it was extremely life-like. He'd got the turn of the nose exactly right, and something of her mocking eyes. But what shocked me was her hair. It wasn't obvious at first but then as I looked closer I could see. Not the mane of beautiful golden locks that I remembered but serpents – literally a cascade of snakes was writhing up from Leon's scalp as from the head of a gorgon. Leon's tongue, too, was split with each half ending in another snake's head. I was shocked by the horror of it. To give the man credit he did look a little shamefaced about revealing it. It was both beautiful in its execution and ugly in its content. But how much of it reflected Leon's real character and how much the mason's prejudices? I didn't have time to ask for round the corner at that moment appeared another of the faces from the mason's yard. Not a monument in stone this time but real life flesh and blood:

Prior Herbert.

Chapter Fourteen
A MATTER OF OPINION

'Is there a problem, brother physician?' Herbert asked eyeing the mason suspiciously.

'A problem, brother prior? No, I don't think so.'

'Only we have a schedule to keep to. We mustn't interrupt the important work of the abbey, must we?'

'The brother was just admiring my work,' smiled the man affably.

'Yes, well I'm sure I don't need to remind you that we need to get these carvings finished before the Feast of Saint Valentine,' frowned Herbert looking around at the half-finished carvings.

'Oh I will, brother,' said the man. 'With love in my heart.' He winked at me.

'Just see that you do. Now, Brother Walter and I have important matters to discuss that are not for your ears.'

The mason smiled again, bowed and walked off rolling his eyes to me as he passed. I was beginning to see why he chose to depict Prior Herbert as The Vomiting Monk.

'It doesn't do to encourage these people, brother,' said Herbert watching him go. 'Be too familiar with them and they take advantage.'

'We were only talking, brother.'

'Talk costs money. I don't pay these people to talk.'

I didn't think he paid him at all, the money for the work coming from a special fund set up by Samson. But Herbert was the prior, second only to the abbot himself, and therefore it was every monk's duty, while Samson is incapacitated, to obey him as we would the abbot. Me included, unfortunately.

I have to confess I have always found this particular vow challenging. *Poverty* I can take. *Chastity*, likewise, I have mastered - in deed if not always in thought. But when it comes to *Obedience* I often have the greatest difficulty, particularly to inane directives given by a semi-literate moron with the brain capacity of a flea.

Prior Herbert had been our prior by then for a decade, a fact I still find extraordinary. He was chosen for the job by Abbot Samson on the death of his predecessor, Prior Robert of illustrious memory, and in the teeth of opposition from the rest of us choir monks. We all wanted Master Hermer, the subprior, to get the job - an altogether more suitable candidate. Hermer was both literate and highly experienced in the art of spiritual counselling if a little brash on occasion especially when it came to dealing with fools. But Samson was opposed and by trickery, as usual, got his way.

Herbert at the time had been a choir monk for barely four years, was young, ill-educated and quite unsuited to spiritual leadership. Indeed, one of my brother monks, perhaps a little harshly, described

Herbert as "a block of wood". I wouldn't have gone that far but his appointment as prior was a rare error of judgement by Samson whose estimation of a man's abilities is normally infallible – he did, after all, choose me as his physician. If I were alone in my opinion I might temper my words more, but when a mason who has known Herbert for little more than a few months can come to the same conclusion then I'm inclined to think I might be right.

Usually I don't have much to do with the prior. My laboratorium is located far enough away from the main abbey buildings that I didn't need to go there very often, and I spend a lot of my time with patients out in the town. In the normal course of events mine and the prior's paths rarely crossed. So to see Herbert bearing down now filled me with mild apprehension - and not, it seemed, without cause:

'I'm glad I've caught you, brother. I've been doing the rounds of all the senior obedientiaries. As ever you're the last. You've been away, I gather?'

'On special assignment for the abbot, yes,' I smiled.

'Ah, well it is with the abbot that I am concerned. I'm sure I don't need to tell you - as a medical man - that Father Samson is a little under the weather at the moment.'

A little under the weather. That's one way to describe death's door.

'You've seen the abbot today? I believe I saw you leaving the palace a little while ago.'

'I have. The announcement of his death was somewhat premature. In my opinion – speaking purely as a medical man - he is still very much alive.'

'God be thanked for that.' Herbert crossed himself. 'So what is your prognosis? Will he see the New Year?'

'I have every confidence he will. He certainly intends to.'

'Nevertheless we must plan for the worse. And with that in mind I have been doing my own calculation.'

'Calculation, brother prior?'

'Of his likely survival. Do you not do the same?'

'I didn't think it was possible. Surely only God knows the number of a man's days.'

'But there are signs if you know where to look.'

I raised a quizzical eyebrow, so he explained:

'You take the saint's day on which the patient first fell ill, add to that the number of letters of his name. If the resulting sum is even he will live. If odd …' He shrugged reluctantly.

'And your conclusion?'

'Samson first complained of breathlessness on September 3 – the feast of Saint Regulus. There are seven letters in Regulus, plus six in Samson making thirteen in all. An odd number.'

'But September 3 is also the feast of Saint Hereswitha who as a local saint is far more appropriate, I would have thought, in the circumstances. Hereswitha has ten letters. With S-a-m-s-o-n makes a total of …' I countered them out on my fingers. 'Sixteen.'

Herbert frowned irritably. 'It's not a foolproof method, merely indicative. Be that as it may, Samson is on his sick bed and incapacitated. He will die soon and we have a duty to be prepared. I have therefore taken it upon myself as prior to take matters in hand and request that all senior men remain close by in case they are needed.'

'If he's dead I'm not sure if even my skills will be of much use – as a medical man.'

Herbert smiled graciously: 'It is not for your skills as a mender of bodies that I make my request, brother, but as a counsellor. An abbey without its abbot is like a ship without a rudder. The sail flutters uselessly in the breeze, the oars flail and the ship has no proper direction. If, in addition, one of those oars is missing then it places an unfair burden on the rest of the crew.'

How very nautical. I'd never thought of myself as an oar before.

'I am, therefore, asking all senior obedientiaries not to leave the abbey precinct for the time being but to hold themselves in readiness to defend the honour of Saint Edmund.'

It never ceases to amaze me how Herbert manages to turn a little local difficulty into a major disaster. Yet I could see his point. Samson could pop off at any moment, and if he did we would all need to stick together if only to prevent the wolves in the Church outside and in government from taking bites out of our exposed carcass. During the last vacancy the abbey's finances went from difficult to ruinous. It was only when Samson was elected that matters finally started to be put back on an even keel, to continue the nautical theme, and even then it took him a decade to to do it. And Prior Herbert was no Abbot Samson. It was therefore debatable whether my presence would make much difference one way or the other. Meanwhile I had to weigh Herbert's displeasure against the possibility that my mother might be murdered. It was a close-run thing but I think I came to the right decision.

'I'm not sure I can do that, brother prior. As I said, the abbot has charged me with a duty to perform. It is a measure of the urgency in which he holds that duty, given the state of his health, that he wishes it to be undertaken now. It may well be his last ever project.'

Herbert took a step closer. 'Brother Walter, this is not a request. I would remind you who has the senior rank here. When the abbot dies – which, though regrettable, is inevitable - it will fall to me as prior to take responsibility for the abbey. I shall need all the help I can get to live up to Father Samson's demanding example. If, God and Saint Edmund permitting, I should be elected your new abbot, as in great humility I believe I shall, I will remember those who were my friends and helped me through these difficult times - and those who did not.'

'Assuming you are still brother prior then, brother prior.'

'Assuming that I am.'

'In the meantime you would agree I should try to fulfil father abbot's final wishes, whether they coincide with your own or no.'

'Is that your final word?'

'It is.'

Chapter Fifteen
PAUSE FOR REFLECTION

Sheriff Peter, Reeve Robert, Leon and now Prior Herbert. I was building up quite a gallery of enemies and feeling somewhat isolated. I decided I needed some moral support. There are two people in this world whose council I trust: Solomon, my chaplain at the abbey, to whom I go for spiritual sustenance, and my brother Joseph whose contribution is of a more practical nature. It was to him I went on this occasion. Leaving Prior Herbert, therefore, to quietly seethe and plot my downfall, I made my way up into the town west of Abbeygate street to where the spicers and the charmers ply their trade.

Anyone who has read my earlier entries in this chronicle will know that Joseph isn't really my brother. We just call each other that on account of having grown up together. For those of you new to my ramblings, Joseph's father was in fact a Syrian Arab and his mother a Damascene Jewess – an unusual combination but one that confirmed the prejudices of our English neighbours who couldn't be bothered to tell the difference. Our fathers met during the wars in the Holy Land where they were both medics, albeit on opposing sides. They admired each other's work so much so that when the fighting finished they returned together to my father's house in Ixworth to dedicate their lives to the alleviation of suffering in others. Joseph and I were both born in that house, Joseph first and me three years later. We each inherited our fathers' interest in medicine but while I went on to medical school Joseph, being a heathen, had to make do with potheking. But whatever Joseph did he was bound to make a success of it and he had clients as far afield as London, Paris, Venice, Constantinople and Norwich. I use him myself to stock my shelves - at a discount, naturally, being family although I think he does it mostly to hear the gossip I bring him from the abbey.

Though he'd never admit it, Joseph relishes his image as Eastern Man of Mystery, aided by his Semitic features and dark complexion. He says it's good for business. Actually he plays a variety of parts including, when it suits him, the persecuted Jew, the misunderstood Arab, and the down-trodden Bury shopkeeper. In reality he's no more mysterious than I am. Despite his flowing robes, his conical pilos and his forked beard, he can swear in broad Suffolk as well as any Ipswich fishwife. I think he sometimes forgets that I've known him all my life and can remember running with him through the bean fields as children and later catching him in the hayloft with the inn-keeper's daughter, his britches down and her skirts up.

Having said all that he is as bright as my mother maintains, damn him, with all the wisdom of the east running through his veins. East Anglia at any rate. His shop lies half way down Heathenmans Street which is where the majority of Bury's Jews live these days. I knew he was at home because the Caduceus wand that lies ostentatiously across the shop's entrance when he is away was absent - a pretentious bit of nonsense that he claims impresses his customers.

'God bless all in this house,' I said as I entered and ostentatiously made the sign of the Cross.

'Ahaha, dear brother!' he beamed gliding towards me in his robes with his arms spread wide. 'What a welcome surprise.' We embraced. 'Come through to the back.'

He parted the curtain that separates the shop from his living area. As ever the place was strewn with cushions – a sore point with me both literally and metaphorically. Despite my constant protests he has never replaced them with sensible – and more comfortable - chairs.

'Have you no customers?' I asked flopping down on four or five of the blessèd things.

'Happily the last left just a few moments ago so you may have my undivided attention.'

'How fortuitous. Of course you had no idea I was coming.'

'How could I?' he smiled.

How indeed.

'And no tea either?' I said looking about. 'I see standards have fallen since my last visit.'

He put on a pained expression. 'Alas, I have no servant at the moment.'

'Oh? Is Chrétien ill?'

'No, he is gone – by mutual consent.'

I was surprised. Chrétien had been his assistant and servant for over a decade. He was originally a protégé of my mother loaned temporarily to Joseph but who decided to stay.

Personally I never warmed to the lad. There was something disquieting about the way he always managed to be in the right place at the right time – a quality I found suspicious. But he turned out to be more useful than I ever imagined, once even saving my life. So I put up with him.

'I can't say I'm entirely sorry to see him gone,' I admitted. 'There was something not quite natural about him.'

'It's true he did have a preference for his own sex, if that's what you mean. As a member of a persecuted minority myself I didn't think I had the right to judge another.'

That wasn't quite what I meant but I decided not to labour the point.

'Well, I shall have to see if I can find you another.'

Joseph inclined his head graciously. 'I can make you a beverage myself if you wish.'

'More of your tea? No, don't bother. All that waiting around for it to brew. A man could die of thirst first. It'll never catch on in England.'

He shrugged and sat down on the cushions opposite.

'So,' I said once we had both settled, 'since you've conveniently emptied your shop of witnesses, I take it you know why I'm here.'

'Green children?'

'What can you tell me about them?'

He gave a huge rabbinical shrug of his shoulders. 'I'm not sure I can help. Green is not a colour with which we Jews are very familiar. It is more a shade favoured by my Muslim brethren. The prophet Mohammed famously wore a green turban and cloak. Blue is more Jewish. It is the colour of the threads in the tallit, our prayer shawl, died to represent the sky and to remind us that God is ever present above us watching.' He glanced warily upwards as though expecting a vengeful bolt of lightning to come hurtling his way out of heaven at any moment.

I nearly snorted with contempt. 'Piffle. You don't believe in God. And you can drop the "poor Jew" act. This is me you're talking to.' I eyed him suspiciously. 'Why are you being so evasive? What have you heard?'

Not much goes on in Bury town that Joseph doesn't know about. An occupational necessity, as he was always reminding me. Members of minorities only manage to survive by staying one jump ahead of the rest – and as the son of both an Arab and a Jew, Joseph was doubly minor. I'm never quite sure how he does it but I imagine it must be spies – a trick he probably learned from my mother. Between the two of them they must have this corner of the country pretty much sewn up.

He sighed and threw aside his pilos to give his scalp a good long scratch. 'I am trying, my brother, in my own subtle way to warn you. This is one I think you would do well to give up. There is danger in it. You could get hurt - physically as well as mentally.'

'Too late. I've been attacked once already.'

'Twice,' he corrected me.

'Oh, you know that much, do you? I suppose it was Oswald told you?'

'Oswald did call in on his way back to Ixworth,' he agreed. 'The Lady Isabel likes me to keep a watchful eye on her only true son.'

'Oh she does, does she? In that case you'll understand my difficulty. Abbot Samson has tasked me to investigate without telling me what or why. I'm not sure he knows himself anymore. I've just come from a rambling interview with him. You've heard that he's dying?'

Joseph gave an indifferent shrug of his shoulders. I can't say I blame him. Samson was not popular among the Jewish community of Bury. It was, after all, Abbot Samson who had instigated the expulsion of all our Jews twenty years earlier for being, in his words, "not Saint Edmund's men". This had been taken at the time as tacit approval for a general free-for-all against the Jewish population. Fortunately Joseph got wind of trouble beforehand and tactfully withdrew to my mother's house in Ixworth to wait out the worst. Even so, when he got back he found his shop had been ransacked and he was forced to spend the next decade operating his business outside the town walls. In Samson's defence, it was a time of great religious fervour. Jerusalem had just fallen to Saladin's forces and there was a great desire for revenge enthusiastically endorsed by King Richard. Jews are not Saracens of course, but as the most conspicuous non-Christian community in Bury they were an easy target. Samson may even have been inadvertently responsible for the massacre of dozens of Joseph's compatriots by preaching a sermon against them on Palm Sunday 1190 – a particularly shameful episode in our history.

But Joseph as ever was pragmatic. He had to earn a living among the goy as non-Jews are called, and in due course he returned to his old shop in Heathenmans Street. But he never forgot the lesson.

He kept a keen ear open for every nuance of trouble and built up a network of useful contacts – and a large stick behind the door. If I ever wanted to know what was going on in Bury he was the man to ask. I therefore gave him a brief résumé of what Samson had told me but I got the impression he knew most of it already.

'Have you thought of asking the girl? She, after all, was the one who went to see the abbot. Surely she must know.'

'Leon?' I shook my head. 'She won't talk to me. Not since ...'

He raised a quizzical eyebrow. 'Not since?'

I shifted uncomfortably. 'Never mind. Suffice to say I had my opportunity and lost it. Anyway, it's not Leon I want to talk about, it's the children. Everyone I've spoken to has a different slant on them. They're like the mist in the morning: one moment they're there and the next they vanish. I'm still not convinced they ever existed at all.'

He shrugged. 'Others have borne witness to them. The Lady Isabel for one. No-one is more sceptical then her. But I think you're asking the wrong question. Not whether they were real but what happened to them afterwards.'

I frowned. 'I don't follow you. How can I ask what happened to them before I establish whether they even existed?'

He smiled and pushed his long legs out in front of him – a sure sign that I am about to get a lecture:

'Don't you find it curious that the children seem to have vanished so completely after their first appearance? In my experience people don't just disappear, especially ones who aroused as much curiosity as these did.'

'I don't know that there's much mystery about it. The boy died. The girl married and went to live in Lynn.'

'My parents died, but I know where they are buried. Where is the boy's grave?'

I shrugged. 'In Bardwell churchyard, I presume.'

'Easy enough to check. But I bet you won't find it. And why did the girl move so far away?'

'She got married. Why shouldn't she go to where her husband lived?'

'No reason at all, except people don't usually move to a town two counties away just to marry, especially if they have no family living there.'

I frowned. 'There could be a perfectly good explanation for all of this. And it doesn't tell us whether the children existed or not.'

'Well it seems to me that either the tale is false and the children never existed in the first place, or …'

'Or?'

'Or it contains an element of truth that is so dangerous that those with the power to do so quashed it as quickly as possible.'

'What element of truth?'

'That I don't know. But I'd suggest it is the direction your investigation should be taking.'

Oh he does look so smug when he comes out with these abstruse conclusions. But he was right, there was an element of concealment about the tale. I'd sensed it myself.

'I have to admit I did wonder about one thing Oswald told me. He said Sir Richard had manufactured a false argument between his household and ours. If his intention was to keep us away it worked. I can't remember going there much as children, can you? And that's not the only thing. This business about the children's colour. That's an obvious nonsense. There's no such thing as *green* children. So why invent it? - unless someone is deliberately trying to muddy the water.'

'And who might that someone be?'

'I haven't made up my mind yet.'

'So what do you want from me?'

'I don't know. A little support, I suppose – and approval that I am doing the right thing.'

'You always have that, my brother. But it sounds as though you've already made up your own mind.'

'You're right. I have.' I got up to leave.

He looked disappointed. 'You're going?'

'I know what I have to do.'

'I had hoped you wouldn't do anything.' He became serious. 'I meant what I said, Walter. This is a dangerous business. And it's not like before. I'm alone here now. I won't be able to help you if you get into trouble.'

'You've already helped. And don't worry. I can take care of myself.'

'Famous last words.' He got up to see me to the door. 'You know, you Christians are not the only ones to have mystical beings. We Jews have the Golem - a creature made from mud. Adam was originally a Golem until God breathed life into him. The word itself means "unfinished".'

'An unfinished man,' I nodded. 'You could argue that is an apt description of us all.'

'Now you are starting to think like a Jew.'

183

'Oh, I'll never do that. I haven't the constitution.' I stepped through the curtain but then had a thought: 'These Golem: how would you recognize one?'

'The chief characteristic of the Golem is that it cannot speak and since it has no life it cannot be killed.'

'Then how would you defeat it?'

'There is only one way: by changing its name. The Golem's name in Hebrew means "truth" and is written across its forehead. Remove one letter and the meaning changes to "death". The creature simply sees its own reflection in the pool and obeys.'

'Rather a stupid creature, then.'

'That, my brother, is exactly the point.'

Chapter Sixteen
AN UNINVITED COMPANION

'Nathan, can you saddle Erigone for me please?'

'Are we going somewhere, master?'

'*I* am going somewhere, yes.'

'May I ask where?'

'Of course you may.' I went over the corner to look for my travelling satchel.

He followed me over. 'Only you know Prior Herbert has given instructions that no-one is to leave the abbey?'

'Tell me Nathan, are you working for me or for the prior now?'

He picked up my canteen and shook it. It was empty. 'I'll go and fill it for you, shall I? You'll also need some food. How long for?'

'Enough for two days. But,' I added as an afterthought, 'if anyone asks, tell them four.'

'To give the impression you are going further than you are,' he nodded. 'I get it.'

'I'm glad you do.'

'I get that you are asking me to lie for you, master.'

I stopped and looked at him. 'Nathan, you are my assistant, are you not?'

'Yes master.'

'Vowed to obey me in all things?'

He shrugged.

'Then you will tell others what I tell you to tell them without question or comment – is that understood?'

'As do you the prior?'

'That's different. My orders come from the abbot. Besides, you cannot lie about what you do not know.'

'But if I did know I would be able to lie far more convincingly.'

I had to think about that for a moment. The trouble with Nathan was that he was clever - a little too clever for his own good. Samson thought education wasted on women. A boy like Nathan can have too much of it.

'You're right,' I said. 'I was wrong to ask you to lie for me. Tell the prior whatever you like. I shan't be here to worry.' I started to leave.

'Would you like me to come with you? Then I wouldn't have to tell the prior anything.'

'Didn't you just tell me it was forbidden for anyone to leave the precinct?'

'I'd be no trouble. You'd hardly know I was there.'

'Nathan,' I sighed, 'you are new here so you don't yet know me or how I work. If you wish to continue to be my assistant you will learn that sometimes there are things I have to do alone.'

'I accept that master, but if I am to be of use to you surely it is better for me to see all the functioning of the department and to learn as much from you as I can.'

'Normally I'd agree with you. But the quest I am about at the moment is not part of my normal practice. Apart from anything else there may be an element of danger,' I said remembering Joseph's warning. But instead of putting him off, the mere mention of it lit up Nathan's eyes.

'All the more reason to take me with you, master. A danger shared is a danger halved.'

I could understand his keenness for adventure. Young men always are keen for that. But I didn't know what I was going to find when I got to Ixworth. He thought he was being helpful, but he might actually be a liability. The last thing I needed was a naïve boy getting between me and a killer's knife.

'I'll need someone to mind the shop while I'm away. That is also part of your function as my assistant. There are patients to attend to and potions to prepare. You'll be far more use to me here.'

'Oh, we're completely up to date with potions,' he assured me. 'We had a delivery while you were away – from your brother Joseph's apothecary shop in the town. So you don't have to worry on that score.'

'No Nathan.'
'And as far as the patients are concerned -'
'*No* Nathan.'
'But master -?'
'And that is my final word.'

I set off for Ixworth - alone. But I was scarcely out of the town gate when I heard the sound of galloping hoofs behind me. After my fright the other evening

I'd become nervous of any sudden unexpected noises. I spun round but immediately recognized the outline of my pursuer – the jutting ears, the hunched shoulders, the angular elbows...

'Nathan, what are you doing?'

'Sorry master,' he said panting to catch me up. 'I forgot to mention before you left: that old woman you were treating for her sciatica? She's completely recovered. She came to the abbey two days ago to give thanks to Saint Edmund and to make a donation to the poor box. I thought you'd like to know.'

'And you needed a travelling cloak and full saddlebag to tell me that?'

'Well I just thought, now that I'm here I may as well stay.' He gave a disarming smile.

'Did you now? Well I'm afraid you were wrong. Thank you for the information about the old woman – whoever she is - but you're going straight back to the abbey. Now off you go.'

'But if I went back now, master, I'd stand a good chance of running into Father Prior.'

'So?'

'Well, he's bound to ask what I've been doing and where I'd been and I'd be bound to tell him. Lying for you is one thing, master. But lying for myself - that's something altogether different. You're asking me to perjure my soul.'

'Then don't lie. Tell him the truth: that you made up this ridiculous story just so to try to wheedle your way into coming with me against my explicit orders, but that I saw through your little game and sent you straight back to the abbey with a flea in your ear – as per his instructions.'

'But if I did that, master, I'd have to tell him where I'd met up with you. He'd almost certainly send a fast rider to catch you up and fetch you back to the abbey. Even if you didn't there'd be argument leading to delay leading to more argument and more delay – delay, argument, delay. Chances are you'd never get away again and your trip would have to be abandoned. Much easier just to let me tag along.'

Very clever. But he was right about Prior Herbert who would indeed use any means he could to stop me leaving if only out of spite. I needed to get to Ixworth as soon as possible. At the moment no-one at the abbey knew where I was going. I narrowed my eyes at his grinning face.

'Get in my way, Nathan, and you will feel the strap of my tongue.'

'Oh, absolutely, master.'

'Not to mention the sting of Prior Herbert's birch when we return.'

'Punishment is good for the soul, master.'

'That's confession.'

'That too, master.'

Nathan was something of an enigma to me. In the short time he had been with me he had certainly proved he had some basic knowledge when it came to medicine. And I couldn't fault his enthusiasm. But I didn't really know much more about him. I knew he was the son of a scholarly family from somewhere in middle England and he claimed at his interview that he had specifically asked to be assigned to me. It's always a good tactic to flatter your prospective employer, although it wouldn't work on me, of course. I was not to be swayed by such opaque blandishments. But if I was to be stuck with him for the next few days I might as well try to get to know a little more about him.

'Where did you say you studied again? '

'Oxford master. My father was a don there.'

'Oh yes. Mathematics. Not a subject I'm very familiar with.'

Or very good at, I might have added. But not a bad beginning I supposed. The schools in Oxford were beginning to attract some decent teachers – a few even from Paris. But as a university it was still very young having been incorporated only some twenty or so years earlier and was not yet widely known in the outside world. It would take time to build a reputation of note - if indeed it ever did.

'I'm sure Oxford is a fine place but it hardly compares with the great medical schools of Europe,' I told him. 'I myself was at -'

'Montpellier - yes I know.'

He'd evidently done his homework about me. More flattery. How much of it was true admiration or how much simply to impress was yet to be discovered. I didn't want another Gilbert who was always a little in awe of me. Adulation, whilst pleasing to begin with, can become a little wearing after a while.

'Actually, I was only at Oxford for a short while,' he confessed. 'I never graduated.'

'You didn't reveal that at your interview. Why did you not graduate?'

'I had to leave along with everybody else.'

'What do you mean, "everybody else"?'

'Have you not heard, master? The university is closed.'

I was shocked. 'No, I hadn't heard. This is distressing news indeed. When did it happen?'

He shrugged. 'Two years ago. Surely you know the tale?'

190

'Remind me.'

'There was a murder. A woman from the town was strangled by someone from the university. No-one owned to it so the townsfolk hanged two other students instead.'

This was appalling. Two innocent men hanged for a murder they didn't commit?

'There has long been resentment of the students by the townsfolk,' he explained. 'You know what young men are like. Too much money, too much free time, and far too much ale. This murder was the final straw and the townsfolk took their revenge by hanging two college men willy-nilly. So in response all the staff and students left.'

'I've never heard the like! Are you saying there is no university at Oxford anymore?'

'Not unless the students and staff return.'

I was mortified. Oxford may not be the most prestigious seat of learning in Christendom but it was England's finest. Losing it would set us back decades.

'Does the king know about this?'

'The king approves. Or at least, he doesn't disapprove. Students, as you know, have to be in holy orders in order to study and since his present dispute with the pope King John has been disinclined to defend clerics.'

Yes, that sounded like John. Selfish to the last. If he felt personally slighted in any way he would react like a petulant child and hang the consequences – literally in this case.

'Where did they all go - the students and the teachers?'

'Dispersed to the four winds. Some to Reading, some to Northampton. I myself went with my father to Cambridge.'

'Cambridge?' I guffawed. 'But there's nothing there other than bog and a few eel-catchers.'

'Certainly no medical school, that's for sure, which is why I didn't stay. I finished my studies in Bologna.'

Good Lord. Oxford, Cambridge and now Bologna. The boy was better qualified than I was.

'I think I should be your assistant, Nathan, not you mine.'

'Nothing surpasses practical experience, master,' he grinned.

More flattery.

It took us a little under two hours to cover the six miles to Ixworth. I didn't want to overtax Erigone while she was still recovering from her injury so we went at a gentle pace. As a result the light was already beginning to fade by the time we got to Ixworth Hall. I immediately looked up at the window to my mother's solar and was relieved to see a candle light flickering behind the shutters. Evidently she hadn't been attacked yet. As we rode up Oswald appeared at the door ready with a tray of refreshments.

'All is well my friend?'

'All well, master.'

'Any other news?'

'Nothing further at present, master.'

'What about Father Alan?'

'On advice from the mistress, he has returned to his home town of Peterborough.'

I nodded. 'Good idea.'

I wanted to have another look at the Bardwell priest-house. It would be better if Alan wasn't there when I did. I saw Oswald eyeing Nathan with curiosity.

'Oh, this is my new assistant, Brother Nathan.'

'Good to meet you, brother,' said Oswald offering him a cup of ale. He frowned. 'Have we met before?'

'I don't think so,' said Nathan pulling his hood up.

'You're getting confused with Gilbert,' I told him. 'Look, I just want a quick word with Oswald,' I said to the boy. 'Wait here, will you?'

I dismounted and took Oswald to one side.

'We're not staying, Oswald. I just stopped by to make sure you'd got back safely. But tell your mistress to be on her guard. There's a madman out there. I don't expect any trouble here at the house but keep the doors and shutters closed up just in case. We should be back by this evening.'

'All is in hand, master. There will be hot food waiting for you.'

'Thank you.' I remounted Erigone.

'Walter?'

I turned in my saddle. 'Yes?'

'Take care of yourself.'

'I will,' I nodded and smiled encouragingly back at him. 'Don't worry old friend.'

Walter. He hadn't called me that since I was a child. A portent of things to come? I supposed I was about to find out.

Chapter Seventeen
SUMMONED

'Master, are you going to tell me what this is all about?'

We had been riding for a while in silence, my thoughts on other things. I supposed I should tell him. I hadn't invited him along but now he was here Nathan had a right to know what he was getting into. When I said there may be danger in what we were doing I wasn't joking. There had already been one murder and I had been viciously attacked. Still, I avoided dwelling too much on the gorier aspects of Ivo's murder; there was no need to frighten the poor lad to death. I had to remember his delicate age and the gentle nature of his family. Even so, my words must have made an impression as he went quiet for a while once I'd finished my recital.

'You can still return to Bury,' I told him. 'It's not too late to change your mind. But if you do decide to stay then I must have your commitment that you will obey me in everything. There can only be one general in this army. If I tell you to do something, do it straight away without question – is that understood?'

'You make it sound as though we're fighting a war, master.'

'That's exactly what we are fighting: a war against evil. And an unequal war at that since we do not know who our enemy is, when they will attack or even why we are fighting them.'

'I thought you said it was to prevent a murder?'

'It is, but we don't know who the intended victim is yet. If we did it might have made this business easier.'

'I take it, then, the curate wasn't the intended victim?'

'Ivo? No, I don't believe so. He just happened to be in the wrong place at the wrong time. It's always the innocent who are the chief casualties of war. You'll discover that as you get older.'

The mere mention of Ivo's name filled me with remorse. If I hadn't turned up on his doorstep the other night he might still be blithely fiddling with his water clock and brewing his atrocious "mule" with many more years left for it to rot his liver. However reluctant I might have been at first to take on this business I now owed it to Ivo to bring his murderer to book.

We rode the rest of the journey in silence. I took surreptitious glances at Nathan's face. It had gone a deathly white – no doubt as a result of the graphic description I'd given him of the murder scene. Perhaps I had been too explicit. But it wouldn't do to deceive him. And he would have to get used to dead bodies if he was to remain my assistant. However, I was convinced the next time he spoke it would be to request that he be allowed to return to Bury. In all conscience I couldn't refuse him if he did.

Eventually the dark outline of Bardwell church loomed before us in the gathering dusk.

'Master?'

'My child?'

'When we get to the priest-house...'

Here we go.

'Yes?'

'Will you let me see the body?'

My jaw fell open. 'Appalling child! Is that all you can say? Can you see the body? I thought you'd be horrified but you relish the gore. Dear God, what is the world coming to?'

'Sorry master. It's just that I've never seen a dead body before.'

'No, and I sincerely hope you don't this time. Reeve Wodebite should have removed it – *him* - by now.'

He nodded back vainly. 'Pity.'

Ivo's body had indeed gone but the evidence of his murder was still there when we got to the Bardwell priest-house: the chair he'd been strapped in, the blood caked across the back, the seat, the arm-rests. Sheriff Peter had been right about that. Ivo's blood had gone everywhere. I hadn't really taken much notice the first time, but the murderer must have been drenched in it. We immediately set to work to try to scrub the worst of it away conscious that Alan would have to return at some stage and shouldn't have to confront this alone.

'What I can't understand is why he just sat here and let it happen,' said Nathan returning with his third bucket of water. 'I would have put up a fight – resisted in some way.'

'You don't know what you would have done in the circumstances. Most likely Ivo couldn't believe what was happening to him and by the time he did it was probably too late to anything about it. He couldn't believe any more than I could that one human-being could do that to another. Unfortunately he wasn't dealing with a normal human-being but with a monster.'

Talking about it brought back memories of the expression on Ivo's face. I was sure I was right. He had looked utterly bewildered by what was happening to him. But Nathan was also right about another thing: Ivo had been no weakling. He'd been a strong young man. How exactly had his murderer managed to subdue him enough to tie him up apparently without a struggle?

'And we have no idea who did it or why?' Nathan asked.

'That's what we're here to find out.'

He nodded and rung out his cloth. 'Do you think it could have been that woman? The one with the man's name.'

I stopped scrubbing to look at him. 'What an astonishing suggestion. Why do you ask that?'

He shrugged. 'It's just that you said she attacked you in Coggeshall abbey.'

'That was different. Leon didn't so much attack as defend.'

'Defend against what?'

'Never you mind. Just get on with cleaning and leave the analysing to me.'

I rung out my own cloth and attacked another patch of dried blood.

'You're probably right, master,' said Nathan. 'No woman could have done this by herself. Except…'

I stopped again. 'Except what?'

'Well, women have powers that we men don't understand, don't they? There are plenty of examples in the Bible: Samson and Delilah. Herod and Salome. Women can make men act against their will and against their best interests. Has any women ever affected you in that way, master? Before you took the cowl, I mean. When you were young.'

I threw my rag down. 'You're talking nonsense, boy. No woman has that kind of power over a man. And while you remain protected within the walls of the abbey you're never likely to have to worry about it. And for your information I'm not yet fifty. When I was young, indeed! So just empty that last bucket and then we'll go over to the outhouse. There's nothing more to be done here.'

We went out to the shed behind the house where I'd found the Eustace document. Oswald had put the door back before he left but still the weather had got in and there were documents and books strewn everywhere and sopping wet.

'What a mess,' sighed Nathan looking round the wreck of what must once have been Sir Richard's library. It was disintegrating before our eyes. Parchment was reverting back to skin; ink was being washed into unreadable streaks across the page. It looked as though I'd rescued the Eustace document just in time.

'A lifetime's work destroyed,' I lamented.

'Sir Richard was certainly well-read,' agreed Nathan.

I looked at him with surprise. 'You've heard of Sir Richard de Calne?'

'I don't need to have heard of him, master, I can see for myself. There are books here I remember from my student days.' He picked up a large tome and rubbed the cover. 'It's a pity we can't salvage some of them.'

'Perhaps when this is all over we will.'

He laid the tome down again and looked about him. 'Are we looking for anything in particular, master?'

'Anything that looks interesting or out of the ordinary.'

Something like the Eustace document was what I was hoping for. But it was a hopeless task. I doubted if there was anything left worth salvaging. So engrossed was I with what I was doing I didn't at first notice the figure standing in the doorway. Some movement caught my eye and I looked up to see the man silhouetted against the evening sky.

I was immediately on my guard, my hand going to my knife. Was this the killer returned? Although the man was in shadow I could tell he was short and stocky and he wore a sword at his side on which he kept one hand loosely draped. Instinctively I knew I shouldn't make any hasty movements. But then came a voice I didn't recognize:

'Brother Walter?'

'What do you want?'

'I bring an invitation.'

'From?'

'My mistress.'

'And who might she be?'

'That doesn't matter.'

I could see out of the corner of my eye Nathan's hand surreptitiously reaching beneath his robe for his dagger.

'Tell your young colleague not to try anything silly, brother,' said the man without taking his eyes from me. 'There has been enough blood spilt in this place already.'

'It's all right, Nathan,' I said putting a restraining hand on his arm. 'He means us no harm.' I turned to the man. 'That's right isn't it? You're not here to hurt us?'

'Not if you do as I say.'

'An invitation, you said. To what?'

'That I cannot say.'

'I see. You won't tell me who you are or what you want yet you expect me to go blindly with you?'

'My mistress knows of your quest. I am to tell you that what she has to offer may be of help to you. If you do not wish to accept her invitation I will leave.'

'And I will never know what it is,' I nodded.

'Let me find out, master,' muttered Nathan.

'No Nathan,' I said. 'Leave it.'

'But don't you see?' he hissed. 'That's probably how he did it.'

I knew exactly what he meant. If this man was Ivo's murderer this may be how he persuaded him to to be strapped into that chair. From the look of him this man was quite capable of slitting a man's throat without compunction, but somehow I didn't think he was Ivo's murderer.

'All right. We'll come with you.'

'Master!' Nathan objected.

'Not him,' said the man. 'Just you.'

'So that you can pick us off separately?' scoffed Nathan. 'I don't think so.'

'The invitation is for Brother Walter alone.'

'No chance.' Nathan clenched his fists.

'Very well.' The man started slowly to back out again.

'No, it's all right,' I said to him. 'I'll come.'

'But master!'

'Remember what I said, Nathan. Only one general.'

The man stood aside for me to leave and then backed through the door after me keeping his eyes on Nathan and his hand on his sword hilt. There were two horses waiting in the yard. I got on one while the man mounted the other. I knew Nathan wouldn't be so easily deterred. As we turned to go I heard him emerge from the outhouse behind us. But then he cursed loudly. The man had hobbled our two mules together. It would take Nathan several minutes to separate them by which time we would be long gone.

Chapter Eighteen
GETTING NOWHERE FAST

I'd be the first to admit I am not the world's greatest horseman and I was having difficulty keeping up with the man. I was trying to keep track of which way we were going but with the rain driving directly into our faces it was impossible to see. North I think, but that's as much as I could tell. I hoped Nathan wasn't being silly back there by trying to follow us for he'd have no chance and would only to add to my problems later when I tried to find him. In the event the ride didn't last long and it ended as abruptly as it had begun.

As I recovered my breath I saw that we were in fact in a clearing in the forest with a building of some kind before us surrounded by a banked enclosure. But what sort of building was it? I'd never seen anything quite like it. And what was it doing here out here on its own in the middle of the forest? It wasn't a house – there were no windows, at least not at ground level. I could just make out one shuttered window at the first floor level but nothing below but a single door. The building looked isolated and deserted - an ideal location for a murder?

My companion dismounted and signalled for me to do the same.

'What is this place?' I asked him.

'All your questions will be answered soon, brother.'

'But not by you, evidently.'

He took my rein and then hammered loudly on the door with his fist. After a moment bolts were withdrawn and the door was swung open - it was too dark to see by whom or much of what was inside. But the door didn't remain open for long. As soon as I was across the threshold it was shut and bolted again behind me leaving my companion outside. Whoever my hosts were they were highly security conscious.

It took a few moments for my eyes to adjust but once they had I could see I was inside a space not much bigger than my laboratorium at the abbey, maybe twenty feet square, with a very low ceiling so that I had to crouch. There was also an overpowering animal smell but I couldn't place what animal it was. Not sheep or chickens or anything else domesticated. Then I had it: rabbits. Of course, this was a coney lodge. I'd heard of such places. Rabbit fur was highly valued especially in the past and the animals needed to be protected from poachers. They were thus farmed in places like this much as doves are farmed in dovecotes. The warrener would share his home with his charges, the rabbits at ground level which presumably was where I was now, with the warrener's family housed on the floor above. But there were no rabbits here now nor had been for some time by the looks of the place. And no warrener either, unless it was the man now standing in front of me thrusting a torch in my face.

'Brother Walter?'

I nodded, shielding my eyes from the flame.

'Follow me.'

We climbed a rickety stair-ladder to the upper floor which was, or had once been, the living quarters. But surely no-one lived here now. The place was derelict. At least up here the smell was a little fresher than down below. The ceiling, too, was higher so that I could stand upright. At the top of the ladder was the last person I would have expected to see: a woman in, I'd guess, her seventh decade of life dressed in a gown more suited to a manor hall than a bolt-hole like this. She looked quite incongruously out of place in such surroundings. A question was forming in my mind which she answered:

'Thank you for coming, Brother Walter. I am Margaret de Calne, wife of the man whose shadow you have been chasing.'

'I apologize for having to meet you here under such circumstances, Brother Walter, rather than my home.'

'I have seen your home, Lady Margaret. This place is a palace by comparison.'

She nodded. 'You are right. It is some time since Wykes was any kind of home. I fear it may never be again.'

I resisted the temptation to mention the present occupants who weren't really in a position to complain.

'What is this place, my lady?' I asked looking around. 'Surely not your home now.'

'It was my husband's many years ago,' she smiled. 'The breeding of rabbits for their fur were one of his many enterprises. Few people know of its existence.'

'Which is presumably why you've chosen it.'

'Indeed.' She squinted at me through the torchlight. 'You know, you're very much like your father.'

'You knew my father?'

She nodded. 'Many years ago. You and I even met once, though I don't suppose you remember. It was a very long time ago.'

'I believe there was a falling out between them – Sir Richard and my father.'

'The two men didn't always see eye to eye.'

'Are you talking about the Anarchy now – or the green children?'

She smiled. 'Yes, I realise that is a subject you wish to pursue, but it is not why I have brought you here tonight.'

'Why have you brought me here? And why the subterfuge?'

'We had to be certain you weren't followed.'

'We?'

She hesitated for a moment before moving to one side to reveal another figure who now stepped forward into the light, a young man in his early thirties.

'Brother Walter – this is my son, Richard.'

'I'm honoured, sir. You bear a proud name. I have heard many great things about your father. A truly remarkable man.'

Now, call me old-fashioned but if someone greeted me in such terms my reaction would be to feign modesty while secretly my chest would swell with pride. Not so Sir Richard de Calne's son, it seemed. Quite the reverse, in fact.

He snorted his contempt. 'If you can call the burnt out shell of a house and a ruined estate "remarkable".'

I admit I was surprised. Up till now everybody I'd met had nothing but praise for the man. Well they say a prophet is never welcome in his own land – nor in his own house evidently. His mother seemed less certain:

'Brother Walter doesn't need to hear this, Richard.'

'What do I need to hear, my lady?' I asked. 'Why exactly have you brought me here?'

'Simply this: the enterprise you've been engaged in these past days. We'd like you to stop.'

'Are you sure you know the nature of the enterprise I've been engaged in, my lady?'

'Oh brother believe me, we've been following your exploits most attentively.'

'Then you'll know that a murder has been committed. A particularly horrific murder.'

She nodded. 'Bardwell's curate. A great tragedy. Ivo was a gentle, harmless soul.'

'In which case you'd surely want me to find his killer.'

'No brother. That is precisely what we don't want you to do.'

'Why ever not?'

'Because you won't succeed.'

That annoyed me. It was the sort of thing my own mother would say. I certainly didn't want to hear it from somebody else's mother.

'I hesitate to disagree with you my lady, but I believe I am succeeding. I already have a suspect.'

'Oh?' said Richard. 'Who?'

'That is for me to know,' I said awkwardly.

His lip curled. 'Leon. You think Leon murdered the curate.'

'All the evidence points that way sir, yes.'

He gave a sick laugh. 'Leon didn't kill Ivo, brother.'

It was a relief to hear him say it, but still I had to ask: 'How can you be so certain?'

He just shook his head.

'You do know it was Leon went to see Abbot Samson?' said Lady Margaret.

'Of course.' I didn't, not for certain. But that confirmed it.

'Then you'll also know she told of another victim – or rather, an *intended* victim. Have you managed to identify this victim yet?'

'Not yet. But I will.'

'Then let me help you,' said Richard. '*I* am the intended victim.'

My jaw dropped open. '*You*?'

He nodded. 'Me. And far from Leon wanting to murder me, she is in fact going to be my wife.'

'Your *wife*?'

'It's true,' said his mother. 'Leon and Richard have been pledged since the nursery.'

I turned back to Richard. 'Is that why you despise your father's memory so much? Because he disapproved of the relationship?'

'My father didn't disapprove of our relationship, brother. On the contrary, he encouraged it. And for once I agreed with him.'

'Then I don't see the problem. Presumably Leon wants this marriage too? Is that what this has all been about? Your marriage?' I shook my head. 'No, I can't believe it. There's something more, something you're not telling me. What is it?'

Then realisation dawned on me.

'You know, don't you?' I said quietly. 'The murderer. You know who it is.'

From their exchange of glances and I could see I had guessed right.

'Who? Who is it doing these things?' I waited. 'For God's sake tell me!'

'It's not that simple,' said the lady.

'What's not simple? There's a murderer loose who's killed once and intends to kill again, possibly you next time. Look at the pair of you, homeless, terrified of your own shadows. Tell me who it is and I promise you all that will stop. Surely that's what you want? Surely that's the reason Leon went to Abbot Samson? '

'That was a mistake,' said Richard.

'How?'

But Richard shook his head. In desperation I turned to his mother:

'Lady Margaret?'

For a moment I thought she might speak, but Richard put his hand on her arm.

'We've already told you more than we should,' she said.

'You've told me nothing. '

I looked in exasperation at the pair of them: 'What's stopping you?'

But they just stared blankly back at me.

'Well I'm sorry, I can't do as you ask. This is about more than just the two of you now. It's about justice – for Ivo. I must continue my search with or without your help.'

Richard gave a sick smile. 'I told you this was a waste of time,' he said to his mother.

Lady Margaret turned to me in earnest: 'Brother, please, I beg you. Give this up. For your own safety sake if nothing else.'

My own safety? All I could do was shake my head.

The lady drew herself erect and set her face. 'Then good night, Brother Walter.'

I found myself dumped unceremoniously out in the rain once more with the door firmly shut and bolted behind me. No sign of my soldier guide this time or a horse to carry me home. They were clearly displeased with me. Well, too bad. If I wasn't determined to get to the bottom of this before I was now. Assuming I ever managed to find my way out of this maze of trees and banks, that is. The wind had picked up and the rain was coming down in sheets blinding me. But I couldn't stay here. There was nothing else for it. I pulled my hood up over my head and set off in the direction I thought I had come.

Pretty soon I was completely lost. Out in the forest all paths look alike, I could wander around for days getting nowhere. If that was the de Calne's intention they might well get their wish. It occurred to me that maybe that is what happened to the green children and explained why they ended up in a pit in the middle of a Suffolk field. How ironic if I were to do the same now. But Richard and his mother weren't going to win that way, of that I was determined. I knew roughly the direction I needed to go. From the time it took us to get here I estimated we had travelled about three miles. On a good day it should take me no more than an hour to walk that distance. Even I could manage that. And surely I must come to the edge of the forest eventually. If only there was something on which I could fix my bearings.

And then I heard it. Faint at first but with increasing vigour: the sound of a church bell. Was it the wind playing tricks? One hears of sailors being lured onto rocks by the bells of drowned churches ringing out beneath the waves on stormy nights. But I was miles from any coast. It had to be the Bardwell bell, there was no other church around. The sound seemed to be coming from behind me. No, wait a moment, to my left. No, I was right the first time, it was behind me. I stumbled on wet, cold and angry with the thought of hell-fire beginning to seem very appealing indeed.

Chapter Nineteen
DEUS EX MACHINA

'I couldn't stop it, master!' Nathan yelled above the din.

Ivo's water-clock. Somehow the boy had managed to set it going and now he couldn't switch it off. It was a wondrous sight to behold - chains clanking, wheels whirring, water gurgling and all without human or animal intervention. Remarkable. But my goodness what a racket it made! And the bell - it boomed out into the night like a beacon in the wilderness guiding me back to Bardwell as surely as the Last Trumpet summoning the faithful to Paradise.

'Don't try to stop it! ' I yelled back at him. 'Let it ring out to the Glory of God – and your genius!'

'If you say so, master,' he said standing back and wiping grease from his hands. 'But I doubt the villagers will thank us.'

Fortunately Bardwell's inhabitants didn't have their sleep disturbed for long. The reservoir holding the water soon ran out and with it went the impetus driving the extraordinary engine. I was mildly disappointed as the last of the water trickled away and the clanking gradually slowed and finally stopped.

'Thank heaven for that!' said Nathan as the last resonances of the bell faded and silence descended. 'I thought it would never end.'

'The wonder is that you got it going in the first place. How ever did you manage it?'

'I found this.'

He produced a large sheet of parchment. It was the plans for the clock that Ivo had told me about. Squares, circles, numbers - all utterly meaningless to me. But not to Nathan, evidently. That's what comes of having a mathematician for a father. Why is it the young are always so much better at these things that us oldies?

'It's quite simple really once you get the hang of it. You just fill these vessels with water like this, open this tap here and -'

'No don't set it off again,' I said laying a cautionary hand on his arm, 'or we shall have half the village at the door.'

'It's not working properly. There seems to be a tooth missing from the braking mechanism – just here, do you see?'

'Yes, I remember Ivo mentioning something about that. A monk from Saint Albans is supposed to be coming to repair it.'

'I didn't realise when I set it going and then it was impossible to stop till the water ran out. Sorry master.'

'Oh, don't apologize. Without it I might still be wandering around the forest.'

Nathan gazed adoringly at the thing. 'This is the future, master,' he said in reverential tones. 'One day every church in the country will have a clock like this. Every house, I shouldn't wonder.'

'Don't let's get carried away. One is quite enough for any village. Are you sure it's off now? It's not going to start up again?'

'As sure as I can be, master.'

'Then let's get inside the house before I turn into a block of ice. It's freezing out here. '

With the fire banked-up and a cup of Ivo's warmed-up "mule" in my hand I was soon feeling human again.

'How did your meeting go?' Nathan asked. 'Who was your mysterious host? Not the murderer evidently.'

I could see he was still smarting over being left behind, so I told him about the meeting with Lady Margaret and Richard in the warrener's cottage. By the time I'd finished he was as incredulous as I was.

'They want you to give up?'

'That's what they said.'

'But why?'

I shrugged. 'Lady Margaret doesn't think I'll succeed. Maybe she thinks an ageing monk physician isn't the right person for the job.'

He nodded thoughtfully. 'Possibly. But that's no reason to stop trying.'

'No,' I agreed firmly. 'It isn't.'

He frowned. 'I don't understand this. Are you sure it was the de Calnes?'

'What do you mean? Of course it was them. Who else could it have been?'

'I don't know. But if I knew some madman was out there threatening to kill me, I'd want everyone out looking for him not putting people off.'

'Even an ageing monk physician?'

'Indeed.'

'And his impudent young assistant?'

He grinned. 'Him too.'

'Anyway,' I said, 'it must have been them. Lady Margaret remembered me from when we were neighbours. She said so in as many words.'

'Anyone could say that. Did you recognize her?'

'No. It was a long time ago.'

'How convenient. My God, I wish I'd been there.'

'I'm very glad you weren't.'

'No, but they were very keen to get you on your own.'

I shook my head. 'I don't think you can read anything into that. They were just being cautious. For all their bravado they were genuinely very frightened people.'

'Then why ask you to give up? There must be a better reason than the one Lady Margaret gave you.'

That was my conclusion, too. I was sure there was something they weren't telling me. Whatever it was it was important enough to risk their own lives and go into hiding over it. Evidently Leon didn't agree or she wouldn't have warned Samson. But then why didn't she go all the way and name the killer? It was bizarre.

'So what will you do? Stop searching or carry on?'

I shrugged. 'I told them I would, so I suppose I shall have to.'

'Good,' he said. 'I hate being defeated.'

I seemed to have talked myself into that one. I drained my cup of mule. 'Is there any more of this? I'm acquiring a taste for it.'

While he was out in the yard refilling the jug I glanced again at the plans for Sir Richard's water clock. Not that they meant anything to me although I could appreciate the competence of the graphics. That was Sir Richard's work too, I imagined.

'I definitely think you have missed your true vocation,' I said when he returned. 'These are incredibly intricate.'

'That wasn't all I found. After you left I went through some of the documents in the outhouse and found this.'

He produced a second drawing, not of a clock this time but a plan of Wykes Hall in its heyday. It was as well-drawn as the clock plans and clearly by the same hand.

'That's odd,' I said peering closer. 'It looks wrong somehow.'

'It is wrong. There's a floor missing. That was the first thing I noticed.'

'Of course, the fire. That's why the bodies were stored on the ground floor. It's not really the ground floor but the rubble above the ground floor.'

Nathan looked at me. 'Bodies master?'

I'd forgotten I hadn't told him that bit yet. I described the visit Ivo and I made to the burnt-out shell of the hall with the piles of bodies stacked against the walls.

'You make it sound like a charnel house.'

'That's exactly what it is: the remains of dead villagers awaiting the end of the interdict and a proper Christian burial.'

'In which case I wonder why Father Alan didn't make use of the cellars.'

'Cellars?'

Nathan nodded. 'There's quite an extensive undercroft beneath the building.' He pointed it out on the plans.

'I was wondering how so much managed to remain intact. It must all have been stored below ground and survived the fire. I wonder if there's anything they missed.'

'Be interesting to find out,' he grinned.

The young and their thirst for adventure. I shook my head. 'No. Too dangerous. With all this rain, it'll be our luck for it all to collapse while we're in it. Besides, Ivo was quite clear they'd removed everything of value when the fire took hold and stored it in the outhouse.'

'Not quite everything.'

He went out and came back with a book – or the remnants of one. It was quite a large, leather-bound volume. Fire had destroyed a good two-thirds of it but there was enough left to be readable. Once again it was in the same tight script of Sir Richard's hand. I'd seen enough books being copied in the scriptorium at the abbey to recognize this had been written by the same hand.

'Where did you find it?'

'It was hidden in a secret drawer inside Sir Richard's bureau.'

'Clever boy.'

'Not really. The back of the bureau had been ripped off. When I moved it the book fell out. It seems to be a record of some kind.

I started turning the delicate charred pages carefully one by one.

'This is gold-dust,' I said after a few pages. 'It is indeed a record of all of Sir Richard's work going back decades. The cellar must have been where he had his laboratorium. I wonder if there's anything in here about green children.'

'I thought you said that was a fallacy?'

'Yes I did, didn't I?' I said wistfully turning more pages. 'Oh, this isn't any good. The writing's too small. I can't read it.'

'Let me try.' He took the book from my hands. 'You're looking in the wrong place. Sir Richard wrote in Latin. We should be looking under V for Viridi not G for Green.' He carefully turned to the back half of the book. 'Here we are: *VIRIDI FILIOS.* Green children,' he grinned triumphantly.

Insufferable child. I snatched the book back and tried to read the text underneath the title. But still my eyes failed me. 'What's this? Duo fil … estate ...' I frowned and tutted.

'*Duo filii mei estate operantur captus theoriis ortum determinare si sunt rectam...*' Nathan read fluently. 'It's referring to the year MCXLIV – that's eleven forty-four.' He looked up. 'Does the date mean anything to you, master? Something about sons and daughters of Sir Richard's estate workers?'

I shook my head. 'No, that's not the story of the green children. It wasn't the de Calne estate. The children were found on farmland miles from here near the village of...'

'Wlf-peta,' Nathan read carefully.

I felt a surge of excitement. 'No, not Wlfpeta. Wolfpit – or rather Woolpit. Sir Richard is either being pedantic, or deliberately obscure.'

'This is starting to sound interesting,' said Nathan. 'We should go and look.' He stood up.

'Not so hasty, my intrepid young friend. Can't you hear that wind? It's howling a gale out there. We'll go tomorrow in daylight. Together. Hopefully the weather might have improved by then, too.'

That meant staying the night in the Bardwell priest-house. Spooky to be spending the night in a house where a murder had just taken place. There was no saying the killer wouldn't come back. I was more concerned that we wouldn't be returning to Ixworth having told Oswald we would. Normally he wouldn't worry, but with everything that had been happening recently he might well organize a search party. As it turned out he didn't send a search party, more's the pity. If he had and if I had been paying a little more attention instead of allowing myself to be diverted by Nathan's urging, the impending disaster might well have been avoided.

Chapter Twenty
KILLING BY DEATH

There is something about the bed-bugs in Bardwell. They seem to have bigger teeth than the ones in Bury. Either that or they have a particular liking for monk blood. They didn't leave my ankles alone all night. What with them and Nathan snoring in the bed next to me, I didn't get much sleep.

I could have done with the water clock to tell me the time and had to estimate the hour. My brother monks, I knew, would be in the choir reciting the office of prime about now so I mentally joined them whilst trying to collect my thoughts for the day ahead. Not easy. My head was still fuzzy from the previous day's activities – and rather too much of Ivo's mule. I managed to stumble my way through the office and then rose from my knees to fan the embers of the fire into life. I then lifted the window shutter and gazed out onto the awakening Suffolk day.

The rain had eased off at last, *Deo favente*, and the watery moon was trying to emerge from behind the cloud above Wykes Hall. But there was an ominous rumble in the clouds far away. Was there ever a December as wet as this? If I were superstitious I might wonder if it was a conspiracy of weather spirits to confound my efforts. I said a quick prayer to Saint Medard who is supposed to favour good weather having sheltered as a child beneath the wings of an eagle. I looked up into the sky above the ruin. No sign of an eagle, but plenty of rooks.

What would we find down there, I wondered? It was where Sir Richard de Calne had lived and worked most of his life. The man was still an enigma to me. I wondered again why his son should despise him so. I might have expected a knight to oppose his son's desire to wed a commoner like Leon with no dowry to bring to the marriage contract, but that doesn't seem to have put him off at all. Quite the opposite. Yet still his son despised him. There had to be another reason for the bad blood. It was yet one more mystery to add to the growing catalogue surrounding this mysterious family.

Wykes was also where the green children had been taken when first discovered. I could well imagine a man like Sir Richard regarding the arrival of two strange beings as an exciting subject for study. Perhaps that's why the Woolpit shepherd brought them to him so far from where they were discovered, always assuming, of course, that the story was true and not a legend. But legends don't grow from nothing. Something went on here six decades ago, something very curious that suddenly flared up and as quickly disappeared. Frustratingly the part of the notebook where Sir Richard might have recorded his conclusions had been destroyed in the fire. I was hoping against hope that something might have survived the flames and remained to be discovered in the cellars beneath the ruined hall. Well, in a short while we would find out one way of the other.

Behind me I heard Nathan begin to stir. Being half my age, he was naturally unaffected by the previous night's indulgence. He bounced out of bed eager to take on the new day and breakfasted heartily on the stale bread and cheese he found in the larder. I felt sick just watching him. He must have the constitution of a goat.

This being the darkest season of the year, daylight didn't arrive until mid-morning. But as soon as it was light enough we started to make our way across the river meadow to the hall. After so much rain the ground was thoroughly waterlogged with only islands of dry grass rising high enough for us to hop across. We managed to get under cover just as the rain started again accompanied this time by the rumble of thunder. So much for Saint Medard. We needn't have waited for daylight for once inside the building all was as black as night again. Fortunately I'd had the forethought to bring tinder and torch with me.

'By the saints, master, what's that smell?'

'I told you, past inhabitants of the village. That,' I said remembering the table-cloth, 'is Father Alan's maid, Dorcas. Over here is the grave-digger, Hugh.'

'We could do with his services now,' Nathan said pulling a face. 'These people should be in the ground.'

'Try breathing through your mouth,' I told him. 'I find it helps.'

We edged our way further into the building. It was hard to imagine this once being a fine hall hung with tapestries and fine furnishings and filled with light and laughter. Now the place was damp and dark and the only things that filled it were the ghosts of the corpses piled either side of us and making a reproachful guard of honour as we passed.

Nathan had brought along the plans and was scrutinizing them closely by the light of the torch. 'I think it's this way,' he said carefully picking his way over the rubble. I let him take the lead. I never was very good with maps.

'What exactly are we looking for?' I whispered.

'The entrance to the cellar. According to the plan there's a doorway along here somewhere. And there's no need to whisper, master. They can't hear us.' He nodded to the serried ranks of dead.

'Even so,' I whispered. 'It's … disrespectful.'

We carried on inching our way further along the wall. Suddenly a pigeon clattered into life above our heads making me yelp with fright and I instinctively grabbed Nathan's arm.

He chuckled. 'Spooky, hey master?'

'Let's just get on with it,' I said pushing him ahead of me.

On we went clambering through the gap and over further pieces of charred and fallen roof timbers. Nathan stopped to examine his plan again.

'According to this the door should be about here somewhere.' He held up his torch to illuminate the wall, but all I could see were more dead bodies.

'There's nothing here,' I whispered. 'Let's go back. I don't think we're going to find anything.'

'No no,' he insisted. 'It's in the wall behind this lot here. Look.' He indicated the nearest pile of bodies. 'We'll have to move a couple of corpses.'

I groaned. 'Must we?'

'They won't mind. Besides, who's to know?'

'God,' I said. 'That's who.'

He shrugged. 'We've come this far. Pity to give up now.'

We approached the nearest corpse. Without pausing he grasped the head while I tentatively took hold of the feet mentally apologizing for the impertinence. After the third body Nathan gave a whoop of joy:

'Look! A door.'

Sure enough there was a lintel. After two more bodies half the door was exposed. Another two and the entire door was clear.

'Now lets go carefully,' I cautioned. 'We don't want to -'

Too late. He'd already taken a kick and the rotten remains of what must once have been a sturdy oak door fell away like tinder. He held up the torch and waved it inside the opening.

'Yes,' he said excitedly, 'it's the cellar all right. Look - steps.'

I peered into a cavernous black hole leading down to heaven alone knew where – Hell most likely. The light from the torch only lit a few steps but it seemed forbidding. I shivered, and not just from the cold. But Nathan was already through the door and starting to descend his voice echoing back at me.

'I really don't think we should go down there,' I tried to protest. 'We should wait. Supposing we slip? Nobody knows we're here. We could be trapped for days. I really think we ought to go back and come back another time.'

But he seemed not to hear me. What, I wondered, had happened to his promise to obey me in all things? Hesitantly, I followed. But where had he gone? I could no longer hear or see him.

'Nathan? Are you there?'

No answer.

I listened but could hear nothing.

'Nathan, don't play games. Answer me, please.'

Nothing.

I didn't like this. I felt suddenly very alone even though I knew Nathan was just a few yards away. And then another fluttering behind me making me jump. I turned, but this time instead of a pigeon I saw something that made my blood freeze. Dorcas, the maid, was standing a foot behind me with her hands raised high above her head. I gasped. Was this the resentful dead risen up to wreak awful revenge on the sacrilegious living? I tried to cry out but found my voice stuck in my throat. Then the dead maid's hands came down with such force that they knocked my torch out of my hand and sent me careering backwards.

What happened next was too rapid for me to remember in exact sequence. A bright light of pain flooded me as I felt myself falling backwards unable to keep my footing. Instinctively I put out my hand but there was nothing to grab hold of. Then I seemed to be floating through empty space. But I came down with a painful bump to earth – or rather onto the stone steps. It was a long, bumpy journey to the bottom. Fortunately I only felt half of them as part way down I cracked my head on something hard and the world spun away from me into blackness before I could feel the full force of the floor come up and hit me from below.

Chapter Twenty-one
ANSWERS - SOME

I awoke to total darkness. If you've never done that, opened your eyes and seen nothing at all, I can tell you it is a terrifying experience. You think you've gone blind. Even in the pitch black of night it is usually possible to see something, but here the darkness was complete. I was totally disorientated – and in pain. It felt like every bone in my body was broken. I must have fallen the entire length of the stone stairway. My head throbbed and my chest hurt with every breath I took. I was also aware that I couldn't move any of my limbs. And then with horror I realised why. I was in the same position as Ivo had been in when we found him: seated in a chair with my wrists and ankles tied to the chair arms and legs. In panic I tried to free them, but the binding was too tight. Try as I might I couldn't free them.

I struggled for a few moments getting nowhere then stopped as behind me I heard a noise.

'Who's there? Somebody's there, I can hear you. Nathan? Is that you?'

'So, you're awake at last.'

A flint was struck and a torch ignited. That in itself was a relief as I realised I wasn't blind after all.

As my eyes adjusted to the light at last I saw my adversary:

Alberic.

I was at once both surprised and not surprised. I didn't know whether to laugh or cry.

But first things first: 'Where's Nathan?' I demanded. 'What have you done with him?'

He brought the torch down to eye level and I saw the figure of Nathan seated in the darkness in another chair directly facing me. He was tied the same way that I was except he was still unconscious. There was a nasty gash on the side of his head and blood was still trickling down his cheek. He must have broken my fall on the way down and come off worse from the collision. But what concerned me was that his head had flopped forward onto his chest. I knew from past experience that it is impossible to breathe in that position.

'Raise his head, damn you,' I said, 'or he'll suffocate!'

Alberic casually complied, lifting Nathan's chin. The boy immediately gasped for air. With relief I saw that he was still alive.

'You see?' said Alberic. 'He's fine. Though for how much longer I don't know.'

My blood ran cold. 'What does that mean?'

'It's very simple. You tell me what I want to know and our young friend here will live. If not...' He let Nathan's head slump forward constricting his throat again.

'Tell you what?' I said anxiously. 'I don't know anything.'

'Young Richard de Calne.'

'What about him?'

'You went to see him yesterday.'

I didn't reply.

'There's no point denying it. I saw you. I tried to follow but that guard was too quick. That's the third time you managed to get away from me. You really are rather a rather difficult man to track.'

The third time? So it must have been Alberic who had attacked me on the road to Ixworth. That was the second time. But the first? Then I understood. Of course, at the kiln. It was Alberic who attacked me, not Leon. It just looked that way in the confusion. How could I have been so stupid?

'For God's sake raise the boy's head, damn you!' I barked at him.

'Tell me where you went in the forest and I will.'

'The warrener's lodge,' I said quickly. 'We went to the warrener's lodge.'

He paused. 'Hm. I take it from your willing reply that he isn't there any more.'

'I don't know. Probably not.'

'But you know where he went.'

'I don't. I told you, I don't know anything. I only met him for the first time yesterday. It was his mother who summoned me.'

'Lady Margaret? Now that's interesting. What did she want, I wonder?'

'Nothing.'

'Oh come. That's a lot of trouble to go to for nothing. She must have wanted something.'

'She wanted me to stop my investigation.'

He frowned. 'Why would she do that?'

'I don't know. And Nathan knows even less. So let the boy go. He's no use to you.'

'On the contrary. So far he's been very useful. Loosened your tongue.'

'He won't be if you kill him.'

Alberic glanced down at the boy and raised his head again. Still unconscious, Nathan sucked in a great lungful of air. I found myself breathing with him willing him to stay alive.

'What do you want with them?'

He looked at me with surprise. 'Don't you know? I thought after all your questions that you'd have most of the answers by now.'

'I keep telling you. I don't know anything.'

He looked at me incredulously, but shrugged. 'Very well.'

He stood for a moment as though composing his thoughts like a priest preparing to deliver a sermon. But this was to be no homily.

'Tell me brother, when you woke just now, what could you see?'

I frowned. 'You know perfectly well I could see nothing until you lit that torch.'

He nodded. 'Quite so. Well, imagine living in a world like that all the time. A world where there is no daylight. No difference at all between night and day. Not even knowing there was a difference. No bird song. No feeling of wind in your face or rain or sun.'

'What you're describing is a prison.'

'That's exactly what it was. A prison.'

'And where was this supposed prison?'

He spread his arms wide. 'You're sitting in it.'

I looked about me and saw what I hadn't noticed before. It wasn't just a cellar we were in. There were bars and grilles. This was indeed a dungeon.

'And who was the prisoner? I suppose you're going to tell me it was you.'

For answer he just smiled.

'Why?' I asked. 'What had you done?'

He shrugged. 'Nothing.'

I shook my head. 'You must have done something. People don't get put in prison for no reason.'

'They do if they are born there.'

'I get it. What you mean is it was your *mother* who was the prisoner.'

'Oh, we never knew our mother.'

'We?'

'My sister and me.'

His words started a faint alarm ringing in my head.

'You're telling me you and your sister were imprisoned here in this cellar? But that would mean… '

I stopped. No, it couldn't be. Was it possible? It was half a century ago. But half a century ago Alberic would have been a child. I let out a gasp.

He smiled with satisfaction. 'Got it at last.'

'No, wait a moment,' I said shaking my head. 'That's not what happened. Sir Richard didn't imprison those children. They were brought here from Woolpit.'

'Yes. After.'

I frowned. 'After what?'

'After we escaped.'

My head, already painful, started to throb. 'No, that's not right either. The boy died, it's in the record – Abbot Ralph's chronicle.'

He scoffed. 'Abbot Ralph.'

'I don't believe you. Sir Richard wouldn't have done that. Imprison two children? Why would he?'

'In order to watch us, of course.'

'Watch you doing what?'

He shrugged. 'Everything. Eating. Playing. He would sit for hours just where you are now, watching us. Oh, and games - that was the other thing he liked to do. Sir Richard did love his games.'

'What sort of games?' I asked not sure I wanted to know the answer.

He grinned. 'Oh, not those sorts of games. He wasn't that kind. Other games. One of his favourites was to starve us.'

'*Starve* you?'

'Only for a few days. Just long enough to get us really hungry. Then he would feed us - but only if we asked to be fed. I say "ask" but of course we didn't have the words to ask. How could we? Nobody ever taught us, not even our angels.'

I couldn't believe what I was hearing. I could understand Sir Richard wanting to study two unusual creatures discovered from a foreign land. But what Alberic was describing was more than that. He was suggesting they – Alberic and his sister - had been deliberately incarcerated from childhood like experimental subjects. I'd heard of rats being bred for experimentation. I'd done as much myself. But *children?*

'I don't believe any of this.'

His smile vanished. 'Then don't. It's all the same to me.'

He made another move towards Nathan. I'd antagonized him. It was a mistake. What I needed was to divert him. Keep his attention away from Nathan.

'These angels you mentioned,' I said quickly. 'Who were they?'

He paused. The smile flickered back. 'They were the only ones to treat us like humans. They fed us and took away our filth. Oh, not real angels of course, that's just how we thought of them. To us they were magical beings. They seemed beautiful - angelic. But even they never spoke to us. Not one single word in all those years.'

'How many years?'

'In my case, eight.'

'And your sister?'

'Ten.'

That agreed with what I'd been told about the green children.

'All right, let's say I believe you. You said just now you escaped. How? Two young children, ignorant of the world and its ways. How would you escape from a place like this?'

'There was a storm. The river is right behind that wall over there. The cellar began to flood.'

'So you didn't escape *per se*. Sir Richard released you.'

'No, Sir Richard wasn't the one who released us. He would have let us drown. It was one of our angels set us free.'

'As simple as that?'

The smile faded again. 'No brother, not as simple as that. Nothing was ever as simple as that. We were suddenly freed. Can you imagine it, seeing the sky for the first time in your life? Up till that moment the only sky we had ever known was this stone roof. We didn't know such a thing as a sky or anything else existed outside or that there even was such a thing as "outside".'

I still wasn't convinced. 'You were discovered miles away from here in Woolpit village. Explain to me how you managed to get there since you knew nothing of the world.'

He shrugged. 'We followed the river. A long silvery road of water.'

The Blackbourn. The river that flowed past my mother's house in Ixworth and rose somewhere in the south of the county. Woolpit was south of here. If he and his sister really did follow the river they could conceivably have ended up in Woolpit. That too was possible. Everything he said was possible. But was it true?

'So you got to Woolpit. What happened there?'

He rubbed his brow. 'A day passed. Then another. We grew hungry. We found some meat in a field.'

I nodded. 'Bait on top of the wolf pit trap.'

'We took it, fell in and couldn't get out.'

'But you were found - by a shepherd.'

'He took us to his house. His wife fed us. But they couldn't cope with us. We were too wild.'

'So the shepherd took you to Sir Richard?'

'His priest advised him to do that.' He laughed. 'Of all the people to choose. Don't you find that amusing? We couldn't speak English so we didn't realise what was happening to us - until it was too late.'

Despite my doubts I found myself wanting to believe him. It was too elaborate a story to have been made up. I found the story immensely compelling and immeasurably sad.

'But why? Why would Sir Richard want to incarcerate innocent children? What possible reason would he have?'

'Well, now you've asked the question, haven't you brother. I suppose the simple answer is that he

232

did it because he could. There was no-one to stop him. None of his servants would dare, nor Lady Margaret. Not even your father who might have done had he known what was going on. But Sir Richard made sure he kept away.'

'By manufacturing a false feud between the two households,' I nodded. 'That tells me how he did it. My question was why?'

'Only one person can answer that one. Sir Richard himself.'

I thought I was beginning now to understand other things better. Oswald's description of the episode in the Wykes' piggery. The children tortured those poor creatures not because they were evil, but because they knew no better. No-one had taught them right from wrong any more than they were taught anything else. They simply didn't understand that the animals were suffering. Under those circumstances I could believe they might well have found the animals' squeals of agony "amusing". It might also explain the girl's lax morality when it came to men.

'When you got back to Wykes, what happened then? Did Sir Richard try to return you to the cellar?'

'How could he? By then the secret was out. The shepherd and his wife; the Woolpit priest. They knew about us. Word spread. Pretty soon everyone had heard about the green children of Woolpit. We were famous,' he grinned.

'Surely the truth about you would have emerged eventually?'

'How? We couldn't speak and Sir Richard wasn't going to tell. Nor was his wife, nor our angels. They were all equally complicit.'

'It was said that the boy – you - died.'

'As you see I didn't. But I might just as well have done. Sir Richard separated us. Agnes – that was the name he gave to my sister - remained here at Wykes while I was sent to live with the Cistercian monks of Rievaulx abbey. That was torture of another kind. You have to understand, we'd never been separated before. And now I didn't know how to get to her. When I did finally learn to speak I was too afraid to say anything for fear of what might happen to her if I did. I imagine she did the same.'

'Did you not try to find her? Later I mean, as an adult.'

'Yes of course I did. But no-one believed me. And can you blame them? The story was too fantastic. The monks accused me of lying and when I persisted they beat me. So I learned to keep quiet. Gradually the memories faded. And Rievaulx wasn't so bad. My life settled into a routine. After a few years I became a lay-brother at the abbey. My former life seemed but a dream.'

'But then you were sent to Coggeshall,' I guessed.

He nodded. 'The monks needed help setting up their sheep farm and the Yorkshire Cistercians are the best sheep farmers in the world. So I and a few of my lay-brothers were sent to help.'

'And there you met Leon. Once you discovered her connection with Sir Richard all the memories came flooding back. You realised it wasn't a dream after all.'

He smiled. 'That's it exactly.'

'So now you want your revenge. Is that what this is all about? Revenge on the family who tormented you? But it's a bit late, isn't it? Sir Richard is dead. And you can't blame his son for the crimes of his father.'

'If you'd asked me that a year ago I might have agreed with you. But not now. Not since I discovered Leon and Richard intend to marry.'

'But why should that bother you?'

'You still don't get it, do you? Leon is my niece.'

I was momentarily stunned into silence by this latest revelation.

Alberic smiled. 'Oh dear, I see I've shocked you. Yes, that's right. Leon is Agnes's daughter. And now she wants to marry Sir Richard's son. Just imagine: the daughter of the only person I ever loved wanting to marry the son of the man I hated more than any in all the world. I couldn't allow it. I *won't* allow it.'

I shook my head. 'No, it's more than that. It's not just Sir Richard's son you want to keep from Leon. It's any man. Any man who ever showed any interest in her. Even me. That's why you attacked me at Coggeshall. That's the real reason you want Richard dead.'

'Believe what you like, brother. But I tell you now, Richard de Calne's son will never marry Leon. Not while I have breath in my body. I will prevent it. And you are going to help me.'

'How? I've told you. I don't know where he is.'

'Then perhaps your assistant does.'

'Nathan?' I'd almost forgotten he was there. 'I've told you, he knows nothing.'

'Perhaps. But he may help jog your memory.'

'What do you mean?' I said, alarmed.

'Oh, don't worry. He won't feel anything. He's unconscious. Unlike your curate friend. He didn't know anything either as it turned out. But it took all his fingers before I was convinced. How many will it take this time, I wonder?'

I watched with mounting horror as he took Nathan's hand and carefully spread the fingers on the armrest. Alberic took out his knife.

'We'll start with the left hand this time, I think. After that the right. See how far we get.'

'No. Alberic, please. This is barbarous.'

'You know what you have to do to stop it.'

'I can't tell you what I don't know.'

He shrugged. 'So be it.'

He took hold of Nathan's right thumb and began to slice into the skin just above the knuckle making the blood flow freely.

'All right! I'll tell you! But in the name of all that's holy, stop!'

What I said next I had to explain later. I know it was wrong of me and I was placing my mother and Oswald in terrible danger. But I had to say something quickly. If I hadn't, Nathan would have been hideously mutilated.

'He's at Ixworth Hall.'

Alberic frowned. 'Your mother's home?'

'Where else? My mother and Lady Margaret are old friends - neighbours. They've known each other for years. Decades. Why else do you think I got involved?'

He thought about that for a moment weighing up my words. But I could see he still wasn't entirely convinced.

'So why did you go to the warrenry?'

'To fool you, of course. Lady Margaret and Richard knew you were following me even though I didn't. It was to draw you away. They thought they could outwit you.'

He didn't like that. The idea that someone should think they were cleverer than him – it was like throwing down the gauntlet. But would he pick it up?

To my intense relief he released Nathan's hand.

'Very well. I will go to Ixworth Hall. It will be easy enough to verify if you're telling the truth. You're not going anywhere. It's impossible to get out of here without help – I ought to know. But if I find you've been lying I will return. And then you will discover just how determined I am.'

Chapter Twenty-two
NARROW ESCAPE

'Nathan wake up!'

No response.

I was leaning as far forward in the chair as I could and shouting at the top of my lungs, but he was deaf to all my entreaties. He was still out cold. That crack on his head must have been worse than it looked. There wasn't much blood but I knew that even minor head injuries can be dangerous. He could wake up at any moment or he could remain as he was for ever. Alberic had left a torch burning so I could at least watch the boy's life slowly ebbing away. In the meantime I had sent a killer to my mother's house. How had I done that? Out of desperation, that's how. If I hadn't Nathan would have been mutilated by that madman. But at least it bought us a little time. Of little use though to either of us trussed up here.

'*Nathan!*'

I calculated we had about half an hour before Alberic returned: a third of that for him to ride the two miles to Ixworth; another third to decide I had been lying and Richard de Calne and his mother were not at Ixworth Hall; and the final third to ride back again – assuming he didn't delay in order to perpetrate some new atrocity by way of revenge on my mother and Oswald. In that time Nathan and I had to free ourselves from our bonds, escape from the cellar, climb the steps and stumble out into the Suffolk day. It seemed an impossible task in the time available. And to add to my problems water was now seeping into the cellar. It must be from the storm outside, rain swelling the river. Alberic said it was the other side of the wall. It was certainly coming in fast. A minute ago it was lapping the soles of my boots and already they were under water. I gave a sick laugh. At least Alberic wouldn't be able to murder us. By the time he returned we will both have drowned. How ironic. This must be what happened to Alberic and his sister all those years ago, only this time there was no "angel" to free us. Which is why it was vital to wake the boy:

'*Nathan!* In the name of God, *wake up!*'

Now the water was up to my thighs. Detritus was beginning to float about – straw mattresses, a couple of wooden crates. Even the rats were scurrying for higher ground. There was no window in the cellar and only the one door at the top of the steps, we were well below the level of the river-bed. At this rate it wouldn't matter if Nathan woke or not for we would both soon drown. I could almost envy him. At least he would know nothing about how he met his end.

The water was coming up to the chair arms now. Pretty soon it would be up to my chest, then my neck. Was this going to be how I ended my days? Drowning alone in this forgotten cellar? I refused to accept it. In my frustration I rattled the chair again.

And then it happened. The first indication was a low rumble like distant thunder followed by an ominous silence. Then a sudden roar and a crashing like the four horses of the Apocalypse stampeding through the wall as a torrent of freezing water burst in knocking me sideways and swamping everything. The torch was immediately extinguished rendering us in complete darkness, water pouring over me. In the next few moments it would be over my head and I would have breathed my last. I took a gulp of air and held it.

But the river wasn't going to let go that easily. The water wasn't rising smoothly like a bath filling up but violently as over the wheel of a millrace. I was being tossed this way and that like a rag doll one moment up high and the next cast down again beneath turbulent rips. Each time I rose I managed to gasp another lungful of air while being tossed around like a piece of flotsam. I managed to take one last gulp before disappearing deep beneath the water and everything went suddenly silent. I don't know how long stayed down there. It seemed like hours. My lungs were bursting, my head throbbing. The need to breathe is an overpowering urge yet I knew I dare not. But then just as I thought I could resist no longer I was suddenly thrust upwards once more. It was as though a giant had scooped me up in his hand and was playing with me. He tossed me this way and that and then in a great billowing swirl of water and air he spat me out. I looked up amazed to see daylight and I found myself being dumped ignominiously on the river bank the force of my eviction smashing the chair to splinters around me. Water roared about me and then subsided leaving me high if not exactly dry. On all fours now, all I could do was breathe and choke and fill my lungs with God's sweet air.

But now where was Nathan? He was less fortunate than I. He too had been flushed from the cell but his chair remained intact and he was now in the middle of the river still strapped in his seat and upside down with his head completely under water. I knew I had to reach him quickly. I managed to free myself of the remainder of my bonds and started across the river to him. But it was flowing too quickly and pushing me back. Several times I lost my footing and was nearly swept away in the torrent. I wanted to hurry but knew I had to tread carefully. It was painfully slow going as each time I thought I had him another swell forced me back again, the river swirling between us. At last I managed to get hold of the chair and turn it right way up lifting the boy's head out of the water though with little hope he was still alive. His skin was cold and wet like a dead fish. No time to cut him free of his bindings. I dragged him still strapped into the chair to the riverbank. I could hear no breath sounds, no sign of life at all. But just as I was about to give up hope he coughed and a great slough of filthy water erupted from his mouth.

'Nathan?'

He opened his eyes. 'Master?'

'Nathan! You idiot! What do you think you're doing frightening me like that? No, don't you dare close your eyes again. Breathe, damn you, breathe!'

Seeing my face glaring down at him he smiled - then puked all over me. I was never so happy in all my life to see vomit. I laughed like an imbecile and hugged him to my breast. He was alive! By God's holy grace we both were.

We both lay exhausted beside the Blackbourn, that once friendly little stream of my childhood that had now turned into a raging deluge. I couldn't remember seeing it so full before. It had completely burst its banks and flooded the fields on either side. But thank God it did for it saved our lives. I looked back and could see that the walls of the cellar had collapsed under its pressure. It was clear now what had happened. The river had quickly filled the space between like a drain and flushed everything – us included – out through the gap. There would be no more cellar beneath Wykes Hall and, God be thanked, no more prisoners either.

The rest of the building fared no better. Two of the walls that had been standing this morning were completely gone. Only a few remnants of this once great house still remained standing. But what was this now floating past? Dear God, some of the bodies that had been stacked in the hall. Someone in Thetford was going to get a nasty surprise in the morning.

By there was no time to think about that. Nathan was recovering, sitting up and looking disconsolately at the cut on his hand.

'It's only a flesh wound,' I told him. 'Don't worry, it will heal.'

I didn't want to tell him the truth, that he had been within moments of being hideously mutilated and possibly having his throat slit open. I wrapped the wound as best I could. It could benefit from Oswald's embroidery skills but would have to wait for now. We had already spent too much time here and with each second the danger increased. We couldn't delay any longer. We had to get to Ixworth Hall as fast as we could.

'Come on,' I said to him. 'Time to go.'

But even as we scrambled across the fields and back up the slope to find the mules I feared we were already too late.

Chapter Twenty-three
A MINOR HICCUP

We set off at a frenetic pace. Poor Erigone didn't know what hit her. But I had other more important matters to worry about. Even so I didn't hold out much hope that we'd get to Ixworth in time to save the day, but we had to try.

Despite the urgency of the situation we still had to proceed with caution so as not to alert Alberic of our presence - surprise was our main, our *only* weapon. The intention was to get to him and overpower him before he had the chance to do anything precipitous. To achieve this we decided to mount an assault on the house in the best traditions of a siege. This would not be easy with just the two of us.

I've never before had cause to describe my family home in any detail, but if you are to understand the scale of out task I must now. Ixworth Hall was built by my grandfather, another Walter, during the peaceful reign of the first Henry, King John's great-grandfather. My father did strengthen its defences during the lawless days of the Anarchy - I believe a moat was added, but later filled in. After that it reverted to what it had originally meant to be and was now: a manor house.

The layout is in the shape of a letter H with the great hall at the centre straddled by a suite of smaller rooms at either end. The west wing is the service area with pantry and buttery and kitchens separate while the east wing is where the private rooms are located. Originally these would have been on one level but my father added a second floor when Joseph's parents came to live with us in the late forties. Eventually when everyone else had died or moved away and my mother was the only one left she turned the upper floor into her private solar. Crucially, there are just two entrances to the building: the main south door to the hall itself and another at the end of the passageway running between the buttery and the pantry.

Nathan and I arrived just as dusk was beginning to descend. We took the precaution of dismounting well away from the house so as not to give our presence away. Nathan was still looking weak but he assured me he was up to the task. I had no choice but to take his word for it. There was no time to summon extra help. Speed was of the essence.

We decided to split up in order to cover both exits at once – a two-pronged attack. Nathan, not knowing the layout of the building, I sent via the most direct entrance into the hall while I took the more complicated route through the servants' quarters. Stealth and silence were to be our watchwords. Our problem was not knowing where in the building Alberic was, and with the light fading fast every shadow was a potential threat. But he had to be making his way to the solar.

Nathan entered the hall first with me a few seconds later. He shook his head to indicate he had seen no-one. No torches burned in the hall but there was just enough daylight filtering in through the shuttered windows. We surprised one of the scullery maids who was just coming in with a large brass bowl. She let out a slight yelp on seeing me, but as soon as she recognized who I was she curtsied. I silently waved her on out of the building. A flicker of light showed beyond the screen at the far end and I signalled to Nathan that we should move towards it. He nodded and together we crept forward. It was then as we approached the screen that we heard the high-pitched scream coming from above our heads.

'The solar!' I gasped to Nathan. 'Quickly!'

Another scream, more sustained this time and higher-pitched. Dear God, what unspeakable crimes was the fiend perpetrating? All thoughts of stealth now flew from my mind as I grabbed a candlestick that was to hand and mounted the stairs three at a time. Yelling 'No!' at the top of my lungs, I burst into the room -

And stopped.

Instead of the bloody carnage I was expecting, the scene before me was one of appalling domesticity. Seated in her usual chair before a blazing fire was my mother looking as though she was at a country fair with Oswald standing at her elbow. Facing her on the opposite side of the hearth sat another woman and between them both stood a short middle-aged man with his back to the fire. All four were silently staring at me with various expressions of incredulity and surprise on their faces. And I suppose I was a sight. Dishevelled, sopping wet, covered in weed from the river and grimacing with candlestick poised above my head, I must have looked like an escapee from an insane asylum – or possibly another Wild Man of Orford. But most bewildering of all to me were the creatures running around the floor at their feet: children – I counted five – had halted their noisy game of chase to gape in amazement at the maniac who had just invaded their world. I instantly recognized them as the family I had stayed with in Melford: Sir Gilbert Kentwell, his wife Lady Agatha and the Kentwell children.

My mother's expression of astonishment turned rapidly to annoyance as she recognised me. 'Walter! What the devil do you mean bursting in like this? Look at the state of you! You're dripping all over the floor.'

'But!' I gasped breathlessly. 'You! He!'

My mother tutted and shook her head. 'What are you blathering about? And where are your manners? You know Sir Gilbert and Lady Agatha. They are here as my guests for the holidays. Lady Agatha,' she said turning to her. 'I can only apologize for my son. This is unusual behaviour even for him.'

'Holidays?' I repeated.

'Yes, holidays,' she tutted tapping the floor with her stick. 'Don't you even know what day it is?'

I shook my head.

'It's Christmas Day.'

'Ho-ho-ho, a very merry Christmas to you, dear Brother Walter,' cooed Lady Agatha putting out her hands to me. 'This is a welcome surprise indeed. We didn't expect to see you again so soon. Are you well?'

I just stared silently at her.

'Well answer Lady Agatha,' said my mother. 'And for heaven's sake put that candlestick down before you hurt somebody with it.'

'Yes, I'm very well thank you Lady Agatha,' I said gingerly lowering the candlestick and taking her hands in mine. Oswald gently relieved me of it and placed it on a trunk.

'Er – thank you Oswald.'

'Been in the wars have you lad?' chuckled Sir Gilbert nodding to my wounded shoulder.

I'd forgotten about that. My robe had slipped exposing my naked shoulder and Oswald's stitching.

'Yes sir – no sir,' I said trying to pull my robe back up. 'But -' I tried again.

'But nothing,' frowned my mother impatiently. 'You're making a complete ass of yourself as usual, showing me up like this.'

By now Nathan had made it up the stairs and barged past me into the room only to slip on my puddles and land flat on his arse. He lay on his back gazing up at my mother.

'And who is this?' she demanded. 'Another drowned rat by the look of him.'

'Nathaniel de Villeneuve, Lady Isabel. Master Walter's assistant.' He tried to rise but slipped back again.

'Well you're better looking than your predecessor, I'll give you that. And you're injured too, I see.' She tutted and shook her head. 'What have you two been up to? You look as though you've been swimming in the river.'

I didn't know what to say. I was speechless.

'Well,' said my mother still addressing Nathan, 'since it doesn't look as though Walter is going to do it, I suppose I'd better make the introductions. This gentleman is Sir Gilbert de Kentwell and this is his wife, Lady Agatha. And these loathsome little tykes,'

248

she said indicating the children, 'are creatures from the forbidden land of Veridan.'

'Not Veridan, aunt Isabel,' corrected the eldest girl rolling her eyes. 'I told you – *Verdinan.*'

'My mistake,' smiled my mother. 'Well?' She cocked an eyebrow at me. 'What do you think of them?'

I looked at the children's faces. I hadn't noticed before but they were all painted with some kind of dye.

'They're green,' I said stupidly.

'I'm glad your eyesight isn't as bad as your hearing. I presume that's the reason you thundered in here like a demented banshee. Did you think it was me screeching?'

'We don't *screech*,' objected the same little girl placing her hands on her hips.

'You do and long may it continue,' my mother said to her. 'Children don't screech nearly enough in my opinion.' She frowned at my gaping mouth. 'Oh dear. Walter is confused about something.'

'I thought …' I began.

'*What* did you think? That I was being murdered by that insipid little monk?'

'Alberic!' I said urgently. 'He's here? You've seen him?'

'Is that his name? Yes, he was here. Not for long, though. He became somewhat confused by the children. I can't imagine why, can you?' she smiled pointedly. 'But it was all right. Between them Sir Gilbert and Oswald managed to subdue him.'

'Fellow was an out and out bully,' frowned Sir Gilbert. 'Coming in here brandishing a knife. I told him: it's not the done thing, not these days. Knives are left outside. We soon had it off the curl. Not a friend of yours, was he Walter?'

'Where is he now?' I said to my mother. 'What have you done with him?'

'Locked him in the piggery,' she replied with satisfaction.

'The *piggery?*' I shot an anxious glance at Oswald.

'Yes master. He is the same boy who tortured the pigs all those years ago. I recognized him instantly.'

'Yes, well Lady Agatha and Sir Gilbert don't want to hear about such unpleasantries,' sniffed my mother.

'*Unpleasantries?*' I gaped. 'Do you know what he's done? Tortured and murdered one man, tried to do the same to Nathan here, half-strangled me then locked us both in a flooded cellar to drown.'

'Oh my gracious!' said Lady Agatha visibly shocked.

'Good Lord!' said her husband.

'That's enough now, Walter,' my mother insisted. 'You're frightening the children. We'll discuss these things later.'

'We'll discuss them *now*.'

She glared at me but I was determined.

'Would you excuse us, Lady Agatha,' she said calmly. 'My son wishes to speak to me alone. It is rather important. Oswald has a treat for the children down in the kitchens. We will meet again at supper.'

Lady Agatha rose gracefully from her seat and together with the other six Kentwells, followed Oswald down to the kitchens.

'Erm, would you like me to leave too, master?' Nathan whispered hopefully.

'No. Stay here. I may need you.'

'How dare you embarrass me in front of my guests like that,' my mother growled at me once the door was closed.

'You knew didn't you? That's why you invited them. To confuse Alberic. That was very irresponsible of you.'

'Fiddle-di-dee. Do you think I'd have had the children here if I'd thought there was the slightest possibility they'd be in danger?'

'Nothing you did would surprise me. Was it your idea to paint them green?'

'That was their own idea. But,' she added with a little chuckle, 'you have to admit it was a stroke of genius. He wasn't expecting that. Completely out-foxed him – as I knew it would.'

'You had no idea how he'd react,' I said angrily. 'He had a knife. He could have done anything with it. It's the most irresponsible thing I've ever heard.'

'He's an old man,' she said tapping her stick irritably. 'Oswald and Gilbert easily overpowered him. And it was just an innocent game to the children. They loved dressing up.'

'As creatures from a fictitious land. Except these weren't fictitious, were they? The green children really existed. You knew that. And one of them had grown up to be a butcher. How long have you known Alberic was the murderer?'

'I didn't for certain. Not till today. I thought it was the niece.'

'Leon? Why?'

'You said it yourself, she attacked you.' She snorted. 'Beaten by a mere slip of a girl. Anybody else and I wouldn't have believed it.'

'I don't fight women,' I said defensively. 'And besides, it wasn't Leon attacked me. That was Alberic too.'

'Oh? Why?'

'Because he thought Ivo had told me where the family were.'

'That was the second time on the road from Bardwell. I meant the first time. At the kiln in Coggeshall. Why did he attack you there? You didn't know anything about the de Calne's then.'

I was dreading this question coming up but there was no avoiding it:

'It's because he was deluded,' I bluffed.

'Deluded in what way?'

'He thought that Leon and I …'

'Hm?'

'Somehow he got the impression that we …'

'Yes?' she smirked.

I looked with embarrassment at Nathan who was watching us with inscrutable eyes.

I pouted. 'Well he was wrong, that's what matters. Leon made that perfectly clear in his hearing – deliberately, so that there was no mistake. She has only ever had feelings for Richard.'

That was why she was so dismissive of me in Abbot Ralph's study, I suddenly realised. She knew Alberic was outside the door listening and knew what he was capable of when jealous. She wanted to leave him in no doubt that there was nothing between us - which of course there wasn't. But it meant she wasn't as contemptuous of me as she made out. She found my attentions "unpleasant" she said. No she didn't. Not really.

My mother shook her head at me. 'For a moment there I thought you were almost human.'

'Never mind all that. How did you know Alberic was the green boy? Everyone else thought he was dead.'

She shrugged. 'It seemed a reasonable deduction. Once I'd realised Sir Richard was Leon's father.'

My jaw hit the floor. 'What? You think Sir Richard and Leon's mother …? That he and she …? That they ...?'

She tutted. 'Such a prude. Yes Walter, I'm suggesting they had *sex* together. In case you hadn't heard that's how children are made. Think about it. Why else would he be so interested in her, training her up, getting her work with Abbot Ralph? Look at you with your mouth open. Such an innocent. I told you what sort her mother was, lifting her skirt for any man around. Leon too, by the sounds of things. Like mother like daughter.'

I was outraged on Leon's behalf at this malign slur on her character. Nor could I believe it of her mother - in this case at any rate. Richard had been adamant when I met him in the warrenry that his father not only approved but encouraged his relationship with Leon. Would he have done that if he was father to both of them? No. There had to be another reason why Sir Richard was so generous to Leon.

'Go and ask the monk,' said my mother. 'You know you want to. I'd go myself if it wasn't for this blessed hip.' She kneaded her thigh. 'Go on, confront him before the sheriff's men get here. You may not get another chance.'

I supposed she was right about that at least. Alberic would soon be taken back to Bury under armed guard where he would remain in the sheriff's custody, be tried and almost certainly hanged without my ever having the chance to see him again.

'All right, I'll go. Nathan, you come too.'

'No,' she said placing a hand on Nathan's arm. 'He can stay here with me. You go alone.'

'Why?' I asked suspiciously.

'He's more likely to open up to you if you're on your own. Don't worry, you'll be quite safe. Oswald's put two of our biggest hay-wards to guard him. Go and quiz him. Use your charm – you're good at that. When you come back, we'll talk again.'

My trouble is I'm too easily persuaded. I didn't hear the nuances in her voice. But I did go down to the piggery to speak to Alberic. And I went alone. Fool that I was.

Chapter Twenty-four
EXPLAINING THE UNEXPLAINABLE

In my time as abbey physician I have confronted many murderers - far too many - but none as cold-hearted as Alberic. Experience tells me that there is usually some emotional trigger for what these people do – anger, fear, jealousy. But with Alberic none of these seemed to be the case. He killed calmly and casually as anyone else would swat a fly with no compassion or sympathy whatsoever. To me this is as baffling as it is exceptional. The only explanation I can come up with was that it was the result of the unique situation he grew up in. Left to his own devices, devoid of a loving family or a Christian upbringing, he had no-one to guide him or show him right from wrong.

But if that was the case then why was his sister not affected the same way? She'd had the same upbringing as Alberic, for longer than him in fact since she was two years his senior. Yet by all accounts she had recovered - sufficiently at any rate to have married and borne a child. Maybe it was her sex that made the difference. Possibly the female is more susceptible to sentiment than the male.

Alberic, by contrast, didn't seem to have advanced at all from that monstrous child that Oswald described torturing pigs with such heartless cruelty. He then went on to do something similar to poor Ivo and would have done the same to Nathan if he hadn't been stopped. And he made no secret of the fact that he would calmly murder Richard de Calne given the chance. I wanted to know what it is that makes one human being regard another as a mere obstacle to be removed as one would kick away a stone from the path. Despite my abhorrence of the man I wanted to try to understand Alberic for I believed that only by doing so would it be possible to recognize another like him and hopefully prevent the same thing happening again. It was for this reason more than any other that I agreed to my mother's request and went down to the outbuildings to speak with him.

The piggery is the only stone-built structure in the barnyard which is presumably why my mother chose it for Alberic's incarceration. Even so it is not the most secure place to hold a man; but then my grandfather never designed Ixworth Hall to be a prison. Being Christmastide, there was just one sow left in one of the pens. Alberic occupied the other squatting on the bare earth floor with his hands and feet secured by rope to a metal ring set in the wall, and he was being guarded by a couple of sturdy-looking farm-hands.

He made no response as I entered but sat placidly watching his gaolers, mute and impassive as a caged animal would watch its keepers. It was evident from the way his guards were lounging around and joking that they didn't think much to their charge. Looking at Alberic it was not difficult to see why. After all, how much of a threat can one aged, crippled monk be? But looks can deceive. I was quite sure that given the least opportunity Alberic would be free of his restraints and away leaving carnage in his wake. Angry, therefore, at their slovenliness and fearful for their safety, I slapped the two young sapheads to attention.

'He can't escape, master,' replied the boldest of them indignantly warding off my blows. 'We have him bound tight.'

'Really? Then show me your knife.'

'My knife, master?'

'Yes, master, your knife, master. Give it to me.'

The man reached inside his smock only to find it wasn't there. He searched frantically and even threw an accusing look at his companion. I then revealed it to him having already removed it myself from his waistband a few moments earlier.

'If I can do it so can he,' I told the man handing him back his knife. 'Now leave us both of you, I want to talk to the prisoner alone. But don't go far. I may need you again.'

The two men slouched out shoving each other and muttering as they went.

I turned to face Alberic. Remembering the scene in the cellar and the even worse one in the priest-house, I gave an involuntary shudder. He was watching me now with a mixture of cold detachment and amusement. I realised now why I'd disliked him so much that first time we met in Coggeshall Abbey. There was nothing behind his eyes. He was a mechanical as Bardwell's water clock. Even so, he wasn't a machine. He was still a human being with a soul. There had to be some way to reach it.

'Are you comfortable?' I asked him as normally as I could. 'Have you everything you need? Food? Water?'

'Everything except my freedom, brother. Can you give me that?'

'You must face the consequences of your actions.'

'Hanging you mean.'

'If that's what the courts decide, then yes.'

He nodded. 'What if I were to tell you I regret my actions? That I've seen the error of my ways and wish to repent?'

I was taken aback. This wasn't what I was expecting at all.

'I'd like nothing more – if that repentance is sincere.'

He then did something quite extraordinary that I certainly wasn't expecting. He began to whimper. He got up onto his knees and held his hands out to me in an attitude of prayer.

'Oh brother, I've been sitting here thinking about all the terrible things I have done. I realise now I've been so eaten up with jealousy and hate that I couldn't see the truth. It was as though the Devil himself was sitting on my shoulder. But you changed me. Yes brother, you did that. Our little chat in the cellar – it was a revelation. I'd never told my story like that before, no-one ever wanted to hear it. It was as though I had lanced a boil – you can understand that being a medical man. The poison that had been festering inside me all these years was being drawn out. I could see that I was wrong. Now I want only forgiveness and the chance to return to the right path. Can you forgive me brother?'

He held out his manacled hands to me, imploringly, pathetically. It was an extraordinary performance. He was very convincing and for a moment I was almost tempted to believe him for I did so want it to be true. His face was contorted with grief. But there were no tears. Emotion, yes, but his eyes were dry, as cold and calculating as a cat's. In the end I just shook my head.

As soon as he saw that the emotion vanished as quickly as it had come.

'No,' he smiled. 'I didn't really think you would. But it was worth a try.' He returned to his place and sat down again looking at me with those cold, inhuman eyes.

I shivered as though the temperature had dropped.

'So,' he sighed, 'you escaped from the cellar. I'm impressed. My sister and I tried for years but we never managed it.'

'You did eventually, by God's grace.'

He snorted. 'God? What's he got to do with it? Oh, I get it now: you've come to save me. Well I'm afraid you're wasting your time, brother. I'm beyond redemption.'

'No-one is beyond God's mercy, brother.'

'I am. God abandoned me years ago.'

His words truly shocked me. Despite his crimes he was still a lay-brother of Holy Mother Church.

'For heaven's sake, man, you spent five decades living with monks. Did they teach you nothing?'

'Deceit, brother, that's what they taught me. How to hide my true self. And that, I think you'll have to agree, I managed rather well. I even had you going there for a moment.' He gave a wry smile. 'I certainly fooled Abbot Ralph as well as the brothers of Rievaulx abbey.'

'Are you quite sure about that?'

'Oh, they tried. They beat me when I rebelled and rewarded me when I complied. I soon learned how to stop the beatings.'

'How?'

He shrugged. 'By becoming whatever they wanted me to be. Gentle, compliant, considerate. All these were useful tools.'

I gasped. 'Is that all they were to you? Tools to be used?'

'They taught me other things too. How to work. Cistercians don't like to get their hands dirty. They'd rather pray and let others do that. So I did the jobs nobody else wanted. If you want anything done, ask Alberic. I was very popular. And I was a pretty child. If any of the brothers wanted … *special* … favours, I gave them too. It was a small price to pay.'

'For what?'

'Trust, brother. Once you have that you have control.'

I'd never heard anything so blatantly cynical.

'Is that how you deceived Abbot Ralph?'

He laughed. 'Oh, Ralph was easy. His headaches – so debilitating. Easily brought on with the aid of a little wormwood as I'm sure you know. Lie down, father abbot. Close the shutters, father abbot. Let me unburden you of your travails, father abbot.'

'And that's how you progressed in life, is it? By manipulating others as though they were pieces on a chess-board. People are not pawns, brother. They are flesh and blood.'

He snorted. 'Oh, I know all about flesh and blood.'

That was certainly true. I now tackled the subject that pained me more than any other:

'Tell me about Ivo.'

'The curate?' He sighed, bored. 'I thought he had some information I wanted. That was all.'

'Which was?'

'What I always wanted. To know the whereabouts of Richard de Calne.'

'And when you realised he didn't have that information why did you then not release him? Why murder him in that grotesque manner?'

He shrugged nonchalantly. 'He'd seen my face. He could identify me. It was just a matter of wiping the platter clean.'

I felt a rage rising in me that was difficult to suppress. To dismiss a human life so casually was beyond comprehension to me. Tears of anger welled in my eyes. It was all I could do not to stride across the barrier and strike him down like the dog he was. Maybe that's what he wanted. To provoke me. He was still playing games. In the end all I could say was:

'I pity you.'

'He doesn't need your pity, brother.'

I turned to see who had spoken. Leon. Of course. That was why my mother wanted me to to come down to the piggery alone. She knew Leon would be here. Seeing her now made my heart leap again in spite of myself. After the chilling void of

Alberic it was good feel the warmth and softness of her presence.

'Then what does he need?' I asked her. 'What do you do with someone born so morally deformed except put them down?'

'Alberic wasn't born. He was made.'

'By Sir Richard de Calne?' I shook my head. 'I don't accept that. Your mother wasn't like that. But even if it were true it doesn't alter the fact that it was he who committed those dreadful crimes. Crimes for which the law demands payment.'

'He's not responsible for his actions,' she insisted.

'Then who is? Explain what it is I'm missing, because as Christ is my witness from where I stand it is all too clear.'

Alberic was watching this exchange with an amused expression on his face.

'Not here,' said Leon, and she stepped outside. I followed her out ordering the two estate workers back inside as I went.

By now the storm that had caused so much damage earlier had moved away leaving a clear, crisp night in its wake. In Leon's presence I was still captivated. Maybe she understood that too. She kept her face turned away from me gazing instead out across the wet meadows glistening under the stars. But my feelings for her were the least of what was on my mind. Was I now finally to hear the explanation for all that had gone on?

She flicked her eyes briefly at me then away again: 'You never knew Sir Richard but I think you admire his reputation. You believe him to have been a man of learning, of limitless capacities. Am I right?'

'I had thought that, yes. But I'm beginning to have my doubts.'

'Do not doubt it. He was all of those things. But more than that, he was also something of a missionary.'

'That's an odd word to use.'

'But an accurate one. You have to understand, Sir Richard saw the world differently from the rest of us. He understood so much more. He could see so much further with far clearer eyes.'

Philosophers through the ages had thought the same, I felt like saying, and very few if any had been proved right. But I wanted to hear her out. She was one of the last connections with the man who seemed to be at the root of all this. I held my tongue and let her tell it in her own time.

'Sir Richard bewailed the condition of the world. He thought humanity had corrupted it and been corrupted by it. He believed it was possible to recover that time of lost innocence, to get back to the original Garden of Eden. He even thought there might be a natural language.' She laughed. 'He thought it might be Hebrew. That was why no-one was aloud to speak to the children. To see what language would develop naturally. Except they had no language, unless you call their wordless grunts a language. Oh, they had words for things like "cold" and "hungry", but little else. There was no natural language.'

'And this he was to achieve by locking children in a cellar?' I said incredulously. 'Deprived of family, friends, any form of human contact. This is your own mother and uncle we are talking about.

Your own flesh and blood. How can you defend that?'

'He did it in order to preserve their natural purity,' she insisted.

'Really? And what was he going to do with this new found purity?'

'Study it. Learn from it. Teach it to others.'

'What about their mother? Presumably they had one. Did she have no say in this? In fact, who was their mother?'

Leon shrugged. 'Some vagrant woman. Very likely a prostitute. In any case someone with no right to be having children. What does it matter? If Sir Richard hadn't taken them away from her they would in all likelihood have died anyway. What he did was to give them a gift, perhaps the greatest gift of all: the opportunity to live and not just any life but the perfect lives God had intended for all mankind. And just think if he had succeeded. A world of perfect human beings, free of wars, free of disease.'

'But he failed. Instead of two perfect children he created two monsters. But having realised that, instead of freeing them he continued to keep them incarcerated. Why?'

She lowered her eyes. 'What else could he do? That cellar was the only world they knew. They would never have survived on their own outside it. It would have been a greater cruelty to let them go.'

'But then fate intervened. There was a storm and the children escaped.'

'Yes,' she darted a look at me. 'And look what happened to them. It proved Sir Richard had been right.'

My God, how completely he had her in his thrall.

'What did happen to them? After they were re-captured I mean.'

She looked away. 'Alberic was the problem. He couldn't adapt. Sir Richard sent him away to the brothers of Rievaulx and told the world he had died. It was the best thing for him. He lived well there. They gave him the security and discipline he needed.'

'That's not quite the way Alberic tells the story.'

'Of course it isn't. He blames Sir Richard for everything.'

'Do you blame him? What about your mother? She married didn't she? How?'

She frowned. 'What do you mean, "how"?'

'I mean how did she meet your father? I don't imagine it was at the village stomp.'

She looked away. 'It was arranged.'

'By Sir Richard?'

'Yes.'

'To an older man?'

She lowered her eyes. 'Yes.'

'And doubtless with a little money just to help lubricate matters.'

She shot me an indignant stare. 'I know what you are suggesting. But Sir Richard wasn't like that. Quite the contrary. Don't you see? He was trying to make amends. That's why when my father died he brought my mother and me back to Wykes. He adopted me, trained me. I owe him everything.'

'For which you are naturally grateful,' I nodded. 'And now you are to marry his son – who incidentally doesn't quite share your admiration for his father.'

'He doesn't understand Sir Richard as I do.'

'His own father?' I shook my head. 'Maybe he understood him better than you think. Where did you get all this from in any case? Sir Richard, I suppose?'

'Mostly. Some came from my mother before she died. The rest Alberic and I managed to piece together between us.'

'So I was right. It was Alberic coming to Coggeshall that was the catalyst for all this.'

'That was the purest chance. Neither of us knew of the other's existence. I knew I had an uncle but like everybody else I thought he had died as a child. It was a shock for both of us when we discovered we were related.'

'And that was when he decided to take his revenge,' I nodded. 'Tell me, how soon did you realise?'

She frowned. 'Realise what?'

'How soon did you discover that Alberic was becoming attached to you?'

'I don't know what you mean.'

'Oh, I think you do. Alberic wanted you for himself. I'm guessing he made a pass at you. Naturally you rejected his advances – he was your uncle. At that stage any normal man would have backed off. But Alberic wasn't normal. He couldn't tolerate rejection - or competition, even from a silly besotted monk. I was easily dealt with. But Richard was different. He was a threat, a very real threat. And given who he is, this marriage is the final insult for Alberic. The son of the man he loathed about to marry his niece. He couldn't tolerate that. He was determined to prevent it any way he could, even as far as murder. You knew that. But you couldn't bring yourself to stop him yourself which is why you went to Abbot Samson.'

Tears were flowing down her cheeks. 'I couldn't. You don't understand. It's not his fault. He shouldn't be punished.'

'No you're right, it isn't his fault. It's yours. The attack on me. Ivo's torture. His hideous death. You could have prevented it all if only you had spoken out.'

'She's right, you know. You may as well hang a dog for biting you when you kick it.'

I turned round to see my mother standing behind me.

'Alberic is not an animal, mother. He's a human being with free will who has committed the most heinous of crimes. His victims deserve justice.'

'Leon doesn't want it.'

'Of course she doesn't. He's her uncle.'

'And neither do others.'

'Ah,' I nodded. 'That's the real reason you're so concerned. I thought you were taking more than your usual detached interest. This is to do with your little conspiracy against the king, isn't it? I should have realised as soon as Samson sent me to you. It was too much of a coincidence. And who's that I see lurking in the shadows behind you? Nathan? I thought Oswald seemed to know you. What is he, mother, one of your spies? Well, go on. I've heard everything else, I may as well hear the rest. What's your part in all this?'

Nathan looked at my mother who nodded.

'I told you about Oxford, didn't I master?'

I had to think for a moment. Oxford. 'The murder of a local woman. Yes, I remember.'

'What I didn't tell you was that those two students who were hanged were friends of mine.'

'And you blame King John for that?'

'I blame him for not preventing it. Those students were entirely innocent. The law should have protected them – or at least brought to justice those who broke it. But King John respects no laws other than his own. He thinks he is above the law.'

'He *is* above the law. He's the king.'

'Then he shouldn't be. The king should should be subject to the same law as everyone else.'

I nodded. 'Well congratulations, Nathan. You have just committed high treason. You could hang for that.'

My mother rounded angrily on me: 'You and your moral outrage. I sometimes wonder whose child you are for by Christ you surely aren't mine. You think you are so superior. Well let me tell you, you are not. It's people like me and Abbot Ralph and this young man, we are the true guardians of England's freedoms, not Richard de Calne, not King John - and certainly not you. There is a cancer growing in the body politic of England that needs to be cut out before it can infect the whole.'

'And you're just the woman to do it. That was really why you sent me to abbot Ralph, wasn't it? Rather than talk to anyone else. You wanted to keep it in the family – the cosy little family of conspirators. And it was why Ralph was so keen to play down the existence of the green children. Shroud it in mystery. Puff it away with the breeze. Why? Why was it so dangerous?'

And then I had it:

'The year the children were found. It was the same year that Prince Eustace was poisoned.' I looked at her. 'The document. The one I found at Bardwell. Where is it?'

'Somewhere safe.'

'Destroyed more like.'

Her lip curled. 'Why would I do that? It proves John to be the illegitimate upstart we always knew him to be.'

'But it does more than that. It shows how you blackmailed Sir Richard into poisoning Eustace in return for being allowed to continue with his vile experiments. That document was his surety that you and your fellow conspirators would keep your word and leave him free to carry on tormenting those children. Mother, how could you?'

She set her jaw defiantly. 'How? Easily. Because the alternative was years more of civil war. Oh, it's easy for you, you weren't around, you don't know what it was like. Nineteen years we endured. Nineteen years without peace, without law; gangs of armed men roaming the country murdering at will, burning crops, raping, plundering. By with one stroke of the pen all that was ended.'

'In return for the suffering of two innocent children.'

'Did they suffer? I mean *really*? They knew nothing else. That cellar was their world. They had food, they had security. Children die daily on the streets of every town in England for lack of either. If it hadn't been for that storm -'

'If it hadn't been for the storm they would have died in that cellar.'

'But they didn't die. The girl married and had a child – Leon.'

'And the boy became Alberic.'

She pursed her lips. 'Mistakes happen. I'll not be blamed. There was no alternative. It was for the greater good. I won't have it otherwise.'

'Easy platitudes when you're not the one suffering. And now you want to do it all again. Tear down the old order and replace it with – what? A new government? A new king?'

'Any is better than this one,' said Nathan.

'And what if someone else doesn't like your choice of king? Will you agree to his being murdered too? That sounds a lot like anarchy to me. I see now why Samson summoned me. A dying man's contrition. He wanted to expose you all and he thought I might be the one to do it. Well don't worry, I won't. Your secret's safe. I don't give two pins for your petty conspiracies. For me it is much simpler: a man has broken the law, committed a dreadful murder and must be punished for it.'

'And he will be,' said my mother.

'How?'

'Abbot Ralph is sending him away.'

'Back to Yorkshire?' I scoffed.

'No,' she said smugly. 'Scotland as a matter of fact. To the isle of Kintyre.'

'Why? What's there?'

'Not much. A few crofters, some sheep. And an abbey recently founded by some monks from Ireland. They're a pretty fierce bunch those Irish monks. They won't put up with any nonsense from Alberic.'

'But out of reach of English justice so that your little conspiracy remains hidden,' I nodded. 'What if he escapes again? What's to stop him carrying on where he left off?'

'As soon as he crossed the border he'd be arrested. But I doubt he'll make it that far. Kintyre is virtually an island, isolated. We're not fools you know. There's just the one land exit and that's controlled by the monks. No, I think you'll find that once he's lodged on his Scottish islet we'll have heard the last of the green children.'

'That's what you thought last time.'

We were interrupted by a noise outside.

'What was that?'

She cocked an ear. 'I heard nothing.'

'Ssh! Listen.'

Somewhere an owl hooted. But then there was another bump followed by a muffled cry.

'Alberic!' I said, and before I could think again I was running.

Chapter Twenty-five
TRUTH FINALLY OUT

The scene in the piggery was one of mayhem. The sow had escaped from her pen and was blocking the door with her bulk, it took a lot of shoving and coaxing to move her. When we finally managed to get inside we saw that Alberic was gone, naturally, the spot where he'd been sitting empty and the rope that had tethered him to the wall cut. Outside came the sound of hooves on the cobbles - Alberic making good his escape no doubt. But for the moment I had other priorities.

Both the men I had sent to guard him were down, the one nearest me staring wide-eyed and motionless and reminding me again of the expression on Ivo's face when I found him. I went quickly to him first but apart from looking bewildered he seemed all right. Nothing appeared to be physically wrong with him. I left him for Nathan to attend to. The other man I was less confident about. He was the one I had chided earlier about losing his knife and sure enough it was missing from his sheath again. He was kneeling on the ground with one hand gripping his throat, his face a deathly white staring wide-eyed up at me. Dear God, I prayed, not again.

'I warned you!' I said dropping to one knee. 'Didn't I warn you? But no, you wouldn't listen. Bring light someone!' I barked. 'Quickly!'

Leon grabbed a torch and held it closer.

'I'm a doctor,' I told him gently. 'Let me see.'

Reluctantly – very reluctantly - he let me ease his trembling hand away from his neck. I could see now his linen neckerchief had been sliced lengthways and blood was soaking the rag either side. With nervous fingers I carefully untied it. Underneath, instead of the blood and sinew I expected to find, there was a second kerchief thicker than the first and made of leather. The blade had gone through this one too. Removing it I found a very neat, very thin red line across the man's windpipe that was oozing a trickle of blood. But he was lucky. The blade had only penetrated the surface of the skin. A fraction deeper and I would be examining a corpse. I put the kerchief back in position and his hand over it.

The man's terrified eyes stared back at me and he swallowed hard. 'Has it … ?' he gasped. 'Am I …?'

'If it had, and you were, we wouldn't be having this conversation,' I told him, at which point he nodded then fainted clean away.

My mother hobbled in on her stick: 'He's taken my best hunter.'

'Which way?'

'North.'

'Back to Bardwell.'

Leon gasped and covered her mouth with her hand.

'What?' I said to her.

Her eyes widened. 'I didn't mean to tell him. I thought he was secure.'

I frowned. 'What? What did you tell him?'

'The priest-house. It's where Richard and his mother have been living.'

Of course they had. How stupid of me. One of the other outbuildings behind the priest-house. Where else would they have gone? Bardwell was their home. All their possessions were there including all Sir Richard's documents. They wouldn't have abandoned them. The de Calnes hadn't gone away as Ivo suggested. They hadn't gone anywhere. They'd been here all along. Ivo knew it but he never betrayed them even while he was being tortured. My eyes filled with tears. The boy was a bloody hero.

The trouble now was that Alberic knew it, too.

Leon was imploring me. 'Brother, you've got to stop him. If he finds Richard he'll kill him.'

'Take another hunter,' said my mother. 'I'll get Oswald to saddle it.' She started to hobble out.

'No, there's no time.' I turned to Leon. 'Can you run?'

She nodded.

'Then run. Run as you have never run before. Run as though your own life depends on it, for by Christ's wounds, others' certainly do.'

I was getting too old for this. It's only two miles to Bardwell but it felt like a hundred. In daylight the road was as familiar to me as my own face but in darkness it might as well have been a foreign country. I stumbled through puddles I didn't see and leapt over others that looked like bottomless pits. Nathan had joined us but being only half my age he easily outpaced me. I might have thought I could beat a woman but Leon was way ahead of me too keeping pace with Nathan. Somehow I just about managed to keep up. In a few minutes that seemed like hours we were there. I cannot tell you how relieved I was to see that priest-house looming up on the bank beside the road.

There was no need for stealth this time. Alberic would know we were coming. And no plan of action either – there was no time to formulate one or even to catch our breath. Vital seconds might mean the difference between life and death. We would simply have to rush in and hope that between the three of us we would be able to overwhelm him.

We found my mother's hunter by the roadside untethered and bareback, still snorting from his gallop which meant Alberic couldn't be that far ahead of us. Where were they - the outhouse or in the house? I flicker of light behind the house shutter answered that.

'He's inside.' I had to think quickly now. 'Leon, you stay here -'

But she shook her head violently. 'No. I'm coming with you.'

There was no time to argue. I could see the look of determination on her face.

'All right. But make yourself known to him. He won't harm you if he knows who you are. Distract him any way you can.'

I then ripped the hood off my robe, wrapped it round my forearm and made Nathan do the same with his.

'He has a knife. This will protect us,' I said more in hope than confidence.

Finally we armed ourselves with lengths of timber fencing. It was the best we could do. The three of us then ran up the slope, me to the front door, Leon to the back and Nathan at the window. On my signal we burst as one into the house whooping and making as much noise as we could.

It's at moments like this that time seems to slow down and almost stop as the mind races to absorb as much as it can as quickly as possible. The first thing I noticed was Lady Margaret seated at the table, her eyes wide like saucers. Standing beside her was Richard. As I entered he turned to face me. God be thanked, they were both alive. But where was Alberic? I stared questioningly at Richard who simply stared back at me. Then he pointed hesitantly at the corner of the room. I looked. There, cowering on the floor, was Alberic. He was whimpering like a baby, his hands held up in front of him. I almost choked with relief at seeing him. But before I could think what to do Leon rushed over to him. She went down on one knee, took the knife he was grasping and threw it away from her.

'Uncle,' she said softly. 'It's me, Leonie.'

'Leonie?' he said as though seeing her for the first time. 'Is it really you?'

I was completely baffled quite unable to work out what had happened. I was just so thankful that no-one had been injured. It was a miracle.

It was then that another figure entered into the room and strode purposefully across the floor. I thought at first it the soldier I'd seen at the warrenry but with a jolt I recognized Alan. I caught a glimpse of the thing in his hand and in an instant I knew what he was about to do but I wasn't quick enough to prevent it. In my defence I doubt even an army could have prevented Alan doing what he did next.

'This for Ivo!' he yelled.

He raised his arm high above his head and brought the hatchet down with such force that Alberic didn't have time to cry out as his severed hand flew up past my head spattering my face with blood as it went.

Chapter Twenty-six
TWO FUNERALS AND A WEDDING

Out of the chaos from which God configured the Universe, I wonder if he ever took time, when the job was done, to sit and ponder his work awhile; and if he did, were there any surprises? God being God the answer is, of course, no, there were no surprises. He knew all before, during and after it happened. For me, however, in the aftermath of what had taken place within the shadow of Peter and Paul's church at Bardwell there were surprises aplenty. But before I could gawp at any of them there were one or two essentials to deal with.

The first thing I had to do was scotch the flow of blood from Alberic's wrist. I confess I was inclined to do nothing and let him bleed out as nature intended and justice demanded, but my training and my Hippocratic oath prevented me. Not that there was very much blood; there never is with traumatic amputations. The mangle of severed veins and arteries tend to seal themselves and Nathan's knife did the rest. He heated the blade in the fire and used it to sear the stump - to satisfying screams from Alberic. I then daubed it with pitch which added further to his agony, and covered the whole with bandaging. It is a procedure which I would normally perform with the greatest reluctance, but not on this occasion I'm ashamed to say. One thing for certain was that it would put an end to his murderous career once and for all. He'd be hard pushed to wipe his own arse after this never mind slit another throat.

My next concern was for Alan. Having purged his anger for his friend he sat in the corner looking utterly drained with tears flowing down his cheeks. No-one was going to blame him for what he'd done and certainly not me. His quick action doubtless saved several lives and prevented further injury. At least, that was verdict we all gave to Sheriff Peter later when asked. I poured him the last of Ivo's "mule" and put the cup into his trembling hand.

'What's that you're holding?' I asked him.

He opened his other hand to show me. It was his priest's collar, the symbol of his office that Pope Innocent had decreed all ordained clergy should wear. Alan had ripped it from his neck.

'There is no God, brother,' he said.

I didn't upbraid him for his blasphemy. Poor man. He was utterly broken. I could see it would take a while for him to recover from the shock of losing his friend under such appalling circumstances, but I was sure he would change his mind in the fullness of time and come to see that even though we don't always understand why, there is a purpose to everything. His reaction was understandable. As I say, with God there are no surprises.

In truth we were all emotionally as well as physically drained, me as much as anyone else, and I sat down on a bench to try to work out what exactly had taken place. Nathan, Leon and I had all entered the house more or less simultaneously hoping to create enough confusion to disrupt whatever was going on inside. I had anticipated a scene similar to the one I saw the last time I was here – blood and gore everywhere. But to my astonishment instead of Alberic leaning over Richard's murdered body it was Richard bearing down on a cowering Alberic. A complete reversal of what I expected. How had that happened?

'He saw Richard.'

I looked up to see Lady Margaret hovering by me.

'You were wondering how the tables could have been turned so thoroughly. I can see it in your face. I've been doing the same thing. I think I know the answer.'

'Then tell me my lady, for I am baffled.'

'He saw Richard,' she repeated.

I shook my head. 'Explain.'

She sat down next to me. 'We were at supper when he burst in. I knew instantly who he was. It's been decades since I last saw him but there was no mistake. We'd been expecting him for some time but still it was a shock when he appeared. I thought he was going to murder us all and for a moment I was almost relieved. At least the nightmare of not knowing would be over at last. But then he saw Richard and everything changed.'

'Changed? How?'

'You have to understand, my husband - Richard's father - was a very strong personality. Richard is exactly like him - not in the brilliance of his mind I don't mean, but in his looks. It is, after all, through their sons that fathers live on, is it not? Every mother likes to think so. But in Richard's case it's particularly true. It must have seemed to Alberic as though my husband had come back to life.'

I frowned trying to understand. 'You're saying Alberic mistook Richard for his father?'

'Not literally of course, but the resemblance was disturbing enough for him. I can only assume that in his mind he must have been suddenly thrust back in that cellar again of half a century ago. The effect was extraordinary. He crumpled before our eyes. He fell to his knees cowering away from Richard and crawled into that corner where you found him whimpering like a beaten dog. He was quite helpless. And to think this was the man we had been hiding from for so long. All the time Richard had it in his power to humble him.'

Her words reminded me of Joseph's description of the Golem seeing its own reflection in the pool and dying – except it wasn't Alberic's reflection this time but Sir Richard's echoed in his son's face. The irony was not lost on me. I was supposed to save Richard from Alberic, but instead Richard had unwittingly saved not only his own skin but his mother's, too.

'You have only yourself to blame for those years of living in fear, my lady. You and your son.'

'And I dare say you think it just desserts that we should have done so,' she nodded. 'You're quite right of course. I don't try to excuse myself. I imagine you must despise us all. But my husband wasn't a bad man despite what you must think. He only ever wanted to improve the lot of his fellow men. That was the purpose of everything he did.'

'Experiments with bricks and clocks is one thing, my lady. But what he did to those children was unconscionable. And by your acquiescence you are as responsible as he was. You must have known what was going on under your own roof.'

'Yes, you're right, I did and I am as much to blame as he was. No doubt you think me a weak and foolish woman. Maybe I am. But you never knew my husband. He thought his genius was God-given and he had a duty to use it. To him knowledge was everything, more important than wealth or status, even life itself.'

I had to grant her that. They had nothing left. Their home gone, their possessions burned. All of it sacrificed on the altar of hubris.

'Some might say it was indeed just desserts, my lady.'

She sighed. 'Richard had many admirers all around the world. One of them, the King of Sicily, sent him a gift of two African apes, a mother and her baby. These apes lived with us in the house for a while as part of the family. They accepted Richard as one of them. Indeed, Richard thought they might be a type of lost human. He even tried to teach them to speak.'

'My lady, I fail to see -'

She put up her hand to crave patience. 'It never got that far. There was an accident. Somehow the dogs got in and attacked the mother - a moment's oversight by one of the keepers. We were alerted by the screams of the baby. It was frantic. It kept running up to Richard pulling on his arm, imploring him to intervene as the dogs tore its mother to pieces. He could have saved her but he didn't. He thought it would be wrong to do so. His reasoning was that if this happened in the wild he wouldn't be there to save the mother and so he allowed the dogs to kill her. It was heartbreaking but he thought it was nature's way. He thought it wrong to interfere.'

I wondered again if Sir Richard would have let the children drown in the flooded cellar if the angels hadn't freed them – as "nature's way".

'What happened to the baby?'

'It stopped eating. Eventually it stopped drinking. It just lay in its cot and pined away.'

'That's the most horrible story I've ever heard.'

'I tell it to you to illustrate my point. Richard was an observer of life in all its aspects, good and bad.'

'And later he went on to do something similar with those children. But Alberic and his sister were human children not apes, Lady Margaret. Did you never question what he was doing? Challenge him?'

'Of course I did. But Richard was a very persuasive man. For every argument of mine he had a counter argument. He wore me down just as he wore everyone down. In the end I simply gave in.'

'And you paid the price for your compliance.'

'It was a heavy price to pay. Our home destroyed, our fortune gone, living in fear and hiding.'

'But you kept your lives while others did not, so you'll forgive me if I don't entirely sympathize.'

283

'I don't expect you to. Fortunately for us Alan and Ivo were less judgemental. In fact they were our salvation. They took us in when we had nowhere else to go. That was one of the two good things to come out of all this.'

'And the other?'

'Leon and Richard.' She nodded to where they were sitting. 'Look at them. They are complete innocents in all this. They should not have to pay for our mistakes. So I am asking you to allow them their chance of happiness. Not for my sake, but for theirs. And so that Ivo's death should not have been entirely in vain.'

So that was the real purpose of our little chat. Not to keep me informed but to plead the case for her son and Leon to be allowed to marry without having to go through the trauma of a trial and in the process everything coming out. And in all conscience I couldn't disagree. Leon and Richard were indeed innocent despite what I said to Leon. It was obvious to anyone that they were devoted to each other. And in all probability Ivo would have wanted it too.

As it happened Lady Margaret needn't have worried. I had no intention of telling Sheriff Peter any more than I had to. The last thing I wanted was my mother's and Abbot Ralph's nefarious activities dragged into the open. The sheriff already had a low enough opinion of me as it was, there was no point making things worse by introducing guilt by association. I therefore gave him the baldest facts that I could relating to Ivo's murder and let him decide what to do with them. The strict legal position was in any case somewhat blurred by the fact that Alberic was a lay brother and therefore technically still a member of the clergy. He thus came under the jurisdiction of the church which in Bury meant the abbot. But Samson was dying and there was no-one qualified to take his place.

But as often happens in such circumstances fate took a hand and we were overtaken by events elsewhere. Unbeknown to any of us, a few months earlier a plot had been unearthed to murder the king. There had been such plots before. What made this one particularly serious, though, was that it involved senior members of the baronage. Two of the leading conspirators, Robert Fitz Walter of Essex and Eustace de Vesci of Northumberland, fled the country and joined the king's enemies in France. There followed a round of executions and confiscations across both counties which would take years to recover.

Sheriff Peter didn't want anything like that happening in Suffolk. He therefore made a political calculation and decided the benefits of exposing my mother's and Abbot Ralph's minor schemings not worth the cost.

'After all,' he asked me contemptuously, 'just how threatening can an ageing widow and a cleric be to a king of England?'

He'd clearly never heard of Eleanor of Aquitaine or Thomas Becket.

'But rest assured,' he said waggling an expensively-gloved finger in my face. 'From now on I shall be watching your family very closely. Very closely indeed.'

Ivo's body was, despite the proscriptions of the interdict, buried in Bardwell churchyard by a tearful Alan who I am relieved to say had recovered his faith sufficiently to send his friend's soul ringing into heaven as I was sure it would. Alberic was allowed to disappear into his isthmus off the west coast of Scotland closely monitored by those dour Irish monks. Some might say hanging was more merciful. The matter of the green children, along with the Eustace document and all that that entailed, was quietly forgotten.

And there we have it. All that is left is to mention the wedding. This was a painful undertaking for me personally. I know, I know, it's entirely inappropriate for a monk to have such feelings and you are quite right to rebuke me for them. But one cannot help one's feelings. At least marriage would lessen the temptation for wilder thoughts (one hopes). Besides, there never was any chance of reciprocation, I was fooling myself if I ever thought there was. You only had to look at Leon and Richard together to see they were very much in love. Alan solemnized their alliance in the porch of Bardwell Church immediately after Ivo's funeral – again, strictly against the letter of the interdict. It seemed he wasn't such a stickler for rules after all.

All very neat – except for one thing: it turned out that Leon's grandmother was not the anonymous vagrant everyone had supposed her to be and certainly not a prostitute. She was in fact one of Sir Richard's own estate workers. He made the admission himself in the notebook that Nathan found in the Bardwell outhouse leaving open only the question of who Leon's real father was. The part of the notebook that might have given the answer was unfortunately lost, so we shall never know.

As I left the happy couple in the churchyard there was a familiar face sheltering from the rain beneath the lychgate. It was Jocelin.

'It's f-father Abbot, Walter. I'm afraid he's d-dead.'

'What again?'

'N-no. For real this time.'

Thus Samson's was the second funeral during that first week of January 1212. He didn't quite make it to the full thirty years after all, falling short by just fifty-three days. The funeral was a brief if solemn affair. Jocelin grizzled the whole way through, of course. We held a requiem mass at the high altar of the abbey church after which the body was carried solemnly down into the crypt where it would wait for another two years until the interdict was lifted and it could be buried in the floor of the chapterhouse. Nathan and I both declined to join the funeral procession into the crypt. Under the circumstances I think you can appreciate why.

Some days later Prior Herbert collared me. He was looking pleased with himself having finally achieved his goal of being officially in charge of the abbey – at least until the next abbot could be elected, and he was determined to make his mark early:

'What's this I've been hearing about a murder at Bardwell church?'

That's Prior Herbert for you. Ever with his finger on the pulse.

'That's all over, brother prior. Nothing for you to worry about. The sheriff has it in hand. He apprehended the culprit and is dealing with it.'

'So long as the abbey is not involved. We can't afford any scandals at this stage. I also hear you've dismissed that boy as your assistant.' He tutted and shook his head. 'That's the third this year. Just can't seem to keep them, can you?'

'It was a mutual decision, brother prior. He wasn't really suitable.'

'On the contrary, I'd have thought he was ideal. Good qualifications and excellent family connections. Too clever for you, was he?' he smirked. 'Well don't expect a replacement soon. Now that I have the abbot's work to do as well as my own I will be far too busy to spend much time on peripherals.'

Peripherals. I must remember that next time he has a whitlow that needs lancing. In actual fact Nathan had gone off to Toledo in Spain to study the works of Aristotle – in Arabic - which have subsequently been condemned as heretical by the Bishop of Paris. I fancy he took up the offer out of spite. I wonder if clock mechanics were among the interests of the great philosopher? No doubt we will be hearing more of him - if he doesn't get himself hanged first.

I began this chapter with Samson's death and that's where I must end it. There is now a great hole at the heart of our community and the grubbers are already hard at work trying to fill it. We are adrift in uncharted waters. Without Samson's stewardship we are in for a turbulent time.

So what epitaph can I give him? None fitting I don't suppose. Others will find finer words than any I can come up with. He wasn't perfect – only God is that. He made mistakes and got some things disastrously wrong. But taken in the round he left the world a better place than when he found it. Maybe that is enough.

HISTORICAL NOTE

The story of the green children of Woolpit has been retold many times since Ralph of Coggeshall first penned it. Fortunately he gave us only the barest bones of the tale so we can clothe them any way we choose.

There have been many explanations of who the children were. They were children of a lost tribe; they were changelings; they were spirits from the underworld; they were beings from another planet. In a credulous age such occurrences were frequent and readily accepted. Of course that couldn't happen in our own more enlightened times. But when long-dead pop stars are regularly seen on supermarket checkouts, spacemen abduct human guinea-pigs to their laboratories in the sky, and extinct sea-monsters surface in Scottish lakes, maybe we're not as sophisticated as we like to think.

THE COLOUR GREEN

It's curious how often the colour green turns up in mystical tales. There is the Green Man of pagan mythology. Sir Gawain and the Green Knight. In folklore fairies are often coloured green as are hobgoblins and leprechauns. In our own time we have Little Green Men from Outerspace. Green seems to be the preferred colour of anything unusual or mysterious.

ATHEISM IN THE 13th CENTURY

It is often assumed that in an age of ignorance about the natural world everyone must have been a devout religious believer. This was not universally true. A contemporary of Walter's, the emperor Frederick II (1197-1250), was a notorious religious sceptic who shocked everyone with his blasphemies and mockery. He was excommunicated several times and is reputed to have said that the "the world had been deceived by three men, Jesus, Moses and Mohammed". Lady Isabel was not alone in her scepticism.

SIR RICHARD DE CALNE

Not much is known about the man to whom the green children were supposedly taken when they were first discovered. He was the lord of Wykes, or possibly Wyken, one of three manors of Bardwell, a village seven and a half miles north of Woolpit. Why the children were taken there is obscure; Bury is just as close and the abbot there was overlord of both Woolpit and Bardwell. The explanation given in the novel, while hopefully plausible, is entirely fanciful. But if Sir Richard really had incarcerated two feral children in order to study them he wouldn't have been the first or the last. An Egyptian pharaoh, a German emperor, a Scottish king and a Mogul khan all tried the same thing – with equal lack of success.

RALPH OF COGGESHALL

Ralph of Coggeshall was a monk of the Cistercian (white monks) order of Benedictines and one of Medieval England's greatest chroniclers. He was born in Cambridgeshire some time around the year 1160. He was present at the fall of Jerusalem to Saladin's forces in 1187 when he received a head wound from which he was to suffer for the rest of his life. He was elected Coggeshall Abbey's sixth abbot in 1207 but retired due to ill-health in 1218 dying some time after 1227. He oversaw the development of a thriving brick-making industry in Coggeshall, the first since Roman times.

Ralph wrote about the green children of Woolpit in his *Chronicon Anglicanum* having got the story, he claimed, directly from the mouth of Richard de Calne himself. It was Ralph who first suggested that the children were tinged green though not with any great conviction. He was a courageous man and not afraid to express his opinions on political matters. He admired King Henry II and Richard the Lionheart but reviled John whom he thought a cruel and incompetent king and who he was convinced had murdered Prince Arthur, John's nephew and co-contender for the English throne.

COUNT EUSTACE DE BOULOGNE

Prince Eustace was King Stephen's only son and heir. Had he lived he might well have become England's next king after the death of his father in 1154. He certainly tried, rallying an army in the eastern counties and devastating the countryside. Unfortunately he died, reputedly from food poisoning while staying at Bury abbey, a few months before his father thus clearing the way for his cousin, Henry fitz Empress, to succeed as King Henry II.

As usual the characters in this novel are a mixture of the real and the invented. Brothers Walter and Jocelin were real people, as were Abbots Samson and Ralph, Prior Herbert, Sheriff Peter de Mealton, Sir Richard de Calne. Everyone else is fictional.

SWW October 2015

UNHOLY INNOCENCE

May 1199. Richard the Lionheart is dead and his brother John has just been crowned King of England.

John travels to St Edmund's abbey in Suffolk to give thanks for his accession. His visit coincides with the murder of a twelve-year-old boy whose mutilated body bears the marks of ritual sacrifice and martyrdom. This isn't the first time such a thing has happened. Eighteen years earlier another child was murdered in the town in similar circumstances.

Abbot Samson needs to find out if this is indeed another martyrdom or just an ordinary murder and appoints the abbey's physician, Master Walter, to investigate. Walter discovers a web of intrigue and corruption involving some of the highest in the land but unbeknown to him his own past holds a secret which will put his life in danger before the final terrible solution is revealed.

ABBOT'S PASSION

Easter 1201. Following a treaty between King John and King Philip of France, England is at last at peace. Alas the same cannot be said for Saint Edmund's Abbey. The pope's new legate has arrived determined to stir up controversy. For Abbot Samson this brings the possibility of a new ally against an old enemy. But his intrigues lead to disaster with Brother Walter being placed in mortal danger and a full-scale battle in the nearby village of Lakenheath.

In the middle of all this the legate's clerk is murdered and a London merchant is wrongly accused. In desperation the man is granted sanctuary at the abbey's shrine, but it is only a brief respite. The whole weight of the judiciary and the church are against him.

Amid rape, religious bigotry and trial by combat Walter has to find the real murderer before a terrible injustice is done and the wrong man is hanged.

BLOOD MOON

November 1214. King John has returned to England having lost his empire to King Philip of France. Humiliated and desperate for support, he again travels to Bury St Edmunds where Abbot Samson has died and a battle is raging among the monks over who will be his successor.

In the midst of this there arrives in the town a seemingly inconsequential young couple and their maid. The wife is heavily pregnant and gives birth in the night to a baby daughter.

But then the maid is mysteriously murdered and it is soon apparent that the family is not all that it appears. With rebellion looming, abbey physician Walter of Ixworth is drawn once again into investigating a murder and a conspiracy that threatens to engulf the country in civil war and ultimately leads to the final nemesis that is Runnymede and Magna Carta.

DEVIL'S ACRE

January 1242. Brother Walter is dying. He is an old man but the prospect of death does not disturb him - indeed, he welcomes it to meet with old friends and see God in the face. But before he finally joins the heavenly host he is determined to solve one last mystery that has been plaguing him for decades.

But there are dark forces afoot that want to frustrate his efforts and are prepared to go to any lengths to keep secret events that even now could disturb the government of England - even murder.

In his mind Walter returns to those far off times when Abbot Samson took him on a bizarre journey away from the comforting familiarity of Bury Abbey and into the wilds of barbaric Norfolk where the abbot's power is limited and be met by a far greater one in the guise of the Warenne family of Castle Acre - or as some still choose to call it, the *Devil's Acre*.

THE SILENT AND THE DEAD

Winifred Jonah seemed like an ordinary Norfolk housewife, jolly, plump and harmless. Yet her bland exterior concealed a sinister secret. At fourteen she had already murdered her aunt and uncle and forty years later it was her husband's turn to die. Even so she might have made it to her own grave without further incident if she hadn't met Colin Brearney. He thought she was going to be a pushover, but he had no idea who he was taking on. The day Colin knocked at her door was the beginning of a nightmare that could only end in blood, silence and death...